DOROTHY DREYER

PHOENIX DESCENDING

CURSE OF THE PHOENIX

BOOK ONE

Edited by Cheree Castellanos
Cover design by Deranged Doctor Design
World map and character illustrations by Sora Sanders
Takumi illustration by Kimberley Wack
Design framework created by Freepik
Published November 2017 by Snowy Wings Publishing

For Humanity
For Equality
For Peace and Love

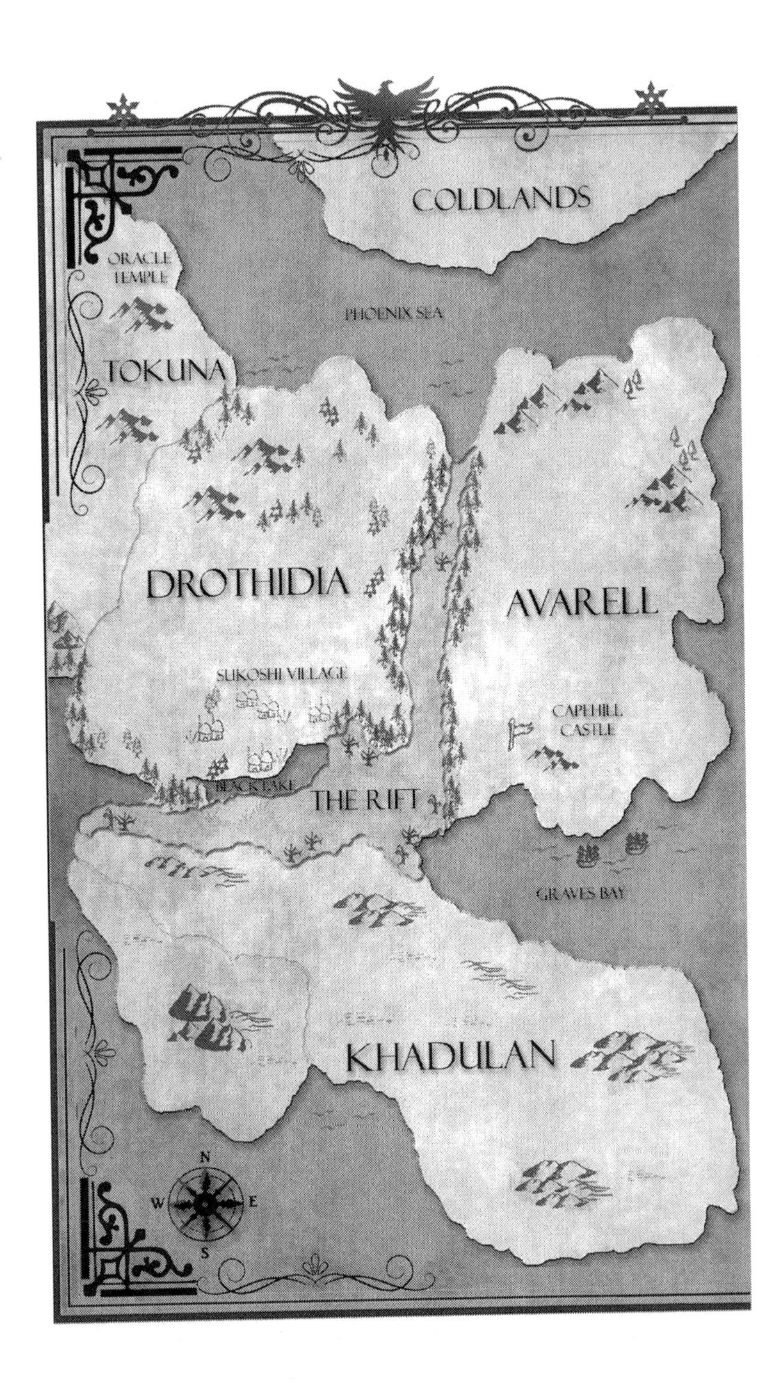
COLDLANDS
ORACLE TEMPLE
PHOENIX SEA
TOKUNA
DROTHIDIA
AVARELL
SUKOSHI VILLAGE
CAPEHILL CASTLE
BLACK LAKE
THE RIFT
GRAVES BAY
KHADULAN
N
W
E
S

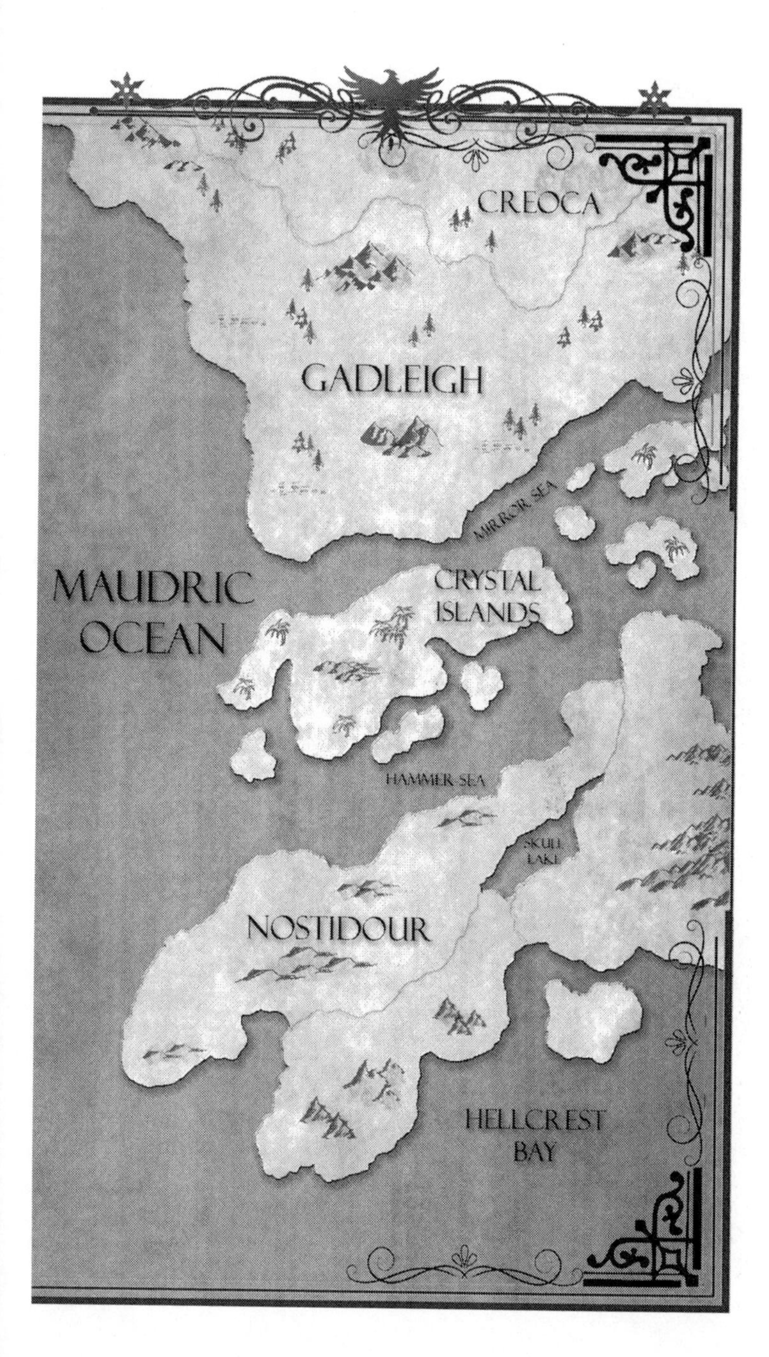
CREOCA
GADLEIGH
MIRROR SEA
MAUDRIC
OCEAN
CRYSTAL
ISLANDS
HAMMER SEA
SKULL
LAKE
NOSTIDOUR
HELLCREST
BAY

CHAPTER ONE

THE DOGS BOUND FORWARD with purpose, their snarls and angry, sharp barks echoing in the winter air.

Bramwell struggled to keep up with the group. He was lucky to be invited on the hunt at his young age, and it would do no good to disappoint his uncle. If he fell behind or complained, he might not be invited again.

"Look alive, Bram," Logan called from yards ahead. "Your legs are long but weak."

Bramwell bit back a sneer and pumped his legs harder, righting himself as his feet threatened to slip out from underneath him.

"Careful," Logan said with a smirk. "You don't want to fall into the Rift."

Bramwell expelled a curse on labored breath as Logan—his lifelong friend—picked up speed, his laughter pricking Bramwell's ears. Of course he wouldn't be so foolish as to fall into the Rift. Children's nightmares were made up of the creatures who dwelled there—the Undead—who endlessly trod the dank and grimy dell that served as a border between the Queen's city of Avarell, the forest lands of Drothidia, and the mining country of Khadulan. Bramwell had never seen an

Undead, but he'd heard the stories. There was even tell of children who had wandered into the Rift, became trapped in the gullies, and were either feasted upon by the creatures or became infected from the bite of an Undead and turned into one themselves.

With a shudder, Bramwell ran faster, his bow laced snug around one shoulder and his quiver of arrows strapped to his back. At least his uncle had trusted him to handle the weapon. How proud he would be of Bramwell should he take down a deer or a wolf. They wouldn't be laughing then. They would celebrate him. And all the praise in Bramwell's name would wipe that impish smirk clear off Logan's face.

There was a turn in the path where it split in two, and Bramwell hesitated. He could no longer hear the dogs, and there was no sight of the others on the hunt. Which way had they gone?

Bramwell looked to the sky, attempting to determine his direction based on the location of the sun. He studied the dirt on the paths, but both trails were equally kicked up. There was no telling which one the Queen's Guard had taken. A flutter of leaves up ahead on the path leading left caught his attention, and he took it as a sign.

He dashed forward, his jaw tight. Logan would never let him live it down if he were to get lost. Thirty seconds into his run, the path narrowed. Thirty more seconds, the path dwindled into nothing but a dead end. Heat flooded his cheeks and neck. He'd chosen the wrong path. Adjusting the strap of his bow, he turned on his heel and ran back the way from which he came.

The harsh shadow of wings suddenly swooped through the air before him, causing him to skid to a stop. A shriek so loud he had to cover his ears resonated through the woodlands around him. Spotting the huge bird, Bram ducked in fear. A phoenix. It was rare to see them in Avarell, but here, on the border of the Rift, it was not uncommon. He'd only seen a few in his sixteen years of living, but never one this close. Recent word was the birds were now contaminated with some kind of disease, and phoenix fever was rumored to be spreading through Drothidia. There were no reports of the epidemic reaching Avarell. In fact, many claimed that the rumors were not true.

The phoenix swooped in an arc and landed on a nearby tree, its orange-gold feathers ruffling as it clasped onto a branch with its sharp talons. Bramwell stared at the glorious creature, and he could have sworn it was staring back. It didn't look diseased. On the contrary, it was quite stunning. The bird cocked its head to the side, and then it spread its wings and dove from the branch. Bramwell gasped as he realized the phoenix was headed straight for his head.

He moved swiftly, side-stepping as he crouched, but his foot caught some ice and he was propelled farther sideways. He landed on his arm, but the snow beneath him gave way, and Bramwell lost his breath as he toppled down into a ditch beside the path. His head caught the bark of a tree on his way down, and the snow that fell with him clouded the air, but his journey wasn't over. This wasn't simply a ditch; the ground here had eroded to a sharp drop. His body rolled farther down, his arms and legs connecting with rocks and branches on the way. His arrows spilled around him, and the string from his bow cut into his shoulder. He landed in a gully with a thud, the air knocked out of his lungs and his ankle throbbing.

At first, he couldn't move; he simply lay there attempting to catch his breath. As blood from the cut on his head slowly streamed beside his eye, he knew he had to get up. He was in the Rift. And it was only a matter of time before the Undead would smell his blood.

He winced, struggling to pull himself to a sitting position. Fog drifted over the snow in the gully, obstructing his view. He looked upward, trying to see where he had fallen from, and more importantly, if there was a way to climb back up. Latching his hand onto a nearby branch, he pulled himself to his knees. But the movement sent firebolts of pain into his ankle. He dropped back onto his bottom, sucking in a breath to keep from screaming. Noise would only attract the creatures in the Rift.

He scooted forward on his backside, using the nearby foliage to get him closer to the embankment. But everything he grabbed on to came loose from the earth and snow, until he sat there with handfuls of twigs and roots but had made no progress.

A branch snapping behind him made his head swivel around. He held his breath, searching the foggy surroundings for movement. The sound of heavy, ragged breathing and dragging of feet caused his heart to thrash in his chest. Every muscle and nerve in his body went rigid as the form of an Undead appeared through the mist. At the sight of its gray pallor, empty eyes, and the way its decaying mouth hung open, Bramwell wanted to gag. The monster drew nearer, and Bramwell fought to untangle the bow from his body. His hands pounded against the ground, fingers searching for one of his lost arrows. There had to be one nearby. His mouth went dry as the Undead dragged itself closer still.

With no luck finding an arrow, Bramwell held the bow firmly in his hands, resigning to use it as a weapon. If he struck the creature hard enough, he might be able to kill it—or at least ward it off.

Bramwell's breaths came in sharp bursts as the Undead reached for him. He held his bow at the ready, but it shook as he trembled. The monster swiped his hand out, grabbing the other end of the bow. Bramwell wanted to scream, but he clamped his mouth tightly shut and yanked the bow back to himself. The creature was strong and pulled at the bow again. Bramwell couldn't pry it away from his attacker, and his heart felt as if it was going to explode.

A swift hiss sounded, and the Undead let go of the bow, his body bent to the side. Bramwell's jaw dropped when he spotted the wooden shuriken—a weapon some called a Throwing Star—embedded in the creature's temple. The Undead let out one last moan before it crumpled to the floor.

Too in shock to track the movement around him, he found himself being dragged backward from his chest. He glanced down, noticing delicate hands of a female wrapped around him. Whoever she was, she was strong. She dragged him farther until he was hauled into a dark place obscured by hanging branches. The small cave was cold and wet and smelled like rotting leaves.

As his rescuer set him against the wall of the cave, Bramwell finally got a look at her. Though the light was dim, there was no missing the young girl's eyes. The exotic slant of them told him she was Drothidian. She was petite, and Bramwell measured her to be about fourteen. Her wrists and ankles were wrapped in tight cloth, her tunic and boy's trousers a green hue that matched the woods, and her black hair was pulled into a knot. He watched her, amazed that this tiny person had the strength to drag him to safety.

"Thank you," he said.

She held a finger to her lips, signaling for him to keep quiet. She didn't smile, and she didn't look at him longer than she had to. Bramwell sat in stunned silence as the girl reached outside the cave and gathered a handful of snow. She crouched down next to Bramwell and slapped the snow against the wound on his head. Only when he winced and let out a slight whimper did the hint of a smirk fly across her mouth. But it was gone as quickly as it had come.

"Where else are you hurt?" she whispered.

Though taken aback by her voice, he pointed to his leg. It wasn't the only place he ached, but it felt the worst of his injuries. "My ankle."

Without hesitation, she withdrew a dagger and ripped back the leg of his trousers to expose his ankle. The skin was red and swollen, a laceration exposing blood and flesh. Bramwell's eyes widened, and he swallowed hard.

The girl blew out a breath, a look of disappointment ghosting over her face. She reached into the satchel that was laced at her side and pulled out what looked like a spotted leaf. "Here."

"What am I supposed to do with that?" he asked.

"Eat it."

"Why?"

"Trust me."

He watched her for a moment, studying her face. Her cheeks looked soft and smooth, and he was half tempted to reach out to feel them. Instead, he took the leaf from her hand.

She stared at him, waiting for him to do as she said. He didn't know why he should trust this girl, except for the fact that if she meant any harm to come to him, she would have left him for the Undead. He twirled the leaf between his fingers, gazing into her eyes a moment more before he popped the leaf into his mouth and swallowed.

❦

His head buzzed and his eyes itched as he came to. He had no idea how long he had been unconscious, but it was still light out, so it couldn't have been too long. Unless he had slept through an entire night, in which case, he had completely missed out on the hunt.

Remembering where he was, he straightened, his back cold from sleeping against the wall of the cave. Whatever that leaf was, it had knocked him out quickly. He frowned as he realized the girl was no longer there. Moving his leg slightly, he hissed through his teeth at the buzz of pain. He reached for his ankle and then froze. A black zig-zag was threaded through his skin, pulling the wound closed. Leaning forward, he delicately touched the thin silk floss. The flesh there was tender, but the bleeding had stopped, and the swelling had gone down slightly. The girl was not only strong, but crafty as well. He smiled and shook his head in wonder.

"Bram!"

Bramwell's eyes widened, and he struggled to crawl out of the cave.

"Bram! Where are you?"

He clawed at the dirt, pulling himself forward despite the pain. "Here! I'm here."

"Bramwell?"

"Yes! Logan, I'm here!"

With every muster of his being, he crawled to the foot of the embankment. The tiny spot that was Logan's head appeared at the top of the wall of soil and snow. Bramwell waved, relief washing over him.

"Hiding out in the Rift, I see," Logan called. "Your uncle won't be pleased. Hang on, then."

Logan disappeared, and ten seconds later a rope was lowered to the spot where Bramwell kneeled.

"Wrap that around your torso, and snake your arms through as well. The men and I will pull you up."

"All right." Bramwell grabbed the rope and tied it around himself. As he looped it around his arm, he looked back toward the cave. If his rescuer was there, he wanted to thank her once more. Perhaps ask for her name. But he saw no one. There was a small pinch in his chest, but he brushed the feeling away and concentrated on being lugged out of the Rift.

"Ready?" Logan asked.

"All set."

"Well, you may not have scored any game, but I bet you have one hell of a story to tell when you reach the top."

Bramwell smiled to himself. "Indeed, I do."

CHAPTER TWO

TORI WATCHED FROM THE CAMOUFLAGE of bushes as the boy rose out of the Rift. She had almost come out when he looked around, as if sensing he had been searching for her, but she couldn't risk being seen by the Queen's Guard. She waited until long after the boy was lifted out of sight before leaving her hiding place.

All the better, she thought to herself. She was raised to avoid contact and interaction with people from the other realms. There was a long history of disaccord between them.

But she couldn't simply let an Undead kill the boy. She saw no harm in saving him. Perhaps there wasn't the need to tend to his wounds; he would have survived his injuries without her aid. But she couldn't help herself. It seemed cruel to let him suffer.

With her dagger gripped in her hand, she glided through the foliage as silently as possible. She had already gathered the supplies she needed, and it was crucial she get out of the Rift before dark. The Undead always seemed hungrier under the light of the moon. Aside from that, she didn't want her mother to be concerned. She had enough troubling her without having to worry about Tori's wellbeing.

She kept her grunts and murmurs to a minimum as she climbed over large rocks and slipped between heavy masses of trees. When she reached the creek that marked the halfway point in her journey, she climbed a great cedar that stretched out over the water. The bough was big enough for her to walk on. Holding her arms out to her sides, she kept her balance and strode along the length of the bough in her waxed canvas shoes. Toward the end of the bough, it forked off into two smaller branches, one of which hovered over a patch of wildflowers. Crouching down and grabbing hold of the branch, she swung her legs down and prepared to let herself drop.

As her fingers clung to the limb, her feet swinging below her, she heard an unsettling sound. Her throat closed up, and her temples and neck dampened with sweat as she realized it was too late to pull herself back up. Her jaw clenched to the point of aching when she spotted two Undead stagger toward her, their hungry moans filling her ears. She dropped to the bed of flowers, her feet barely touching the ground before she pulled two shuriken from their leather pouch. The first one she threw hit the closer Undead in the inner corner of his eye. The creature stumbled back with a loud moan, arms flailing as it fell. Tori swiftly hurled the second shuriken, which caught the remaining Undead in the decaying flesh near its ear. The creature floundered, spinning in a circle before crumpling to the ground and growing silent.

Tori let out a shuddered breath, letting her shoulders fall. She was usually good about avoiding the Undead, only resorting to using her shuriken when needed. It took her four days simply to carve one. Each one was treated in deadly nightshade overnight, the wood soaking up the poison, which would, by design, leach into its target upon impact. When handling the shuriken, she protected her hands with gloves, and when she was out in the Rift she covered her skin with a special salve made from wax and sap, though the nightshade only took effect when contacting broken skin.

Today alone, she had used three of the Throwing Stars—two weeks' worth of work gone in a matter of hours. She didn't dare retrieve the weapons from the corpses. Certainly, she could clean them off, re-carve any damaged parts, and re-treat them in more poison, but Tori made a point not to go near an Undead, fallen or not. There was simply no telling if one would rise again—though she'd yet to see that happen. And besides, the shuriken had served their purpose and taken down the Undead, and she was glad to be alive.

The sky was bathed in a pinkish hue as she finally reached the border of Drothidia. Climbing the familiar Sakura tree that sat at the embankment between the Rift and the outskirts of her village of Sukoshi, she took in the heartwarming sight of her homeland. Coming home from the Rift always filled her with two conflicting emotions. On one hand, she was glad to be home, unscathed and out of harm's way. But the very reason she had to venture into the Rift at all filled her with sadness, a hollow feeling in her gut that left her with hopelessness. The Rift was the only area where Sweetwood Root grew. And Sweetwood Root was needed to ease the symptoms of the phoenix fever—the disease from which her sister suffered.

As she trudged along the road that led to her home, she passed the homes and people of her village, every once in a while spotting a symbol painted on a door in red paint: a straight vertical line which split at the top into two curved lines. The mark represented a phoenix and was a warning to anyone who might want to enter the house that someone inside had been infected. It was the same symbol that covered her own door. It wasn't known yet if the disease could be passed from person to person, but everyone was being cautious, just in case.

It had become a ritual upon her return from the Rift to prepare the Sweetwood Root she had gathered by chopping the plant and then separating it into enough satchels for the infected. The satchels would then be delivered to the families of the ill, where they would be infused in boiled water and served as a tea.

There was no known cure for phoenix fever, but Tori had discovered that Sweetwood Root tea had alleviated most of the symptoms. When her sister Miki would drink the tea, her chills would subside and her stomach cramps would lessen. There were even times when Miki had been able to leave her sick bed and join the family for supper. The fever, however, though dropping a few tenths of a degree, would continue to burden her, and her body remained weak. But even a morsel of relief for her poor, suffering sister was enough reason for Tori to risk the dangers of the Rift.

Her feet felt blistered and sore when she finally reached her door. She only cast the red mark upon it a fleeting glance as she entered the house. Her mother, who stood in the kitchen preparing dough for bread, dropped what she was doing and ran up to Tori.

Placing hands full of flour on Tori's cheeks, her mother studied her with concern in her eyes. "Tori, I was worried. You were gone for moons."

"Sorry, Mama. But I've got the Sweetwood Root." She handed her mother the bag. "How's Miki?"

Her mother pressed her lips together and shook her head. "Her fever went up today. A few cold cloths helped a little. She's sleeping now." A small smile appeared on her face. "She'll be happy to see you."

"I'll be right by her side when she awakens."

Her mother hugged the bag of roots to her chest. "Let's get the tea ready."

Tori followed her mother to their small kitchen and took out a pair of knives. "Are Father and Masumi home from their duties?"

"They returned for supper, but left afterward to help the Saito family with their fence."

Her father and brother were part of the team that built and mounted spiked masts in and around the village to ward off phoenixes. Before the disease, the beautiful birds were a welcome sight, their vibrant plumage a wonder to behold. Now, the fowl were looked upon with abhorrence. There were far too many deaths caused by the phoenix for anyone to look past its stunning appearance.

"And Taeyeon?" Tori asked.

"Out playing with her little friends." Her mother offered her a small smile. "But she will be back soon."

They worked silently for a few minutes, but Tori noticed her mother's eyes on her more than once.

"What?" Tori asked.

"Something happened." It wasn't a question. Her mother always knew when she was hiding something from her.

Tori knew it was pointless to lie, but she also was in no mood to start a quarrel. If her mother found out she helped an Avarellian, they would be discussing her actions for moons. Perhaps she didn't have to tell the entire truth. "There was a Queen's Guard hunt. I had to hide."

"Did anyone see you?"

Tori shook her head. "I was well hidden."

"Good. There's no telling what those savages would have done had they spotted you. They wouldn't lift a finger to help us during the war with the Khadulians. That makes them enemies as well, if my opinion counts for anything."

"I know, Mama."

Tori went to the sink and scrubbed the green off her hands. She remembered the way the boy thanked her. The kindness in his eyes when she offered him the Ledola leaf. The way he did as she instructed and ate the leaf without question. He didn't seem like an enemy to her.

As promised, Tori was at Miki's bedside when she awoke. It was beyond troubling to watch her younger sister suffer. She wished there was more that she could do for her. Taeyeon sat on the floor by Tori's feet, playing a game made up of a ball and six hard berries. The bounce of the ball upon the floor matched the rhythm of Tori's fingers stroking Miki's arm.

Miki's eyes widened upon spotting her older sister, and she reached for her with a trembling hand. "You're here." Her voice was dry, cracking on the last word.

Taeyeon stopped playing her game and stood, watching their exchange.

Tori handed Miki the cup of tea, which had cooled to room temperature. "Drink."

Miki straightened and took the cup, pain evident on her face as she moved. She sipped the tea slowly, and then began to cough. The cup shook in her hand as her coughs grew harsher, and Tori snatched it away, placing it on the bedside table. Leaning forward, Tori reached behind her sister and rubbed at her back, hoping it would help. Tori kept her chin up, refusing to let her sister see the worry that compressed her heart.

Miki's coughs faded, and she placed a hand on Tori's arm, nodding her thanks.

"You weren't back for the midday meal," Miki said. "I was worried."

Tori forced a smile. "You know better than to worry about me. I've been trained in attack and defense by Akihiro Shung, the best warrior in all Drothidia."

"You mean the only warrior willing to train a girl," Miki said with a lopsided grin.

"And that makes him the best." Tori let out a small laugh.

"Maybe he'll train me one day," Taeyeon chimed in, chin high and arms straight at her sides.

With a chuckle, Tori ruffled Taeyeon's dark, silky hair. "He'd be lucky to have you as a student."

A figure moved into the doorway, causing Tori to turn her head. "I thought I heard trouble in here," Masumi said, leaning against the doorframe.

Taeyeon let out a giggle and rushed to his side, wrapping her arms around his waist.

Tori smiled at the sight of her older brother, whose face was smeared with dirt. His clothes had remnants of wood shavings, and he smelled of earth and grass. "You're a mess," Tori said.

Masumi smirked, crossing his arms. "I don't look any worse than you usually do when you come back from the Rift."

Tori smoothed out her plain dress. "But at least I know how to clean myself up. You wouldn't think twice about going to bed in that state."

Masumi shrugged, but the smirk remained. "The girls don't seem to mind."

Miki laughed. "You pig."

Taeyeon let out another giggle, jumping up and down. "Pig, pig, pig." She finished with a few loud snorts.

Masumi pushed himself off the doorframe. "Fine. I'll go wash up."

As he left the room with Taeyeon in tow, Tori looked back at Miki. Tori's smile immediately faltered as she took in the pale pallor of her sister's face. Something was wrong. A sheen of sweat covered Miki's forehead, and she looked as if she was going to vomit. Tori drew closer and propped a hand behind Miki's back, helping her to sit up. She grabbed an old pot that sat by the bed and placed it on Miki's lap. Miki grasped the pot and leaned her head over it, and Tori rubbed her sister's back as she spit up bile.

As the last of Miki's heaving came to an end, Tori grabbed a washcloth that sat in a bowl of water, wrung it out, and placed it on Miki's head. She eased her sister back down to her pillow and took the pot away. She hated seeing her like this. She hated not being able to do more for her than make her tea. There had to be something else she could do to make it all go away.

"Should I get Mama?" Tori asked.

Miki shook her head, barely able to keep her eyes open. She reached out and took Tori's hand. "No. Stay with me."

Tori gave her hand a squeeze. "Okay. I will."

There was agony in Miki's eyes as she stared at the ceiling, her breathing labored and her swallows coming hard. "Tori, you have to promise me something."

"Anything, Miki. Anything at all."

Miki closed her eyes, tears gently falling from the corners. "I know you want this to end. I know you want to find a cure. But you have to promise me: if I die, you'll keep looking."

Tori's eyes grew wide. "Miki—"

Miki locked gazes with her. "You must promise me. Find a way to help the others, Tori. It will keep spreading otherwise. If it reaches Mama, if it reaches Taeyeon… Don't give up."

Tears burned as they rolled down Tori's cheeks. The deepest agony lay in her heart at the thought of her sister dying. She was sure she would want to die herself if that were to happen. But

Miki's eyes were pleading, and Tori knew she couldn't deny her this.

She held her sister's hand, pressing it against her heart. "I promise."

FIVE YEARS LATER ...

CHAPTER THREE

STARS SHONE LIKE GLITTERING JEWELS in the night sky as Tori peered upon the large buildings that dominated the dusty mining town in Khadulan. Her jaw dropped in wonder at the layout before her. She'd never seen so many buildings before, and certainly none so big. Monstrous warehouses sat on the outskirts of colossal factories, all perched high on dust-covered knolls that overlooked the numerous mines that bordered the city.

Tori's arduous journey through the Rift to get to the unfamiliar land left her weary, but gazing upon this foreign city filled her with determination. What she sought was in one of the buildings, and though she wasn't certain which one, she had to start somewhere.

As she hid behind a pallet of crates, her faithful fox Takumi skittered toward the man guarding the first warehouse. Takumi silently drew closer to the unsuspecting guard. The Khadulian man was dressed in a dark sentry uniform emblazoned with silver buttons, his pointed ears—the distinctive attribute of the Khadulian people—stuffed beneath a forage cap.

Takumi had his instructions. Distracting the guard wouldn't be a problem. But if he could manage to swipe the guard's keys, it would make Tori's quest all the more easier.

She had spent weeks calculating this plan, weeks convincing herself she could pull it off. But it had taken her months before that to even think about venturing out, to even think about facing the world at all. Those months were the lowest phase of life she had ever lived through—and she barely did that, distraught as she was by the death of her sister. When the phoenix fever ultimately claimed Miki, Tori fell into a deep depression, not eating for weeks and hardly sleeping. If her family had shut out the world as much as she did, she hadn't been aware, for she had been too lost in the abyss of sadness. Over time, her mother began to show signs of the disease, and the promise Tori made to Miki to find a cure came screaming back to her.

Every day that passed had her paranoid that her youngest sister Taeyeon might show symptoms, and she watched her closely, afraid to let her out of her sight. Her brother Masumi—normally the muscle of the family—didn't seem as agile as he used to be, the usual drive he possessed diminished, and though Tori feared he might have the fever as well, he assured her he was perfectly healthy. Tori, however, believed he was skilled at putting up a front so as not to worry her. Her father, alone, showed no signs of being affected by the illness. But how long would that last?

Fearing for her family's lives, Tori had decided to set out to find the cure. She didn't even know what it was called, but she knew it existed—manufactured and stored in the enemy realm of Khadulan.

Takumi came within a meter of the guard and began to gekker, his high-pitched vocalization coming out in a stuttering flow. The guard started, stiffening with his rifle held out, and turned to see the fox crouched down on his hind haunches. To the guard, the fox must have looked ready to attack, but Tori knew he would never hurt anyone on purpose. The guard's hand hovered over the trigger of the rifle, but his eyes told Tori he was hesitant about using his weapon on the animal. Sensing the guard's trepidation, Takumi shifted suddenly and slithered through the guard's legs at a surprising speed. He bent his body and ran a quick circle up the guard's left leg, then jumped down and away from him. Startled by Takumi's unexpected movements, the guard did not notice that the fox had unlatched his keys from his belt. With one swift jump, Takumi bounded upon a stack of crates and leaped over the roof of the warehouse.

As the guard scampered toward the other side of the building, cursing and grumbling, Takumi doubled back and jumped down to where Tori was hiding. He quickly dropped the keys by her feet and then rushed back toward the guard, kicking up dust with his tiny feet. He had to continue distracting the guard so Tori could find the right warehouse.

Certain they were far enough away, Tori emerged from her hiding spot and approached the first warehouse. The dark night made it difficult for her to make out the lettering painted on the outside wall of the warehouse, but as she got closer she saw it was a storage unit for lumber.

She continued her quiet search, making her way from one building to the next, until she finally found one marked with the word *MEDICAL*. Her heart pounded harder in her chest. This could be it. On the other side of the door could be the answer to her problems. She fumbled with the keys, begging her fingers to stop shaking. She tried the first key with no success. Gritting her teeth, she grabbed the next one. And then the next. When she slipped the fourth key into the lock and turned it, it blessed her with a click.

She pressed her lips together and held her breath as her eyes adjusted to the lack of light. When rows and rows of floor-to-ceiling shelves came into view, she swallowed back the fear of not being able to find what she came here for. Strange-looking machines were lined up along one wall, their ominous metal parts bent in impossible angles.

Footsteps sounded outside. From the sound of them, Takumi was running by with the guard in his wake. She paused for a solitary moment before making her way past the pallets of boxed bandages and skin salves. The rows of shelves were not marked, but when she came upon the section of vials and bottles, she knew she must be getting closer. She read label upon label, her fingers trailing upon the bottles marked for herbs that cured headaches and pastes that soothed rashes. Ultimately, she reached a section of vials that made her pause. The words on these labels were unrecognizable. She had learned a lot from her village's local apothecary, but she had never even heard of any of these medicines, much less pronounce them.

If only she knew what the cure for phoenix fever was called.

A clicking noise echoed in the warehouse. Tori held back a gasp, knowing the guard had finally tired of chasing the fox. But she wasn't certain which vial contained the cure.

The enormous room suddenly filled with brightness. Tori had heard of electricity being used in other realms, but she had never experienced it until now. Trying to contain her amazement at how the building lit up as if the sun shone inside it, she quickly switched her attention back to the shelf. The guard hadn't spotted her yet, so she had to use this opportunity to grab what she could. Scooping two of everything into her satchel, she tiptoed to the end of the row and peered out at the guard. His hand firmly grasped his rifle as he searched the space. He must have known someone was in the building. If only that damned light could be snuffed out, Tori could use the dark to mask her escape.

Tori could see the switch on the wall that the guard had used to turn on the lights. It was clunky and metal and looked as if a strong hand was needed to switch it. She noticed a thick, black cable coming up out of the metal contraption and followed it up to where it connected with the massive glowing bulbs. And the idea hit her.

She quietly reached for a shuriken and took a silent step out from between the rows. She had to be quick, and her aim had to be true. Her jaw tightened as she whipped the shuriken through the air. The guard's head swiveled, unsure of what caused the whooshing sound that flew past him. The shuriken pierced the cable dead on, and the lights went out immediately.

Tori crouched down and slunk toward the door, a tight hold on the satchel to prevent the vials from making noise. She couldn't see the guard, but she heard him stumble into something, his mumbled curse a low rumble in the darkness. Without releasing her breath, she reached the door and glided through it, the night air hitting her like fresh relief.

She clicked her tongue three times—her signal to Takumi to join her—and raced toward the woods from whence she came. Her satchel rattled as she ran, despite her effort to clasp a hand around it. But there was no way to stifle the noise of her footfalls pounding against the dirt.

With gallant speed, she breached the woods, Takumi following close behind and eventually passing her. Once under the cover of the woods, she allowed herself to slow down, but she didn't stop. The moon was bright in the night sky, and she would still need to make her way through the Rift. Instead, she concentrated on sucking in and blowing out her breaths, careful to keep them steady, all the while minding where her footsteps took her and resisting the temptation to check behind her. It would do no good to lose her footing now.

After running for miles, she reached the area of the woods that dropped into the Rift. Only now did she spare a moment to look over her shoulder. Her breath came out in strong currents as her eyes scanned the trees. The dark might have disguised movement, but she was sure Takumi would have alerted her if he heard anyone approaching. Finding no proof that they were followed, Tori bent her knees and jumped into the Rift.

She loathed being in the Rift at all, but especially at night. Nighttime did something to the Undead. It was as if it heightened their senses, made them hungrier. The cloak of darkness helped keep Tori hidden, but nothing could conceal the smell of blood pumping through her body. If she got too close to a den of Undead, they'd smell her in an instant.

Her tired muscles weighed her down, and the heavy satchel full of medicine added to the task. She needed to find a place to rest, just for a few minutes. Up ahead she spotted an ancient fig tree, its enormous branches sure to provide sanctuary for a reprieve. Takumi must have read her mind, for he darted toward the tree and skittered up into the safety of its boughs. Tori pushed herself to follow suit, her muscles screaming with every step.

She latched her hand up onto a steady branch and began to pull herself up. But as she grabbed onto the next branch with her other hand, something pulled her downward. She slipped a few inches, her teeth clenched as she struggled to pull herself up. She didn't have to look down to know that it was the hand of an Undead wrapped around her ankle. Snarls filled her ears along with her rapid heartbeat. Takumi gekkered, pacing back and forth on the branch above her.

Eyes wet with tears of panic, she kicked at the creature, twisting her leg left and right. She just needed to loosen its grip so she could spring upward into the tree. But the creature's hold was strong.

Takumi, letting out high pitched screeches, scampered down the tree and clamped his teeth around the pant leg of Tori's attacker. Tori wanted to cry out in protest, frightened for Takumi's life, but she found it hard to take a breath. Her fox friend must have accomplished what he'd set out to do, however, for the Undead released Tori's ankle enough for her to slip through. She hoisted herself up into the safety of the boughs, her eyes immediately searching for her fox.

Takumi jetted around the Undead in a circle before bounding up the tree to join Tori. Tori's hand pressed hard against her chest, willing herself to catch her breath, willing her heart to slow from its thunderous pace.

The Undead clawed at the tree, moaning in the night as drool hung from its gaping mouth. Tori needed to shut it up or else risk attracting more creatures. Retrieving a shuriken from her pack, she steadied her hand and took aim.

It wasn't until the Undead dropped to the ground, its limbs no longer moving, that she was able to breathe freely again. Takumi paced, continuing to watch the lump of the creature. Tori wiped sweat from her brow with the back of her hand. Along with the soreness in her abdomen, the sides of her neck ached, and she bit back a curse. This was no time to feel sick.

Shifting into a steady yet comfortable sitting position, she closed her eyes and concentrated on taking slow, deep breaths. She needed the rest, yes, but she needed to get home. It would do no good to let her exhaustion give way to fever.

With her eyes still shut, she took in the sounds of the woods. Far off in the distance, she heard the high-pitched caw of a phoenix. This didn't come as a surprise, as the large birds were known to nest more commonly in the Rift. Low hooting told her that an owl was near, and the buzzing insects were on their continuous journeys through the trees. And the shuffle of leaves and the breaking of a twig …

Her eyes popped open and her hands gripped the bark of the tree. She scanned the ground below her for signs of movement, ignoring the sweat that dripped into her eyes. She swallowed hard, cringing at the stinging pain in her neck, and wondered if what she heard was another Undead or if she had been followed by a Khadulian guard after all.

Takumi purred and pawed at her leg. Tori studied him, noting that he wasn't concerned with the noise of the breaking twig.

"I do trust you," she whispered to him. "So if you're not worried …"

Takumi lifted himself up with his hind legs and sniffed at her chin. The strained muscles in her shoulders relaxed a bit. She wrinkled her nose at the feel of his tickling whiskers and let out a small laugh.

Akihiro Shung sat on a wooden chair he had built himself and took a long draw of his pipe. Tori knew she would find him here, even in the middle of the night. He didn't turn his head as she approached, but his eyes met hers. If he was surprised to see her, he didn't show it. His white beard hid his mouth, as always, so she could never tell if he was smiling or frowning.

Tori slowed her pace, not knowing if Akihiro could help her. But he was one of the highly respected elders of Sukoshi village.

Maybe he wasn't the wisest, but he certainly taught her a lot when she trained with him. Not only combat, but also strategy, patience, and inner peace. Now, older and a bit slower to move, he spent his evenings and most of his nights on his porch, watching the stars as he smoked his medicinal pipe.

"Master Shung," Tori said as she climbed the porch. Her voice was breathy, a reflection of her tedious journey. "I was hoping you could help me."

"I know not of what you need, but I, too, hope I can help you, my child."

Her hand went to her satchel. The weight of it was dreadful, but she would have carried more if she could, if only to be certain to have the cure she sought.

"I have some tonics here." She crouched down in front of him and removed the strap from her body, feeling instant relief in her shoulder. "I was hoping you could tell me which one … if one of them might be the cure to the phoenix fever."

His bushy brows lowered slowly, his glassy eyes focusing first on her and then on the satchel. "Cure?"

"Yes, Master Shung. There is a cure for the phoenix fever. The citizens of both Avarell and Khadulan are immunized against the disease. But it's we, the Drothidians, who need it most."

She carefully spilled the vials onto the floor between them, her hand gliding gently over each glass container as if it would call out to her when she touched the right one.

Master Shung placed his pipe on the small table beside him. "Tori, did you steal these?"

Her face warmed. "I did what I had to do."

She bet if she could see his mouth beneath his moustache, she would find a stern frown. At least, that was the hint his eyes were giving her.

A raspy sigh escaped his mouth as he leaned forward, his eyes scanning the pile at his feet.

"I can read the labels," she said, "but I've never seen these words before. I don't know what they are."

She felt as though a boulder was inside her chest, weighing her down, as Akihiro Shung looked over the labels. He turned a few over, in order to see the names better, but his face remained drawn down. Tori had to force her hands to remain at her sides to avoid wringing them.

Clearing his throat, he straightened in his chair and slowly shook his head. "I'm terribly sorry, my child, but I cannot help you, as I do not know what these chemicals are."

"What?" Her voice was a whisper, and she could swear her heart stopped beating.

"These words are not of things found in nature. Perhaps the ingredients were, at some point, but they have been tampered with by man, by Khadulians, into something I'm afraid I do not recognize."

She bit her lip, feeling the blood drain from her face. "One of them has to be the cure."

His expression changed to pity, which made Tori feel even worse. "There's simply no way to know."

She stayed kneeling in front of him for a hundred breaths, each one painful, each one full of sorrow. He could not help her. Perhaps no one could. A sharp pain stung behind her eyes as she bent forward and scooped the vials back into her satchel. Her head buzzed with surrealism, her mind unable to accept the truth.

There was no hope left.

Tori stood and slung the strap of her satchel over her shoulder. "Thank you, Master Shung."

He nodded, picking up his pipe.

It was as if her bones weren't strong enough to support her body, but she forced herself to put one foot in front of the other until she made it to her house. No lights were on inside, and she was glad that her family was still asleep. There was no need to wake them, no need to rouse them from their much-needed rest.

As she opened the door and took a step inside, Takumi let out a hiss. Tori froze in place as a dark figure stepped out of the shadows, his ears raised into points and a stern tightness around his mouth as their eyes locked.

CHAPTER FOUR

TAKUMI SNARLED, HIS TEETH BARED as he bore down on his haunches, ready to attack.

The man's hand moved toward the sheath on his belt. "I'd think twice about doing anything, little fellow."

It was no ordinary sword at his side, but a machete, the hilt of the thick blade catching the moonlight streaming through the window as the man shifted. Tori's breath caught in her throat for a second time.

"Takumi, stop." Her voice was firm, but she did not shout. If her family was asleep—if this man hadn't harmed them in any way—she didn't want to alert them. She didn't need anyone charging into the room unexpectedly when the man before her carried such a weapon.

Takumi tilted his head at her, a small gekker signaling his confusion.

"It's okay, Takumi. Go outside. I'm fine. I can handle this."

Takumi looked between the man and Tori, then padded his little feet around Tori's boots before scampering outside.

The man's bushy brows lowered. "I've never known a person to befriend a fox."

"My family," she said, ignoring his statement. "Have you harmed them? I must warn you: anything other than a no will cost you your head." Her heart beat at an impossible speed, but she forced herself to remain outwardly calm. A million scenarios went through her head as to how she could take him down, but if her family had been taken away somewhere, she would need this man alive in order to tell her. She clenched her hands so tightly her nails dug into her palms.

The man had the audacity to chuckle. "Do not worry."

"Easier said than done."

"They are safe. For now."

She wanted to run and check. She wanted to take this man down and be with her family. Hold them and make sure they were never harmed. But she stood firmly in place.

The man scratched at his beard. "You have something that doesn't belong to you."

Her hand twitched, almost grabbing the satchel to tuck it behind her, but she knew it was no use. He'd already seen it. And even if he hadn't, she had the feeling he knew what she had done.

Reluctantly, she removed the strap from her shoulder and handed the satchel to him.

"Could I trouble you to light a candle?" he asked. "I understand Drothidia has not yet been exposed to electricity, but even I cannot see properly in the dark."

She did as he asked, her mind still searching for a way out of the situation. If it wasn't for fear that her family could be harmed, she would throw the candle in his face and fight him. Candlelight danced upon the man's face as he rifled through the contents.

With a look of confusion, he looked back up at her. "What could you possibly need all this for?"

Her gut told her not to answer him, but her head told her it was of no use. "My mother and some of the villagers are suffering from the phoenix fever. My sister died from it. I know there is a cure. An immunization. I needed to find it."

He stared at her incredulously for a moment. And then, without warning, he let out a low laugh. He reached into the satchel and grabbed a handful of vials to hold up to her. "Nothing you stole would help phoenix fever."

Disappointment washed through her like poison. "I know."

"The cure for phoenix fever doesn't come in a vial, for one."

Hot flames of aggravation scorched her skin. Was he trying to torment her? "If you know what the cure is, why don't you help me? Your people have been immunized. Avarell is free of the disease. Why not Drothidia? My mother claims the Khadulians are heartless. Prove her wrong."

He studied her, his eyes narrowing. "I watched you in the Rift. You're quite clever and handy with your weapons."

"You watched me?"

"Followed you. After you took off out of the medical warehouse."

She had a feeling she might have been followed, but she hadn't seen anyone. She was impressed that he was able to track her unseen, but she wasn't about to tell him that.

"You're quite skilled, and you obviously have a tough head on your shoulders. Perhaps we can make a deal."

Tori almost laughed. "Surely you're joking."

"I assure you, I am not."

"A deal with the enemy? A Drothidian make a deal with a Khadulian? I could never go against my family by making a deal with you."

"Yet you asked for my help when it came to saving their lives."

Tori pressed her lips together, seething.

"Perhaps going against their beliefs is the very thing that *will* save them. Save your mother and your neighbors." He studied her as if he were assessing her. "This war that separated our people happened decades ago."

"You stole our lands." She stiffened when he raised a brow. She'd heard many a tale of the battle in which the Khadulan armies seized the southern lands of Drothidia. Khadulan took everything south of the Black Lake and the western stretch of the Rift. "I was a mere child when it happened, but I still remember the sorrow in my mother's eyes when she told me about what had happened. My grandfather died trying to defend what was ours."

He shifted, his eyes never leaving her face. "Perhaps it is time for a change. For peace."

She was silent for a while, watching him. "What kind of deal do you speak of?"

"First of all, it might be better if we knew each other's names. Perhaps it would break the chilling ice that is apparent between us." He stretched out his massive hand. "My name is Goran."

She hesitated. Forcing herself not to shiver, she took his hand. "Tori."

"Hmm, Tori. It means *bird* in the ancient language, does it not?"

Her brow puckered. She hadn't expected this Khadulian to be familiar with the ancient language. Still, he was right. She was given the name because of the flock of phoenixes that had landed in their garden the day she was born. Thinking back on it now, she wondered if it had been a sign.

"Tori," he continued, not waiting for a response, "I've spent years trying to come up with an answer to my problem. Perhaps fate has given me the alliance I seek."

"I don't know what you mean, and I'm afraid to ask."

"There are a few tasks I need carried out. Tasks that require a skilled, agile, capable person such as yourself to perform. If you are willing, I would need you to go into Avarell."

She laughed, the feel of it abrasive to her throat. "Go into Avarell?"

"I would bring you there myself, of course."

"You expect me to sneak around the queendom and carry out tasks for you? While the Queen's Guard march around, ready to chop a thieving hand and slay any traitor who threatens to defy the realm? I wouldn't last a day."

"You would if you were a member of the Queen's court."

"Ha! Surely you jest."

"I am quite serious. The queen regent is in need of a new High Priestess, as hers was recently found dead."

Tori blanched. "What did she die of?"

"I'm no expert, but I'm quite certain the blade to her ribcage did the trick."

Tori fought to keep her expression neutral. "So, the queen regent needs a High Priestess. But, you see, we've run into our first problem. I am not a High Priestess."

"They do not know that. I can supply you with the robes, the books, everything you need in order to masquerade as a High Priestess of Tokuna."

Something strange stirred and knotted in Tori's stomach—something more than the aggravation she felt toward this man. "You want me to pretend? I've never even been to Tokuna."

"With help, you could pull it off. I have someone on the inside who would serve as your handmaid."

Tori's knees felt weak, but she fought to remain still. She couldn't afford to let Goran see her as vulnerable. "If you've got someone on the inside, why doesn't *she* carry out these tasks for you?"

"Only members of the Queen's court can get anywhere close to the high tower. My person won't be able to do this."

"Why not?"

"She is like me: Khadulian. You know as well as I do that the queen regent does not trust us for more than delivering shipments and performing as servants. And I'm afraid her ears give her away."

Tori's stomach clenched. It was as if her insides were being twisted and torn in half. She thought it was nerves from this encounter with Goran, but now she feared a fever coming on. Now of all times. With her hands balled into fists, she fought off the sick feeling in her stomach and kept her back straight. Sweat beaded at her temples, but still, she remained stoic.

He took a step toward her, concern in his dark eyes. "Are you all right?"

She waved him off. "What's in the high tower?"

"The Queen. At least, that's what we are hoping."

Fear spread through her veins like ice. If Goran wanted her to kill the Queen, all bets were off. "What do you want with the Queen?"

"We have reason to believe she is not ill, as the queen regent has told the citizens of Avarell. In fact, there is question to whether she is, at all, alive."

When Tori had first heard how the Queen had taken ill four years ago, she had suspected it was because of the phoenix fever. But the queen regent, the Queen's sister Lady Maescia, had assured the court it was an infection in her lungs which required strict bed rest. Until the Queen could recover, her sister would stand in her place as regent. The Queen's daughter, the Princess Wrena, could not take the crown until her mother's death. But if Goran was right, if the queen regent had been lying all this time, deceiving the citizens of Avarell and denying Princess Wrena the crown, then there was no telling what her true intentions were.

"If she is dead—?"

Goran nodded once. "Then Princess Wrena would become Her Royal Highness Queen Wrena of Avarell and take her mother's place on the throne."

"And if she is alive but locked in the tower as a prisoner, then the queen regent would be named a traitor to the crown."

"Resulting in not only her removal from the throne, but also her execution."

Tori blinked, her mind swirling. "I'm still not sure what you want me to do."

"Avarell has gone through a rough amount of change in the last four years," Goran said. "The laws Lady Maescia is enforcing are cruel and merciless. I do not know what you have heard, if news of what happens at the royal court travels as far as Sukoshi, but the queen regent's methods of law and punishment are… cold-hearted at best. She clearly doesn't care for the people."

Tori almost scoffed. "*You* care for the people of Avarell?"

"What happens in Avarell affects my people. It affects Khadulan as a nation." Goran scrubbed at his beard. "We have a trading treaty with the Queen—the real Queen. And my fear is what might happen when the queen regent gets too greedy with her power, which is completely foreseeable, considering her latest methods of governing. She's already been rumored to back out of negotiations with other realms. She may start enforcing her laws unto Khadulan. She may draft our people to serve in her wars. I can't let that happen to my people. We need to stop her."

"Why can't you just charge in there with your army and do it yourself?"

"Because that would go against our treaty, the violation of which could impair our agreements with other realms." Goran lowered his head slightly, his eyes still on Tori. "And because they have my daughter."

Tori's mouth opened, but for a moment she couldn't speak. Her face felt flushed, but she wasn't sure if it was because of the fever or from pity. "I'm sorry."

"They took her when a shipment came in damaged. It was… my daughter Hettie… she was the payment. The reimbursement."

"What do you mean?"

"They did not receive what they paid for, and so they turned her into a servant." There were flames in Goran's eyes. "But they will not tell me who she is working for. She's been gone three years now. I'd say that's more than enough time to reimburse them for the damaged goods. I haven't seen her since. I don't even know if she is alive."

"That's awful. And the queen regent ordered this?"

"Yes." Goran's shoulders squared. "But you can get her back for me."

"Back?"

"I need you to find her, rescue her from wherever she is being held, and deliver her to the docks when our ship is due in."

"That sounds risky, at best."

"So does letting your family die of phoenix fever."

A sudden coldness hit Tori's core, both from his words and the illness spreading through her. Goran's eyes narrowed, as if he was trying to read her mind. She averted her gaze, fighting off the pain in her gut. Battling with the ache in her body was the outrage she felt at being put in this position. This man—this enemy of her realm—was asking her to risk her life to help him. But in return, she could be saving her family. She had been about to give up on finding a cure, but here, standing before her, was a proposition that could solve her dilemma.

"And if I do these things, you'll get the cure to my family?"

"And to you, I gather."

She flinched.

"You can't deny it, girl. I see the signs. You've got it too."

"I'm fine."

"Hmm." He paced slowly, as if going over a list in his head. "There is one more thing I will need."

"I hate to ask what."

"There is a grand library in the castle, and in this library, there should be record books."

"Books? What do you need books for?"

"There is one in particular I need." A pained look ghosted his expression. "At the time my daughter was taken, my wife—an extremely bold woman, as the Khadulian females are prone to be—took it upon herself to get Hettie back. She did this without telling me, otherwise I would have stopped her… or helped her. This act was, of course, illegal. And dangerous. I was too late to stop her, so I kept quiet so as not to give her away. But my wife never returned. When I approached the court demanding to know if they knew where my family was, the queen regent told me my wife had been killed. That her body had been thrown into the Rift for committing a crime against the queendom."

Tori wrapped a hand around her middle. "I'm so sorry."

"The problem is, I don't believe it. Wouldn't be the first time a lie was told in the queendom."

"But… what do you think happened?"

"That's what I need the books for. Lady Maescia can lie to my face and lie to the queendom, but if my wife's disappearance served as any financial gain to the queen regent, then it would be in the record books. Contracts must be kept, you see. A proof of sale to prevent a dispute between realms."

"Sale?"

"I believe she was sold into slavery. To whom, I don't know. That's why I need the book noting the sale."

"So you can find her."

He didn't answer. "I need you to find the book and bring it to the ship as well. I don't expect you to do all of these tasks at once, of course. We have a number of deliveries due in to Avarell in the next few months. When I sail in with the shipments, you can meet me at the docks."

A few months. Did her family have that much time? Did she?

"You must promise me you'll give my family and the others infected in Drothidia the cure."

"If all is delivered, you have my word."

Tori clenched her fists, both from frustration and from the pain in her body. "But they are suffering *now*. I can't leave them knowing they could die while I'm away."

"I can give them medicine that will alleviate their symptoms."

"I've been doing that with Sweetwood Root."

He narrowed his eyes. "Ah, but too much Sweetwood Root is damaging to the heart. You replace one illness with another. I can give them something twice as effective to get them back on their feet. And when you complete your tasks, I will provide the cure for all who suffer. Including you."

Tori stared at him, unsure. Could she pull off what he wanted her to do? She had to. What other way was there to save her family and the ill in Drothidia? And, aside from that, she had promised her sister. She remembered the look on Miki's face as she begged Tori to keep looking for a cure. The feel of Miki's hand squeezing hers. And the abysmal loss she felt when Miki had died. Tears filled her throat, but the presence of Goran made her swallow them back.

"Do you accept?" he asked.

She held her hand out and shook his. "I do."

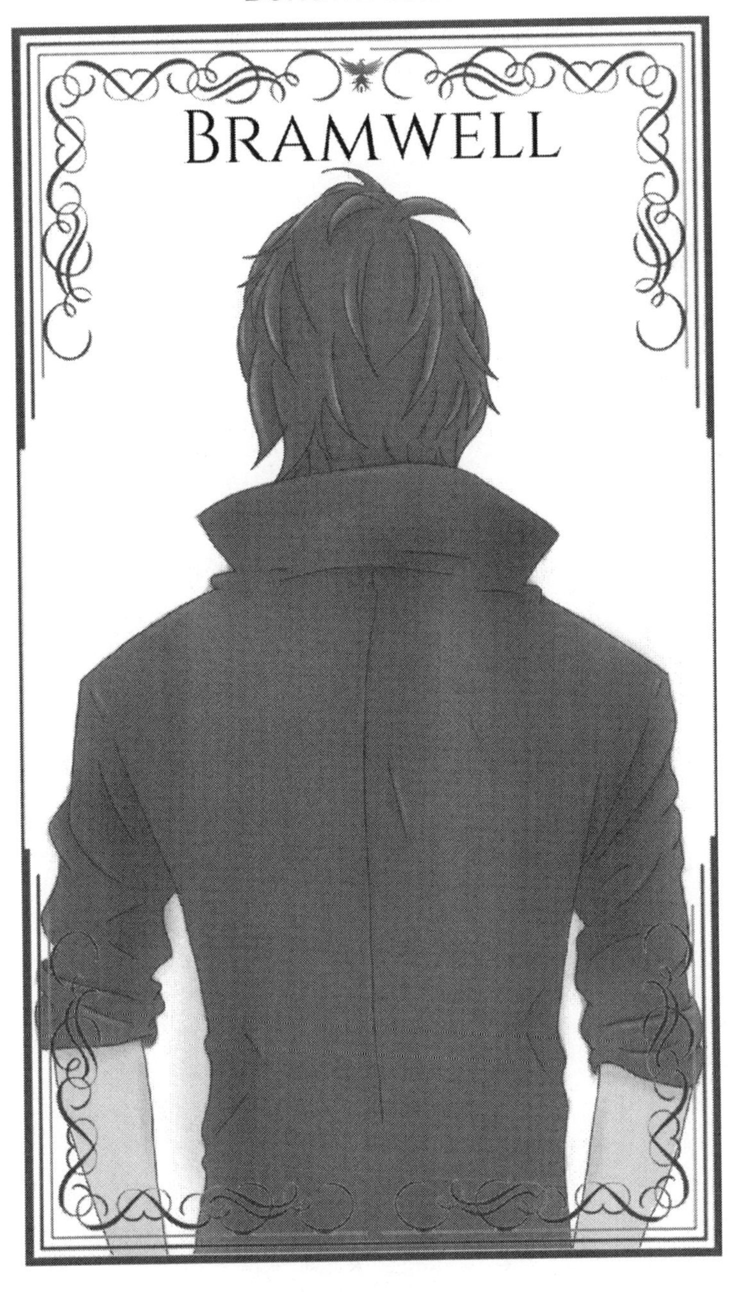
BRAMWELL

CHAPTER FIVE

BRAMWELL STORMBOLT SHOOK the sweat out of his eyes, his grip tight on the hilt of his sword. A loud crack sounded in the training hall as steel smacked against steel, Bramwell's training weapon overpowering his opponent's. He'd been training for over an hour, but he wasn't about to give in to exhaustion. Logan had tricked him in their last match, landing Bramwell a bruised cheek, but this time he was going to get even, best friend or not.

Logan pointed the tip of his sword at Bramwell, the corner of his mouth inching up into a smirk. Bramwell blocked Logan's thrust, feigned a jab, then surged forward with a crouch, the blunt tip of his training sword catching Logan in the side.

With a wince, Logan nodded, then gave Bramwell a wink. "Good one, Bram."

But Bram wasn't done. As Logan limped by him, Bram nicked him in the stomach with the hilt of his sword. Logan let out am oomph that ended in a chuckle.

"Sorry about that, my friend." Bram slapped Logan on the back. "Just making up for my bruised cheek."

"You won't get a promotion by killing me, Corporal," Logan teased. "Duke Grunmire would be rather distraught to lose one of his best men."

"I wouldn't dare." Bram handed his training sword to a page, who carried it away to be stored in the casemate. "But not because of Duke Grunmire. What Azalea would do to me if I were the cause of your end is of greater concern."

Logan looked over at the training match on the other side of the hall where his love, Azalea Clayborne—whom they often called Ace—swung her heavy sword with ease, successfully blocking her opponents attack.

"She's been out here as long as we've been," Bram said. "How does she not look tired?"

"Trust me." There was a cheeky twist to Logan's smile. "It takes a lot to wear her out. I suspect after training I'll be rather busy for the next few hours. She mentioned having some moves she wants to show me in private."

"I'd be careful if I were you," Bram said. "She's quick with a dagger as well."

"Then I'll just have to make sure her hands are busy elsewhere."

Bram shook his head and laughed. "I don't know how she stands you."

"Because I treat her like a lady." Logan nudged Bram in his side. "Maybe if you weren't such a prude and spent more time with Raven, you'd know how relationships work."

"I'm not a prude, but I'm also not a scoundrel."

"I'm not a scoundrel. At least not since I've met Ace. I remain tried and true to her, and I am justly rewarded for my loyalty."

Bram let out a chuckle. "Then I wish you a pleasant afternoon, dear friend."

Logan separated from Bram, approaching Azalea, who removed her helmet, allowing her shoulder-length locks to fall graciously upon her armor. Her smile matched Logan's as he came near enough to kiss her. They refrained from doing so, however, because Duke Grunmire was keeping watch over the training area.

As Captain of the Queen's Guard, the duke was a strict leader, whose priority lay in maintaining a strong, effective army. King Henry Bracken of Avarell had appointed the position to him decades ago, perhaps an indication of his trust in the duke, or perhaps as a favor, since the duke was the King's cousin.

Seven years ago—though the memory was still fresh in Bram's mind—the King mysteriously toppled from a high window of the castle. Rumors were that he was drunk, but others say he was unhappy and jumped. Whatever the reason, the widowed Queen Callista Bracken kept Duke Grunmire on as Captain of the Queen's Guard. And four years ago, when Queen Callista had taken ill, her sister, Lady Maescia, ruling as regent, not only had Duke Grunmire maintain his position, but often sought his counsel in matters of court.

Bram eyed the duke. He had been dwelling on bringing up the matter of a promotion with his captain but had yet to find the proper time to do so. He wondered if the duke had seen his sparring with Logan. Perhaps now would be a good time to approach him. But just as Bram started heading toward him, the duke was approached by Tiberius, the head executioner of the Queen's Guard. Bram quickly readjusted his footing to leave for the barracks. There was no need to compete with whatever Tiberius had to say to the duke.

As he stepped out of the training hall, exhaustion and hunger weighed him down. He made his way down the arched walkway that connected the training hall to the barracks, where the members of the Queen's Guard had their chambers. A fresh breeze blew into the walkway from the courtyard, clearing Bram's head.

As he rounded the corner, he nearly collided with a petite, dark-haired figure of the same slightly-olive coloring as himself. They both stopped short and let out a small laugh.

His cousin Aurora brushed a lock of curls off her shoulder. "Bramwell. I didn't see you there."

"The fault was mine," Bram said with a slight bow. "Where are you off to?"

"The princess sent word that she would like to play a game of cards." Her pink lips curved into a smile. "She is becoming quite skilled and says I'm a worthy partner."

"How generous of you to give her the time."

"Of course. She is the princess, after all. We ladies of the court do have our duties to attend to."

"I imagine your duties will increase tenfold once her engagement to Prince Liam is finalized."

Aurora's gaze fled to over Bram's shoulder. Following her focus, he caught sight of Princess Wrena speaking to Eleazar, the duke's son. The princess stood rather close to him, his head inclined as if she was whispering.

"Are we sure her engagement to Prince Liam will withstand her friendship with Eleazar?" Bram asked.

"What do you mean?"

He looked over his shoulder. Though he was certain the duke was still in the training hall, he didn't want to risk him hear Bram speak of his son. "They seem rather close. Has the princess spoken of him?

"What is there to speak of?" Aurora's tone held sudden irritation.

"I do believe he's taken her on a picnic once or twice, but I am unsure if it means anything."

Aurora shook her head, giving him an annoyed look. "Bram, they have been friends since they were mere babes. Is it unusual for life-long friends to accompany each other on a picnic? Is it unusual for life-long friends to remain just that?"

"Perhaps they are more than friends now."

A wrinkle formed between Aurora's brows. "What do you care? Do you fancy the princess?"

"No. Not that it would matter in the end. The treaty in place to see her wed to Prince Liam of Gadleigh is certain to be finalized soon."

"Yes, I know," she mumbled.

"What is it?"

For a second, Aurora's brow rose. "Truth be told, I'm just not particularly fond of arranged marriages."

"Arranged marriages have been tradition in houses of royalty for centuries."

"And you approve of that? What if you had to marry someone you didn't love?"

"You don't know if they would or would not love each other."

Aurora's gaze dropped momentarily. "Maybe not. But neither does the Queen, or in this case, the queen regent."

"What are you on about? Do you have something against Prince Liam? Or Eleazar, for that matter?"

"No."

"Then what is troubling you? Are you worried for the Princess? I hear Prince Liam is a decent man."

She dipped her head, studying her wringing hands. "Yes, I'm sure he is. I just don't like the idea of people being forced into situations they don't want to be in. I certainly don't want to be told to whom I should be married."

Bramwell smiled at his cousin and stepped closer, putting his arm around her. "Uncle Samuel is a kind-hearted man who only wants you to be happy. I'm sure he would let you choose your suitor yourself."

Bram's uncle, his mother's brother, took Bram in when he was a child. His father had died in battle, and his mother brought Bram to Avarell, where her brother lived, as she did not have the means to support him on her own. Shortly thereafter, Bram's mother died as well—some said from a broken heart. Bram's uncle and aunt raised him then, until his aunt passed away from illness. It was around that time his uncle became injured during battle and was forced to retire from the Queen's Guard. Since then, Bram helped care for Aurora. Though they were cousins, they grew up together as if they were siblings.

She pressed her lips together and let out a *hmm*. Bram couldn't tell from her expression what she was thinking, but he'd always known his cousin to be quite opinionated, and brushed it off as one of her stubborn rants. Aurora straightened, and Bram noticed the princess approaching.

"As lovely as it is to see you," Bram said before the princess was within earshot, "I reek of training and do wish to have a bath."

"Yes, you do put off a stench," she teased. When he laughed, she gave him a playful push. "Of course, cousin. I will see you at dinner."

Content that Aurora no longer appeared angry, Bram relaxed and continued on his course to his chambers. Exhaustion weighed heavily on his shoulders. Upon his return, he was quick to loosen his belt. He sighed as his muscles relaxed. He shrugged off his waistcoat, which was stained with sweat. He opened his door to call a page to fetch hot water for a bath, but was met with a messenger who had a parchment in his hand.

"A letter for you, Master Stormbolt."

"Thank you," Bram said, noting the Gadleigh seal on the envelope.

Though he was born in Gadleigh, he hadn't visited the land since his father died. He had a notion of what words he would find inside the letter, as it wasn't the first time he'd received communication from his birth home.

As he expected, the Captain of the Gadleigh army was requesting that Bramwell reconsider their offer for him to return and join their army. His father had served with them as Commander, and they highly respected him. They had reason to believe Bram would prove a good man and an excellent soldier, just as his father had been. With the union of Prince Liam and Princess Wrena in sight, the eventual unification of the Gadleigh and Avarell armies was inevitable. Captain Thornwood was offering Bram a chance to leap ahead in ranks and lead a brigade of his own.

Back when Bram had come of age, the Captain of the Gadleigh army had sent him a letter asking if he might consider coming back to Gadleigh and joining their ranks. Though it took him some time to reflect upon their offer, his final response was to thank them but rescind. A year and a half later, when a number of their Corporals were killed in battle, they corresponded with him again, stating that they needed to rebuild their army and would be honored if he reconsidered their offer. At the time, he had just been promoted to Corporal and didn't want to muddle his chances in the Avarell army.

Besides, he couldn't dream of leaving Aurora and Logan. He had made a home in Avarell, and he held on to the hope of climbing the ranks in the Queen's Guard. Ultimately, he declined

Gadleigh's second offer, but made certain to keep things on amiable terms. Yet here he stood, years later, with another offer to join Gadleigh's army—including a promotion to a rank higher than even Logan and Eleazar. Would it be betraying his friends to take such a position? Would he be able to achieve it on his own merit? Uncertainty twisted his insides.

If circumstances had been the way they were when Queen Callista reigned, he wouldn't have been considering taking Gadleigh up on their offer. But things were different now.

Since the Queen's illness, the realm had been in transition, the citizens adjusting to the queen regent while feeling insecure about the fate of the Queen. Bram had his doubts on more than one occasion as to how Lady Maescia was ruling the queendom, but he was also a man who believed in second chances and giving people the benefit of the doubt. His utmost hope was that the Queen would fare better soon, regain her strength, and take back the reins from her sister before more damage was done.

But not knowing if that would happen, Bramwell Stormbolt stood at a crossroads.

CHAPTER SIX

HER ROYAL HIGHNESS PRINCESS WRENA lay in the comfort of her bed, her legs wrapped in a tangle of silk sheets as she stared wistfully at her lover. They were sure to be quiet and meet in secret. If anyone found out, there would be a scandal, and not just because she was promised to Prince Liam from Gadleigh.

That marriage arrangement was strictly political, anyway. Some pact her mother made to smooth over ties between Avarell and Gadleigh, as the two realms had gone back and forth on forming an alliance. There were rumors that the neighboring realm of Nostidour, which sat to the south of Gadleigh just beyond the Crystal Islands, was becoming increasingly hostile and growing their army. Some even said they had sent out their savages to battle the forces of the infamous pirate queen, Hira Kaliskan, leader of the Crystal Islands, who in her own right was known to sooner slay those in her path than hear their pleas. Word was their battle ended in bloodshed. However, an alliance between Avarell and Gadleigh would strengthen their numbers, creating a combined army that could not only hold back the forces of the Nostidour army, but defeat them.

She understood why the Queen had signed the deal and why she was expected to uphold her duty, but her heart wasn't in it at all.

Wanting to forget the rest of the world for now, she reached out and played with the small hairs at the nape of her lover's neck. How she wished she could stay like this forever, here with the person she loved without anyone telling her what to do. What good was it to be the princess if all she felt like was a pawn in a game?

A light knock came at her door.

"A moment, please."

She shook her lover's shoulder. "You have to go," she whispered.

Her lover roused, gazing upon her with loving eyes, and took her hand and pressed a kiss upon it before rising from the bed.

Fighting back the urge to ignore the caller at the door, Princess Wrena rushed to dress, as her lover did the same. Her heart pounded from the exhilaration of almost getting caught.

With a gentle touch on a specific spot on the wall, a secret panel opened to a hidden passageway. Princess Wrena sucked in a breath, an ache in her heart at having to part with her lover.

Hearing her soft sigh, her lover turned to her and blew a kiss her way. Princess Wrena pretended to catch the kiss and held her fist to her heart as her lover slipped away into the secret passageway.

Tightening her sash, Princess Wrena opened the door to her chambers, finding a page waiting patiently.

"Your Grace," the page said, "His Highness Prince Theo requests your presence in his chambers."

"Yes, of course. I'll be there at once."

She closed the door and went to her mirror, not wanting to leave her rooms with her hair out of sorts and her clothing crumpled. After making sure everything was in order, she left her rooms and ventured off to find her brother Theo.

She found him on the floor of his rooms surrounded by piles of old trinkets and items she hadn't seen in a very long time. Though Theo was tall for a boy of nine, he appeared quite small amongst the jumble of junk around him.

"What's all this?" Wrena asked.

"I found something," he said, ignoring her question. "I'm not sure what it is."

She wormed her way around the pile of things and took a closer look at what he had in his hands. A sad smile crept upon her face as she realized what it was.

"It's mother's kite." She ran her hand along the material that was formed in the shape of a phoenix. The bright colors of the kite resembled fire. "She made this."

"She made it?"

"Yes. You know, phoenixes were her favorite animal growing up." She moved her fingers along the middle of it until she came to a splintered piece of wood. "But it is broken and no longer flies."

For a moment, Theo merely stared at the kite, the painted eyes of the phoenix gazing back at him. Then suddenly, he turned to Wrena. "Why can't I go see her?"

"What?"

"They let you see her. I'm older now than when she first got sick, and I can handle it."

Wrena reached out and stroked his golden strands of hair. "I know you can, dear brother. But they are not aware of how clever you are, so they only let me see her."

"But I want to see her too. I hardly remember her."

She stroked his head. "I know. It is unfair. But if there's anything you want to know about her, you can ask me. I still remember everything about her. The way she used to be, in any case."

"What was she like?"

"She was beautiful and just. Strong-willed. And she was very good at building kites."

His eyes flit along the features of Wrena's face, and she waited as he absorbed her words. With a sigh, he lifted the kite, studying it. "I'd like to think I've inherited her talent."

"You most certainly did. From what I've seen of the little boats you put together to swim on the lake, you've got a talented hand indeed."

"I'd like to try to make a kite."

She took his hands in hers, squeezing them. "It will be the best kite Avarell has ever seen."

He gave her a warm smile, which twisted at her heart. She leaned in and embraced him, wishing it could have been different, wishing her little brother hadn't had to grow up without his mother, wishing she was strong and well enough to care for them both instead of constantly wondering if she would be strong and well enough to live.

CHAPTER SEVEN

KHADULIANS PROVED TO BE PROFICIENT. Tori hadn't been sure Goran could pull off everything he said he could, but so far, he'd been true to his word. The first evidence of his veracity took place when he brought Tokuna holy transcript books to Sukoshi for her to study. Along with this delivery, he had brought medicine. Not the cure for phoenix fever, but capsules that those affected had to ingest twice a day—morning and night—to keep the symptoms at bay. Tori had been doubtful, but the very next morning, she found her mother in the kitchen, making bread, livelihood in her step and color returned to her face. It was a bittersweet moment, for Tori knew the effects would only last as long as the pills did.

Tori steadied her footing on the bow of Goran's ship, running her hand along the damask cloak draped over her shoulders, the wide hood hanging down her back and the hem almost brushing the floor. Goran had described the color as glaucous blue, but she had only ever seen this hue in the twilight sky after a storm had cleared. The material was as soft and smooth as cherry blossom petals, and she had to force herself to stop stroking it so as not to look like an obsessed fool.

"It's quite lovely, isn't it? It's the traditional cloak of High Priestesses of Tokuna," Goran explained, seemingly proud of himself. Tori wondered if he had gone to a great amount of trouble to get it. She wouldn't put it past him to have stolen it.

"I've read about it," Tori said, her gaze set upon the land the ship was approaching. "I'd just never seen one up close."

"You'll find the trunk we've prepared for you is equipped with a few dresses—the usual garb the High Priestesses don—and in a secret compartment beneath the main one is an entirely different outfit."

He didn't have to explain about that one. She couldn't very well sneak around Avarell at night in her High Priestess clothing. She would need something that would conceal her in the shadows.

"There's also this." He detached a leather pouch from his belt and handed it to Tori. She loosened the ties and peered inside to find it contained over a dozen metal shuriken. She took one out and studied it. "Though your wooden carvings of the weapon are impressive, the metal is sturdier and stronger than wood."

Tori turned the shuriken in her hand, the shiny surface catching the sun. Careful not to touch the sharp tips, she rubbed the weapon between her fingers, noting how finely they had been welded. The edges looked as if they could slice through bone.

"How do you like them?"

She regarded him. "They're magnificent. I may need to practice throwing them, as they are heavier than what I'm used to."

"I'm certain you have the skills to master them in no time. There are also two kunai in the trunk with your hidden outfit."

"Kunai?"

"They are steel daggers, forged of iron, with sharp, leaf-shaped blades. They can be thrown, or you can use them as hand-held weapons. Most Khadulian soldiers strap them to their thighs for quick access. I've supplied sheaths in the trunk as well."

Tori nodded, wondering if she would need to use all the weapons Goran gave her.

Asleep on the deck, Takumi let out a purr, lulled by the movement of the waves. When Tori brought him with her, Goran's first instinct was to protest. But Tori explained that he was able to get in and out of places she would be unable to, and that they had been partners for a long time.

Sea water spritzed up onto the deck, and the rocking of the boat caused Tori's stomach to swirl. As she held a hand to her midsection, Goran walked over to a nearby basket and pulled out a green apple.

"The sea is choppy today," he said, handing her the apple. "It helps with the sea sickness."

She took it from him gladly and sunk her teeth into it, closing her eyes as she waited for the fruit to do its magic.

Though it hadn't been a terribly long journey across the bay to the docks near Capehill Castle in Avarell, Tori was relieved when the deck hands began to call out to each other as they prepared to pull into port. As the men scurried about, Goran turned to her. Though she didn't know the man well, she could swear that it was concern she read in his eyes.

"You've been studying the books given to you on the rituals of High Priestesses and the history of Tokuna?"

"Yes. Thoroughly." Her sister Taeyeon helped quiz her on every topic in the books imaginable, making sure she had memorized as much as she could.

Thoughts of Taeyeon caused a stir in Tori's heart for her family. It pained her to leave them behind, but she had to carry out this mission to save them all. She hoped the medicine Goran supplied them with would continue to relieve their symptoms.

She didn't take stock of the supply he'd left them with, and she had to hope that it was enough until she could secure the remedy. There were too many questions and uncertainties in her head, and she only had Goran's word to go on.

As the ship's anchor dropped, Tori's gaze went upward. The high tower of Capehill Castle could clearly be seen from where she stood. The stone stronghold was adorned with emerald green banners flying in the wind, the Bracken symbol of a growling bear embossed on each one. There weren't many ships in the harbor aside from Goran's, as the treaty in place named Khadulan as Avarell's main source of goods, but fishing boats floated nearby.

Tori bent down and opened her large, sturdy canvas bag. "Takumi," she called.

He opened his eyes and gave out a yawn.

"Time to go," she said, giving him a nod.

At that, he skittered to her, leaped into the canvas bag, and curled into a ball. Handling the bag with care, she wrapped the strap around her shoulder, glad that Takumi remained still while being carried.

Her legs practically wobbled beneath her as she disembarked, her feet uneasy after being on the water for so long. The salty air tossed her hair and her cloak upon the wind, the strong smell of fish wafting about her. She waited as Goran signed in with the dock masters. The ship hands began to unload cargo, and Goran's footmen carried Tori's trunks and other belongings to one side of the dock.

Goran approached her when his business had been attended to. He retrieved a glittery object from his tunic pocket and took Tori's hand. The small locket was cold as it hit her palm.

"You must find Hettie first," he said, the grief from missing his daughter apparent. "This will convince her that you were sent by me to rescue her, for Hettie was never one to trust a soul. It belonged to her grandmother Delores who cared for Hettie for a month when her mother fell ill. I doubt anyone else would know about it. But if you tell her this, she will know you speak the truth. Please find her."

Tori dared not promise out loud. She simply nodded and tucked away the locket.

"We will be back in a week's time with the next delivery. I will be quite disappointed if you don't have a delivery for *me* when I arrive."

"I'll do my best."

One of his men walked up to Goran and handed him a small box.

"Ah, yes." Goran took a velvet pouch out of the box. "There is a pocket on the inside of your cloak. Put this inside."

"What is it?"

"This is in case your heart starts to give out from the phoenix fever."

"Wha— But you've given me my supply of medicine."

"Yes. Be sure you take that every morning and evening. As effective as it is, there is still the chance your heart could fail."

Tori resisted the urge to hold a hand to her chest, as if pressing it there would keep her heart safe. "What's in the pouch, exactly?"

"It is a syringe. Inside the barrel is a powerful chemical that will restart your heart, should the phoenix fever pitch your body into shock. Should your heart begin to fail, the needle must be inserted directly into your heart, and the plunger will deliver the treatment into your blood."

As Tori stood with her jaw agape, Goran's attention shifted to someone approaching over her shoulder. Tori turned to see a thin, older woman about the same height with dark skin.

"Good morning, Goran," the woman called, her voice a raspy tenor.

"Finja," he said to her plainly.

Tori recognized the name. Goran had explained that Finja was his person on the inside, a Khadulian like himself. Her job was to be handmaid to the High Priestess. She had served the last one in the castle, and it was she who had found the Priestess stabbed. The perpetrator, however, was nowhere to be seen. The court covered it up, of course, claiming her food must have been tainted, the ultimate cause of her demise, with no mention of the stab wound in her chest.

"This is Tori Kagari, hereafter to be known as Her Holiness Lady Tori."

Finja did not smile, though somehow Tori did not expect her to. As Finja turned her head to take in the sight of Tori's baggage, Tori noticed a scar that ran across what remained of Finja's left ear, where the pointy tip of her Khadulian ear had apparently been cut off. Tori averted her eyes, wondering what foul creature might have done that to her.

"Finja will be able to fill you in on everything from this point on." Goran slapped a hand onto Tori's shoulder. "Don't forget what you've come here to do. Good luck."

As Finja instructed the footmen to load Tori's belongings into the awaiting carriage, Tori stared after Goran, who had already made his way back onto the ship. She rubbed at her arms, feeling a sense of loss. Aside from Finja, who she'd only known a total of two minutes, Tori was alone. Fear of her family dying was the only thing keeping her from backing out of the deal she made. Setting her jaw and letting out a sigh, she turned away from Goran and his ship and set out to do what she came to do.

CHAPTER EIGHT

"LET US AWAY TO THE CARRIAGE, Lady Tori." Finja reached out her hand as if offering to take the canvas bag slung over Tori's shoulder.

Tori tightened her grip on the strap. "I'll keep this with me, if you don't mind."

"As you wish. It's this way." She motioned for Tori to follow her. "Take note of the Queen's Guard at the port exit. They monitor the imports and exports and make sure everything is in order. Not just cargo, but people, too. Goran gave you your papers, yes?"

"Yes."

"Then let this be the first test of your acting abilities."

Though intimidated by the boxy looking men in their armor, Tori straightened her back and put on a confident face. In order to make them believe she was the person detailed in the papers she carried, she would have to almost believe it herself.

"Papers," was all the guard said as he held a palm out to Tori.

She handed the paperwork over, keeping steady eye contact with the guard as he studied her.

"You're a long way from Tokuna. Shouldn't you be coming in from the north by carriage instead of down south by sea?"

Tori kept her chin up but decided to flash a peaceful smile. "I had some business to attend to in the Crystal Islands. Rituals for the dead. If you'd like to see my transcription journals, I'd be happy to provide you with them."

The soldier's face sobered at her mention of the Crystal Islands. "No, that won't be necessary."

"May the Divine Mother bless your house," Tori said with a slight bow.

"Thank you, Your Holiness." He said, handing back the paperwork. "And welcome to Avarell."

Tori and Finja continued toward the carriage, not for a second abandoning their ruse, and it wasn't until they were out of earshot before Finja leaned closer to her and said, "Impressive."

The coach driver opened the carriage door upon seeing her approach. It was a struggle for her to gather the skirts of her dress and the length of her cloak in order to fit through the door, but she managed to do so without knocking her canvas bag about—to Takumi's benefit. Finja climbed in after her, still void of any expression, and kept her gaze out the window.

As they pulled away from the docks, the ride became smoother, and the sound of the horses' hoofs clopping against the road became louder. Where the paths in Sukoshi were laid with dirt and small pebbles, the streets of Avarell were constructed of hard stone. The carriage journeyed through the towering archway of the city entrance. Tori soaked in the sights, marveling at how different Avarell was from Drothidia—and even from Khadulan. The city was thriving, and from the look of all the people gathered at the fish stands, the butcher shops, the taverns, and inns, business was booming.

There were hordes of people everywhere. Tori could hardly believe so many people existed in the world. The colors of the clothes they wore covered a spectrum much wider than she was used to seeing. And the shops along the road sold things she had never even heard of.

"Have you lived here long?" Tori asked, still taking in the view.

At first Finja did not answer, but when Tori turned to face her, she let out a frustrated sigh. "I've served the last two High Priestesses. I was originally hired by Queen Callista, but when Lady Maescia sat regent, I was kept on. The first High Priestess took her leave shortly after Queen Callista fell ill, but no one knows exactly why. Word is she went to look upon the Queen, said a blessing, and headed back to Tokuna. The second High Priestess I served was killed—as Goran must have informed you—but to this day, it is considered an accidental poisoning."

"Did you tell no one what you saw?"

"I'm not a fool. Someone killed that woman. Someone who had not been caught. If I were to speak up, I could be next."

Tori nodded, catching the fear and the scorn in Finja's eyes. "Right."

"Instead, I went to Goran. I met his ship when it next came into port and told him my suspicions that the queen regent was behind the High Priestess's murder."

Tori swallowed back a gritty taste in her mouth. "Why would she do that?"

"I'm afraid I was not present for every meeting the High Priestess had with Lady Maescia, but I do know that their last meeting did not end well. Lady Lyandra was quite nervous after that meeting, and the next time I saw her, she was dead. Not that Lady Maescia lifted the blade herself, mind you; she has enough people under her control to do the dirty work."

"It's a horrible thought."

"It's a horrible truth." Finja scratched at the scar near her ear. "But Goran and I discussed ways in which to bring justice to Lady Lyandra and the Queen. And the citizens of Avarell."

"So, all this time, you haven't seen the Queen?"

"No. She is under medical supervision by Lady Maescia and every apothecary she can find to aid her sister."

"But if the Queen is being held prisoner—or dead, which seems highly unlikely—then why go through all the trouble of bringing in apothecaries?"

Finja narrowed her eyes. "That is a good question among many unsolved."

Tori kept her gaze on Finja, but her mind was spinning with questions. "And what of Hettie? Goran's daughter? Have you not caught sight of her?"

"No. We suspect whoever is keeping her is calling her by a different name to elude Goran or anyone who knows him. If she is still a servant—and still alive—she must be being kept secluded, serving her master without leaving his quarters."

"Like a prisoner."

Finja nodded. "Exactly."

Tori played with the hem of her cloak, mustering the determination to find Hettie. She didn't know how she was going to do it, but Akihiro Shung had always taught her to use her head before she used her muscles. She would figure out a way.

They soon approached the immense doors of Capehill Castle, the stone façade so light grey in the sunlight it was almost silver. Past the doors, the castle was like a magnificent beast, five block towers nesting upon a maze of covered walkways, high stone ramparts that looked out on the city, and on the western wall, the high tower, standing proud in the dancing shadow of the Bracken flag.

The carriage crossed the stone bridge that stood over the Capehill Brook, and as it came to a halt before the main entrance, Tori let out a shuddered breath. She clenched her fists, forcing herself to breathe easier, though inside she was a jumble of knotted nerves and nausea.

"The footman will help you out," Finja instructed, opening the door and exiting before Tori could react.

Tori cracked open her bag. "We're here, Takumi. Be a good boy and stay still and quiet until I can let you out."

Takumi blinked and buried his head in the bag, and she took this to mean he understood.

The footman who helped her out of the carriage did not make eye contact, and Tori wondered if the status of High Priestess was a position that implied she was esteemed. In truth, the footman was her equal, and it gave Tori a strange feeling to be treated as though she was better than anyone else. But it came with the ruse, so she held her head high and followed the footman to the castle doors.

The first thing that caught her eye as she stepped into the atrium were the lights. Electricity was still a fresh, new thing to her, and it fascinated her to see so many fixtures in one room. Above her head hung a circular contraption where hundreds of tiny bulbs were mounted, giving the appearance that the atrium was filled with sunlight. On the walls, crystal sconces lit the way down long corridors.

Below her feet, the marble floors shined as if recently polished. A great oak staircase spiraled in a semi-circle at the end of the atrium, leading to a higher landing, each step cushioned with emerald green carpeting. She had never been in the presence of such luxury, and she was finding it quite difficult to keep from gaping at it all.

Finja was suddenly at her side, elbowing her. "Look alive. Here comes the seneschal."

A woman in a long grey dress with a wimple of light lavender cloth covering her hair came toward her from one of the corridors. "Welcome, Your Holiness."

Tori dipped into a slight bow, unfamiliar with the gesture but hopeful that it appeared authentic.

Out of the corner of her eye, she spotted servants taking her trunks and other belonging to another part of the castle. One of the servants held his hand out to take her canvas bag. Finja, apparently sensing Tori's apprehension of releasing the bag, nodded at her. "Not to worry, Your Holiness. I will personally bring the bag to your rooms."

Tori forced a relaxed face and handed the bag to Finja, hoping Takumi would keep still until safe in her rooms. She watched for a moment as Finja joined the servants in their duties, then turned her attention to the seneschal.

"I am Miss Geneva, the seneschal of Capehill Castle," the woman said. She seemed friendly enough, which allowed Tori to relax a bit. "I'm in charge of the of domestic arrangements and the administration of servants."

"Pleased to meet you, Miss Geneva."

"Lady Maescia asked me to see you in. Do not fret about your belongings; the servants will see them safely to your rooms where I'm certain your handmaid will organize everything for you. Lady Maescia's original plan to meet with you in private has been postponed due to an unexpected trial, so if you would follow me, I can escort you to the courtyard."

"Yes, of course." Tori had a strange feeling in the pit of her stomach. On the one hand, Tori felt she had a little more time to prepare herself to meet the queen regent face to face. On the other hand, her plans were already going off course, which made her anxious.

She kept pace with Miss Geneva, taking in the grand paintings that hung on the walls and luxurious, velvet-upholstered chairs along the way.

"Lady Maescia will meet with you directly, of course—later, in her sitting room for a private interview. I will send a page to escort you as soon as the trial is over."

Tori was about to respond, but Miss Geneva stopped short and opened a large door that led out to the courtyard. Standing sentry just outside the door was a tall soldier with unruly hair. He stood with his back to them until they approached, at which point he turned to face Tori. Something inside of her fluttered, like a surge of adrenaline tingling through her body. His face was so familiar, but Tori couldn't put a finger on where she might have seen him before.

"Master Stormbolt, this is Lady Tori, the High Priestess who has come to interview with Lady Maescia."

Master Stormbolt bowed. "Your Holiness, I'm afraid the timing of your arrival isn't optimal. The queen regent is about to announce a verdict in a criminal trial."

"Yes, of course," Tori said, every ounce of her resolve concentrated on keeping her front. "Court business must be seen to. I understand."

Miss Geneva bowed to Tori. "If you'll excuse me, I must see to the kitchen staff."

"Thank you, Miss Geneva," Tori said, returning her bow.

"We have a place for you to sit," Master Stormbolt said. "I'm afraid it isn't with the rest of the court, for the seats filled rather quickly. But it's comfortable and not too crowded. It will only be until the verdict is announced."

"Of course. Thank you, Master Stormbolt."

He led her to a section of chairs where citizens were seated, one spot left empty for her. The people seated around her were dressed in elaborate garb, and Tori gathered they were Lords and Ladies of the realm. Each of the nobles had a sour-looking expression on their face as they looked upon a young woman standing before the queen regent. Master Stormbolt gave Tori a slight bow, and then returned to his post at the entrance to the courtyard. Studying his profile, she knew she had seen him before. But it wasn't as if she had seen many citizens of Avarell in her life. In fact, the last time she came into contact with an Avarellian was…

Could he really be the boy she saved in the Rift? He would be about twenty-one if she had guessed correctly that the boy had been approximately sixteen back then. She would estimate Master Stormbolt to be that age. She could be wrong, but there was a chance it was him. Of course, it didn't change her mission or affect it in any way. There was no use pondering over it aside from nostalgia and the phenomenon of chance.

"Please state your name for the royal court." The magistrate's voice boomed through the courtyard, the bass of it pulling Tori's attention to the trial at hand.

"Allwyn Mowbray," the woman said. She had a plain beauty about her. There was a slight tang to her voice, giving her words a strange, nasal sound.

Across from her, perched in elegant thrones which sat on a dais, two women studied Allwyn Mowbray. In the bigger, more elaborate throne, sat a woman with dark blond hair swept up with jeweled pins, a decorative nest for the gold crown upon her head. Tori took in the sight of Lady Maescia, the queen regent of Avarell. Her mouth sat in a straight line, and the look in her eyes was a mixture of contempt and boredom. Beside her, a younger woman—approximately Tori's age—clasped her hands upon the silk skirts of her gown as she sat bone-still on the smaller throne. The dainty crown upon her head was only slightly more golden than her hair, which was partially sectioned into a perfect braid, the remainder of her glorious locks flowing down to below her shoulders. While the queen regent focused intently on the woman being questioned, Princess Wrena's eyes tended to travel elsewhere, as if scrupulously taking in all the faces in the crowd.

"Miss Mowbray," the magistrate continued, pacing between Allwyn Mowbray and the royals. "You are being accused of theft of property belonging to a Lord. How do you plead?"

Allwyn Mowbray wrung her hands. "I didn't want to do it, sir. I was made to do it. I was made to do it all."

"Made?" The magistrate looked her over.

"Made by whom?" The voice was quite shocking to hear, and Tori leaned forward a bit in her chair to take a closer look. The queen regent, Lady Maescia herself, had asked the question.

Allwyn Mowbray looked over into the crowd, her gaze landing on a man twisting his cap between his stubby fingers.

"The queen regent has asked you a question, Miss Mowbray." The magistrate joined his hands behind his back. "Will you deny her an answer?"

"No, sir." She scrubbed a hand across the back of her neck. "It… it was my father."

"Your father made you steal from Lord Varcarry?"

"Well, he…"

"Answer the question, Miss Mowbray." The magistrate's voice became significantly louder.

"Yes, sir. He made me do it. You see, Lord Varcarry, he was hinting that he wouldn't mind some intimacy between us. At first I wasn't interested. I don't much care for older men. But then my father caught wind of it, and—you see—he told me that if I did what the old man wanted, I'd have access to his riches. That an old guy like that would most likely sleep like the dead after the deed was done, and I'd be off with his things, quick as a whip."

More than once the crowd let out gasps and murmurs. Tori was appalled. Not only because the woman would give up her innocence over some gold, but that her father encouraged her to do so.

"Miss Mowbray, do you have anything else to say before receiving your sentence from the queen regent?"

Allwyn Mowbray swallowed visibly, her eyes darting between the magistrate, the queen regent, and her father in the crowd. "N-no, sir."

The queen regent shifted in her chair, her gaze never straying from the woman. After a moment, she looked over at her niece, Princess Wrena, and then to the tall, brutish-looking man standing guard near her throne. Tori assumed the man to be the captain of the Queen's Guard, Duke Grunmire. Though he was her advisor, the man said nothing, merely awaiting the queen regent's word. Tori wondered if his eyes were delivering whatever message Lady Maescia anticipated. After a second, the duke turned to face the accused woman, but remained sentry at the queen regent's side.

Allwyn Mowbray twitched as Lady Maescia dropped her gaze upon her. The entire courtyard was silent.

"Miss Mowbray," the queen regent said. "For the crime of theft upon a Lord in the realm of Avarell, you are hereby sentenced to the Rift."

"No!" It was the woman's father who had shouted. Allwyn's head dropped into her hands, sobs blurted out through her fingers. "No, she should not be punished," her father yelled. "It was my fault. Punish me instead. It was my doing. I beg of you, Your Grace!"

As the man pushed himself forward, Duke Grunmire unsheathed his sword and pointed it at the man. "I'd stop where I stood if I were you," the duke said.

The man stopped short and raised his hands. "I surrender myself, my Lord. Please." With a shaking bottom lip, he faced the queen regent and the princess. "I beg of you. Take me instead."

Lady Maescia raised a hand, her face remaining stoic. "Silence."

The crowd, which had begun its mumbling and murmuring again, grew still.

"Mister Mowbray, what kind of ruler would I be if I were to let every thief, every criminal in Avarell, decide what sentence they receive for their crimes?"

The man simply stood there quivering, wringing his hat in his hands.

"I do like your idea, however," Lady Maescia said. Allwyn's head surfaced from her hands, her red eyes wide. Her father's jaw dropped, his bottom lip still quivering. "Mister Mowbray, you are hereby sentenced to be dropped into the Rift."

"Father!" the woman shrieked as the Queen's Guard seized him.

"And as for your daughter," Lady Maescia continued, a brow arched, "she will be hanged."

Allwyn practically collapsed to the ground, but two of the Queen's Guard were quick to pick her up, dragging her away to the gallows. The men who held her father dragged him in the opposite direction, their hold on him strong despite his flailing and kicking.

CHAPTER NINE

TORI COULD BARELY BREATHE, for the outcome of the trial shocked her so. Goran had said that the queen regent had strange and cruel ways of dealing with criminals, but never had she imagined something like this. Still, she didn't have a moment to dwell on it. Before her stood Master Stormbolt, who gave her a slight bow.

"Your Holiness," he said. His voice didn't seem as strong as it did before he seated her. Perhaps he was also surprised by the outcome.

She offered him a small smile and stood.

"If you would follow me," he said.

"I was told a page would escort me to the queen regent's sitting room," she said, following him out of the courtyard and back into the castle.

"I can escort you myself, Your Holiness. It is no trouble."

"Thank you. And please, call me Lady Tori."

"Lady Tori," he repeated, bowing his head slightly. "So, you've arrived from Tokuna?"

"Actually, I came by sea," Tori answered, knowing the port records would show she arrived at the docks. It would do no good to start with such an easily-checked lie. "I was called upon to lead a holy service in the Crystal Islands."

Tori noticed how Master Stormbolt's eyes widened. The Crystal Islands were notorious for being inhabited by pirates, and anyone who even came near to the likes of the infamous pirate queen, Hira Kaliskan, was likely to be courageous.

"From there I came by ship, courtesy of the Khadulian shipping company."

"Then you must be exhausted. That is quite a long journey."

"Yes. It was. But I am bound to my duties, and I am grateful for the opportunities presented to me."

"How long have you been a High Priestess?"

"I was brought to Tokuna when I was twelve." This lie she knew he couldn't check. Tokuna did not keep record of High Priestess study durations, only certificates of study completion, which Goran took care of.

"Twelve? So young. And you knew it was your calling from that age?"

"Yes. The Divine Mother called me to her house." Tori was prepared for these questions, thanks to the book Goran had supplied and Taeyeon's constant quizzing.

He stopped in front of a set of white double doors adorned with gold leafing. He nodded to the two guards stationed at the doors, then turned to Tori. "This is the royal sitting room. The queen regent will meet with you inside."

"Thank you."

The guards opened the double doors for her, and Tori stepped inside. The sitting room was equally luxurious as everything she had seen of the castle so far. How could anyone have so many riches? And where did it all come from? Plush chaise lounge chairs formed a seating area where the queen regent's ladies-in-waiting sat, though Tori wondered if the ladies were actually those of Queen Callista's, literally waiting for her to be on the mend. Two of them were listening to one with thick, silky, black hair go on about a soldier she fancied, the three of them sipping wine from gold goblets.

In the biggest and most decorative lounge chair sat Lady Maescia. Up close, she appeared younger than Tori imagined she would look, with smooth skin and rich, full lips. Or perhaps it was wealth and positions of power that bought the secrets to keeping your youth. Two handmaidens combed and pinned up Lady Maescia's hair as another applied a powder to her face. The princess rested on a nearby chair, reading a book.

"Ah, Your Holiness," Lady Maescia said, sitting a bit more upright but not standing. The handmaidens continued their work. There wasn't an actual smile that surfaced on Lady Maescia's face, but one side of her mouth curved up unnaturally. Perhaps the lack of expression was so she would not ruin her powdering, Tori thought.

The ladies-in-waiting all turned to see Tori enter. They rose to their feet and curtsied, all the while studying Tori's gown and cape. And perhaps the slant of her eyes.

Tori placed her hands together as if she were praying and gave a slight bow. As she took a few steps closer to the queen regent, she fell into a full curtsey. "Your Highness." She straightened, nodding her head once. "Please call me Lady Tori."

"Thank you, Lady Tori. And you can address me as Lady Maescia. I'm afraid 'Your Highness' is reserved for my sister, the Queen, or my niece, the Princess Wrena." She motioned to the princess. Princess Wrena looked up from her book and gave Tori a polite nod. "Though 'Your Grace' is acceptable."

"Yes, Your Grace."

"What luck we have that we can be honored with your presence at this particular time. Our former High Priestess unfortunately passed on due to an allergic reaction. Something she ingested, according to the court coroner."

A coroner who was most likely paid a handsome sum by the queen regent. Goran had told Tori that the last High Priestess had been stabbed. Did Lady Maescia's lies mean she was involved? Or was she simply trying to keep the reputation of the queendom impeccable?

The ladies-in-waiting shook their heads slowly, remorse apparent on their perfect features.

"We were quite saddened by her death," Lady Maescia said as she waved away the perfume one of her handmaidens sprayed in her direction. "Lady Lyandra held eloquent liturgies, and since her death, the court has felt rather lost. The people have been expecting a replacement for their holy prayer assemblage. Their connection to the Divine Mother is very important, and they need a solid bond to Her. And a Queen's court is never complete without a High Priestess. Not having one is like inviting demons into the castle."

Tori nodded once. "I would be happy to supply that bond, Your Grace."

"You must stay on a few days while I make my assessment of you. It would be unwise for me to take you into the court without knowing more about you. You do understand?"

"Of course. It is very wise of you, Your Grace."

One of the ladies made a noise, and Tori turned to see that the dark-haired lady-in-waiting had spilled wine on the lounge chair she was sitting on. The look on her face when the queen regent turned her way was one of horror. "Oh, my stars, Your Grace. I'm terribly sorry."

Lady Maescia set her jaw and took a long breath in through her nostrils, her brow raised at the young woman. "Would it have been the first time you had this accident, I would have understood. But no, Raven, this is the third time. If you cannot be trusted with wine near the royal furniture, you may not be invited to sit with us at all."

Princess Wrena looked up again from her book. "Raven, it's quite all right."

"I would think your mother would say differently," Lady Maescia said to the princess. "I was with her when she went to the trouble of picking out the perfect fabric for these chairs."

The princess twisted her lips, but whether it was from knowing her aunt was right or a reaction from her aunt overdramatizing, Tori could not tell.

"Your Grace," Raven said, snatching a serviette from a nearby table and attempting to blot up the wine. "I'm terribly, terribly sorry. I'd only become excited to welcome Her Holiness to the court."

"Do stop your blubbering, Raven. It's embarrassing."

Raven closed her mouth and stood, curtseying. "My apologies, Lady Tori. Lady Maescia."

Almost rolling her eyes, Lady Maescia turned to Tori. "My apologies as well, Lady Tori. I have just realized that you've arrived after supper was served. You must be hungry."

"No, your Highness." What Tori felt more than hunger was exhaustion. "The Divine Mother often has us fast. We've gone days without eating, so I've grown accustomed to skipping meals. But I do appreciate your considerate nature."

"Fasting for days? How diligent." Lady Maescia shooed away her handmaidens. "We shall speak more tomorrow. For now, you must be weary from your travels."

"Shall I escort Her Holiness to her rooms, Your Grace?" Raven asked, obviously trying to compensate for ruining the furniture. "I believe Miss Geneva is sorting the night staff at the moment."

"Thank you, Raven, but I'd like to stretch my legs a bit. One bad thing about becoming queen regent is everyone automatically thinks I'm suddenly too old to move. I assure you, I still have many years left in me."

Raven blanched. "I'm terribly sorry if I offended you, Your Grace."

She waved Raven away with a dismissive hand. "I will take her myself. Plus, I could use the fresh air."

"Of course, milady."

Lady Maescia stood, her skirts ruffling around her. Tori followed her out of the room and was led down the hall. Everywhere they went, servants opened doors for them. They made their way down an outdoor covered walkway that connected this part of the castle to another building within the castle walls. The entire castle seemed to be made up of a number of stone buildings, sitting safely within the outer wall, all connected by walkways that were open to the courtyard. Above them were the ramparts, supported by stone arcading. A breeze carried the sweet smell of honeysuckle through the air. Tori looked up at the starry sky. It wasn't as vast in the number of stars as it was back home, but it was still beautiful, especially from within the comfort of the castle.

As they walked, Lady Maescia asked the same questions Master Stormbolt had asked, to which Tori rattled off her rehearsed answers. Inwardly, she wondered how many times she would have to repeat the story.

"This is the door that leads to your rooms," Lady Maescia said as she stopped at the end of the walkway.

"Thank you, Your Grace."

"I will see you at morning's meal." Lady Maescia dipped her head slightly and left Tori's side.

She climbed one flight of stairs and came to another door, which was unlocked. Inside, she found a small sitting room with a sofa in front of a fireplace. Behind the room was a bed chamber, and a door that led to a wash room. There was also an archway that led to a small balcony which overlooked the courtyard. She had expected something small to house a High Priestess, but the apartment was huge compared to Tori's home in Sukoshi. She could fit her whole family in it with room to spare. She noticed a lever on the wall near the door, and when she flipped it, the bulbs of light came on in the room. She would still need to get used to being around electricity, she thought to herself. It reminded her of an open flame, and growing up in the woods, they were taught to always be careful of open flames.

The door to the apartment suddenly opened, and Tori turned to find Finja enter the room.

"So you survived your first meeting with the queen regent," Finja said, her expression void of emotion.

"Yes. She was actually kind to me."

Finja scoffed. "Of course she was. Let's see what tomorrow brings. She's going to put you to the test, so keep alert."

"What kind of test?"

"High Priestesses are given the gift of *sight* by the Divine Mother, and Lady Maescia will expect you to have it."

Tori nodded. It was something that had been troubling her, but she had hoped to avoid the subject in the presence of the queen regent.

"Don't fret," Finja said. "Goran and I discussed this. I will help you."

"How, exactly? Do you have the *sight*?"

"Not like that of High Priestesses, no. But I do get visions. I will have to get close enough to the queen regent to lay my hands upon her. If I can get a glimpse of something, you can use it to trick her into thinking you have the sight."

"Lay your hands on her? How will you manage to do that?"

Finja shrugged. "Goran partnered with me because of my ingenuity. I'll think of something."

A thump sounded in the apartment, and Tori noticed movement by her bags on the floor. Finja let out a cry as Takumi emerged and skittered across the room. He made a clicking sound and placed his front paws on Tori's dress. Finja hurried to grab a fireplace poker and raised it as if to strike the fox.

Tori rushed forward and stood between Finja and the fox. "No, don't!"

"You know of this beast?"

Tori held up her hands to stop Finja from swinging at him with the fire poker. "This is Takumi."

Finja's brow puckered. "It has a name?"

"He does. He's my fox."

Finja lowered the poker and snickered. "He won't stand a chance in this castle. You know the Queenshunt sometimes brings home foxes?"

Tori smirked and opened the balcony door. Takumi was quick to run out, jumping upon the railing and disappearing into the night.

"Takumi is no ordinary fox. He'll be fine."

"You're sure he'll be back?"

"He never fails me."

Finja pursed her lips. "I was told Drothidians were a strange breed. Now I see why."

"No stranger than Khadulians."

Finja let out a *hmph* and returned the poker to the fireplace. "Do you need any help getting ready for bed?"

"No, thank you." She considered Finja. "I understand you are under the *false* pretense of being my handmaid, so I don't expect you to perform such duties when we are alone."

"Still," Finja said, rolling up her sleeves, "I should do what I can to keep up the illusion."

"That's fine." Tori held back a yawn. "But if you could leave me for tonight, we can continue our charade in the morning."

Finja nodded, her lips pressed together. Tori could tell by Finja's eyes that she hadn't yet gained her trust. "Goodnight, then, Lady Tori."

"Goodnight."

As soon as Finja was gone, Tori glanced at her trunk. She was curious about the outfit and the weapons hidden there, but exhaustion kept her from taking a look. As dizziness began to cloud her vision, she remembered she needed to take her phoenix fever medicine. Popping the capsule in her mouth, she swallowed it dry, and then went out onto the small balcony that looked over the courtyard. In the distance, the city lights shone brightly. The sun had just set, a subtle glow lining the horizon over the city. Judging by where the sun had set, Tori calculated the direction in which Drothidia was located, and closed her eyes.

CHAPTER TEN

An hour of parrying and lunging, advancing and deflecting, took a toll on Bram's muscles. He stretched out his arms and bent his neck from side to side. Eleazar, the duke's son, was certainly a commendable opponent. And he knew it.

"Had enough?" Eleazar asked, his playful smile taunting Bram.

"Yes, I better quit while I'm ahead," Bram answered.

"Ahead?" Eleazar let out a laugh.

"Yes, well, I am still able to move." Bram turned in his sword and wiped the sweat off his brow. "Truth be told, I found it much harder taking on Azalea."

Eleazar and Bram turned toward Azalea, who was sparring with Logan and winning.

Sharp footsteps echoed in the hall as the duke approached them. "Gather round, troops. I have news from Gadleigh."

At the mention of the realm, Bram tensed. He tried to read the duke's expression, wondering if they had called Bram out—or perhaps someone had found the letter that had been sent to him. But he couldn't decipher anything from the duke's ever-present scowl.

"The stormwatchers predict unpleasant weather within the coming weeks," the duke said as the rest of the men and Azalea gathered around him. "Therefore, the royal court of Gadleigh has moved up their arrival date. They are due to arrive within the week to discuss the final engagement arrangements between Prince Liam and Princess Wrena. I will need twice the guards stationed at all entry points to the castle. We will also have to arrange a Queenshunt in order to provide game for the feast."

Bram's eyes instinctively went to Eleazar. It might have been his imagination, but the duke's son tensed at the mention of Prince Liam. Though Aurora denied there was anything between them, Bram felt that something was being hidden.

As the duke went on briefing his army, Bram realized that the arrival of the royal court of Gadleigh meant that Captain Thornwood would also be in attendance. Bram had not yet returned an answer to the captain's proposal, and Bram had a feeling their written correspondence would turn into a face-to-face meeting.

The duke dismissed his guards, and Bram strode along with Logan and a few others as they headed for the barracks.

"A week early," Logan said. "I bet that didn't go over well with Lady Maescia. You know how she expects her welcoming banquets to be perfect."

Tiberius, the stoutest of the group, clapped Eleazar on the back. "Not to mention how nervous Princess Wrena must be to have her fiancé arrive so soon."

Eleazar cast Tiberius a quick glance. "Princess Wrena is a dignified lady. Nervous though she may be, I'm sure she'll handle herself with charm and poise."

"Is she nervous, then?" Bram asked. "Has she said so?"

"Why ask me?" Eleazar didn't make eye contact with Bram… or anyone for that matter.

"You've been friends a long time," Bram said. "You seem to spend a lot of time together."

"Yes, we are close friends."

"So much that this visit from Prince Liam would… upset you?" Bram prodded.

"On the contrary."

Bram knew better not to push the subject, but his curiosity was eating at him. "Do you know something you are not telling the rest of us, Eleazar?"

Eleazar stopped, finally looking Bram in the eye. "If I did, there would be no reason to divulge it here and now. Why don't you wait until after the Gadleigh court visits?"

"Well, now I'm curious," Logan said.

"Does this have something to do with the Princess's engagement?" Bram asked.

"Bramwell, you ask many questions. You might want to reconsider how you speak to me. You never know how high I may climb one day."

Bram rubbed at the scruff on his chin. "I have a feeling you're not only referring to becoming the Captain of the Queen's Guard one day."

"From simple men come the virtues of kings," Logan said, his head held high in mockery.

Eleazar shook his head and pushed Logan aside.

"If I didn't know any better," Bram said, "I would think you intend on stealing the Princess away from Prince Liam."

"And why not?" Tiberius said, clapping Eleazar on the back again. "She'd be a fool not to fall for him. How could she resist his charms?"

"That's enough," Eleazar said, sounding more tired than upset. "We shouldn't be assuming anything about the princess. What she does and how she feels is her business, not ours."

"Well, maybe some of our business," Tiberius joked as he broke away from the group and headed to his chambers. "Maybe some more than others."

"Idiot," Eleazar mumbled.

"Don't mind him," Logan gave Eleazar a smirk. "He thinks himself funny, but no one has the heart to tell him otherwise."

Bram considered Eleazar, feeling guilty for prodding. He let his curiosity get the best of him, when the truth was it didn't matter if Eleazar was or was not in a relationship with Princess Wrena. As soon as she was wed to Prince Liam, whatever they might have had together would come to an end. "Eleazar, I apologize. I did not mean to offend."

Eleazar clapped him on the shoulder and nodded. "No offense taken, Bramwell."

"Please forgive me."

"You are forgiven. And I bid you a good night."

"I wish you a good rest, my friend," Logan said to Bram, nodding to him as he departed with Eleazar.

As Bram watched him walk away, he heard heavy footsteps coming from the other end of the walkway. He turned to see the duke coming in his direction, his head down and eyes far away. It was as good a time as any to speak with him, and there was no one around to interrupt them. Bram stepped forward and squared his shoulders.

"Duke Grunmire," Bram said, "Might I have a word?"

The duke slowed his pace and regarded Bramwell. "What is it, Corporal?"

"My Lord, I've been meaning to speak with you about applying for a promotion."

"Didn't we just upgrade you to corporal a few months ago?"

"No sir. It's going on two years now."

"Oh, I see." The duke cleared his throat and linked his hands behind his back. "Yes, I have noticed an improvement in your form. You will have to endure the review procedures before a climb to Lieutenant can be awarded, of course."

"Of course, sir."

"I do seem to have in mind that you've been a bit unfocused lately. Could there be any reason behind such behavior?"

"No, sir," Bram fought back the heat that flushed his neck and cheeks. "Nothing, sir. If anything, I feel more focused than ever." Bram hoped the duke could not tell it was a lie. There were so many things on his mind as of late that he rarely got a full night's sleep.

"Very well, then." The duke nodded, his hands unhooking from behind him. "We should be able to schedule a review soon."

"Thank you, Duke Grunmire."

The duke offered him a courteous smile as he continued on his way, but Bram wondered if he would hold true to his word. It wouldn't be the first time his request had slipped through the cracks. Perhaps he would simply have to be more persistent in his efforts this time.

As he passed the courtyard toward his quarters, his attention went up to the night sky. It wasn't the moon or the stars that caught his eye, but a beautiful woman standing on her balcony. His breath caught as he took in the sight of Lady Tori staring out over the city. Her cloak hood no longer sat upon her head. Her dark hair blew freely in the wind. How lovely she looked. And Bramwell Stormbolt could have sworn he had seen her before.

CHAPTER ELEVEN

SUNLIGHT STREAMED IN THROUGH the gauze curtains in her bedchamber, casting a golden glow on everything it touched. Tori felt something cold tapping her arm and opened her eyes wider to see Takumi nudging her with his nose. She had almost forgotten where she was. She stretched, enjoying the feel of the soft sheets against her skin. She had never slept so comfortably in her life.

"Your fox is funny," a small voice said from the foot of her bed.

Tori bolted upright, clenching her covers to her body, then relaxed her face when she took in the small face of a blond-headed boy, about the age of nine or ten. Even if he hadn't been so young, Tori knew he served no threat, for Takumi hadn't made a fuss. Instead, Takumi seemed as interested in the boy as the boy was in him. She could tell by his finely textured clothes that he was not part of the servant staff. Catching sight of his golden ring, which sported the crest of Avarell, she realized she was in the presence of royalty.

"I'm Tori," she said. "What's your name."

"I'm Theo." His voice was small but confident.

The way Prince Theo teetered back and forth on the balls of his feet reminded Tori of her sister. Takumi paced in a circle on top of the bed covers, then sat and stared at the prince. Theo let out a little laugh and reached out to pet him. A small purr thrummed out from Takumi's throat as the prince stroked his head.

"His name is Takumi."

"That's a funny name."

"It means *clever* in the ancient language."

"What's the ancient language?"

"Something that people spoke long, long ago." Her eyes went toward the window. The height of the sun worried her; she needed to get ready for breakfast. "Shouldn't you be in the banquet room?"

He gave a pout, and Tori assumed he was disappointed to leave. "Yes. Will you be there?"

"Yes, as soon as I'm ready."

"And Takumi?"

"I'm afraid he's not welcome in the banquet room."

Theo tilted his head. "Are you staying here from now on?"

"That's up to the queen regent."

He smiled at her, still petting Takumi. "I'll put in a good word for you."

"That's very kind of you, Your Highness. Thank you."

"How did you know I was the prince?"

"You have a very princely manner about you," Tori answered with a smile.

"All right. I suppose I *should* go now." He hesitated, staring fondly at the fox.

"Theo, before you leave, I have a big favor to ask of you."

"What is it?"

"You like Takumi?"

"Yes. He's soft, and his whiskers tickle my hands."

"Well, you can come play with him whenever you want. But, I don't know if he's even allowed to stay." Tori gave him a fake pout.

"I'm the prince. I can allow him to stay."

"Your aunt or sister might have another opinion. So, perhaps we should keep his staying here a secret? Just between us."

Theo's smile was wide. "All right. I won't tell."

"Thank you, Your Highness. I'll see you in the banquet hall as soon as I'm ready."

Theo straightened and then performed a proper bow, which made Tori giggle. He had a skip in his step as he left her chambers. If she had to guess, she would say Taeyeon was probably a couple years older than the prince, but their spirits were practically the same.

A heavy weight pushed on Tori's chest at the thought of her sister. She missed her family so. She hoped Goran made true on his promise to supply them with enough medicine to keep their symptoms at bay. She would do what she must to get them the cure, but it wouldn't do any good if they died before she got back.

Finja opened the door to her apartment with such gusto it made Takumi scramble to hide under the bed. Noticing him, Finja mumbled something under her breath. She carried huge buckets of steaming water to her bathing room. Another handmaid followed with two more buckets, and Tori heard them fill the tub.

"Be sure to take your medicine," Finja said to Tori once the other handmaid left the apartment. Tori stood and stretched in her thin nightclothes. "Can't have you passing out from fever. What good would you be as a lump on the floor?"

"I'd like to think I'd make a rather nice rug," Tori joked.

Finja did not even crack a smile. "Remember to carry yourself like a High Priestess," she said as she laid out Tori's dress for the day. "And watch your words."

"Yes, yes. I know."

Tori followed Finja to the tub and let her nightclothes fall to the floor. Finja averted her eyes until Tori was submerged in the bubbly water. A sigh of wonder escaped Tori's mouth as she settled into the tub. She was amazed that water could be so warm and at how good the soap smelled. Back home, she would make soap from flowers that grew in Drothidia, but these fragrances were new to her, and the scents were almost intoxicating. Delicious, even.

"Have you never had a hot bath before?" Finja eyed her with a cocked brow.

"Nothing like this. This is… well, heavenly."

"Yes, yes, but please, you need to concentrate."

Though her tone was abrasive, Tori was too relaxed by the invigorating hot water to mind. After scrubbing her body and her hair, she was reluctant to leave the bath, but Finja's disapproving scowl prompted her to do so.

As she dried off, Takumi came out from under the bed, sniffing the air. He approached her and wiggled his nose around her skin. Tori laughed from the way his whiskers tickled her leg.

"It's still me, Takumi. Just a bit cleaner."

Tori was finally able to start focusing as Finja helped her with the dress, fastening buttons on the back and pulling the corset tighter. The blue cloak was then added to the outfit, and Tori's hair was brought back into a loose braid. Strapped to her waist but concealed by the skirt of her dress was a leather pouch containing some of the shuriken Goran had given her. She didn't honestly think she'd need them, but she felt better in this foreign land with the pouch strapped to her body, especially not knowing the true intentions of the queen regent.

She travelled down to the banquet hall with Finja following behind and bowing her head as if she was a faithful servant. Finja discreetly instructed her where to go. Luckily, her quarters were not far from the banquet hall, for Tori had discovered her appetite had grown overnight. And even in the halls, the inviting smell of freshly baked bread wafted out to greet her.

Sunlight brightened up the inner corridors. Servants bustled about, cleaning floors and carrying things from one part of the castle to another. A servant with a large tray rushed past her and entered the banquet hall. Tori was still amazed at how many people worked here.

Entering the banquet hall, she was taken aback. There were so many tables, and so many people seated at each one. She wondered if they all lived in quarters on the castle grounds, or if they had to travel from the city to get there. The ceiling was high, painted with murals of seraphim and cherubim so lovely Tori found it difficult to look away.

Spotting the overflowing plates of food upon the tables, she held back a gasp. She was not used to seeing so much food in one place, let alone eating such a meal. The variety of breads alone made her head spin. There were so many different meats, vegetables, and fruit she didn't know where to begin. And the pastries made her mouth water.

"Lady Tori," a voice came from the front of the room.

Tori turned to see Raven, the dark-haired lady-in-waiting, lifting her dainty hand to call her over. She and the other ladies-in-waiting sat at a table not far from the queen regent's table.

Tori gave her a small smile and walked toward the table, sparing a glance at the queen regent, who was almost scowling at her food, and the princess, who was picking up the cloth napkin her brother, Prince Theo, had let slip to the floor. Theo's eyes widened in delight at the sight of Tori, and he gave her an enthusiastic wave as he stuffed a roll in his mouth.

Tori nodded her head to him in greeting as she continued to Raven's table.

"Your Holiness," one of the other ladies-in-waiting said, bowing her head. She had chestnut-brown hair with a lilac pin holding two twirled strands in place. "We would be honored if you joined us."

"Thank you," Tori said. "That would be lovely."

"I realize we haven't been properly introduced," Raven said as Tori settled into her chair. "I'm Raven. This is Aurora—" Raven motioned to the chestnut-brown brunette. "This is Jasmine—" She motioned to the silvery blonde. "And this is Azalea—" The last one she motioned to was a woman in chainmail. "She is not one of the ladies of the court, but a soldier."

"How revolutionary," Tori said, pleasantly surprised. "That explains the uniform."

"I have a penchant for swords and shields rather than petticoats and hair pins," Azalea said. "Not to judge anyone's choices, of course. I mean no offense."

"None taken, Azalea," Raven said, waving a dismissive hand.

"I also prefer to sit with the ladies-in-waiting instead of the soldiers because, well, men can be swine when they eat."

Raven let out a haughty laugh while Azalea shrugged matter-of-factly.

"Tell us about yourself, Your Holiness," Aurora said.

"Please, call me Lady Tori." Tori took a pastry from the serving dish in the middle of the table. She couldn't resist taking a bite before continuing. The delicious flavor overwhelmed her taste buds, and she had to fight not to let out a moan of approval. Upholding her composure, she wiped her sticky fingers off on her napkin. “My story is not different from others of Tokuna. I studied at the Holy Temple from the age of twelve. In the last few years I began travelling the world to offer my services. There isn’t much more to tell, I’m afraid.”

Tori turned her head and studied the head table. Princess Wrena ate her food slowly. There was a sadness in her eyes that could not be missed.

“The princess is a rather quiet person, is she not?” Tori asked, being sure not to speak to loudly.

“Princess Wrena kept to herself for a long while when the Queen fell ill. Slowly she’s come out and interacts more and more with the court, but we all suspect she sulks in worry over her mother.”

“Which is completely understandable,” Aurora added.

“Has anyone seen the Queen since her sickness claimed her bedridden?” Tori asked.

“No one’s seen her except the princess and Lady Maescia,” Raven answered.

“What about Prince Theo?”

“No.” Raven leaned forward in her chair. “He was a mere toddler when his mother took ill. The queen regent doesn’t think he’s quite old enough to grasp the severity of his mother’s illness. That she might—”

“Raven!” Aurora said, her hand quick to grab Raven’s. Azalea slowly shook her head in disapproval of Raven’s words. It was frowned upon to speak of the possible death of a royal. It could even be considered treason.

Raven pressed her lips together and looked over her shoulder, making sure no one had heard her.

“He barely knows her at all, the poor child,” Aurora said.

Tori glanced again at Theo, remembering how sweet he was when he had pet Takumi. Beside the queen regent, the duke sipped wine, barely touching his food. Stern brows sat low above his eyes as his gaze swept over the many tables in the banquet hall, as if surveying the scene and keeping watch for any danger.

"What about the duke?" Tori asked. "Isn't he related to the deceased King?"

"Yes, Duke Grunmire is a distant cousin," Azalea explained. "He is the captain of the Queen's Guard, in charge of all the soldiers." She motioned to the table of men in uniform.

Tori's eyes went to the table where a number of men sat, including Master Stormbolt, who so vigorously cut into his meat that his roll flew from his plate. He looked around, cheeks reddening in embarrassment, as he retrieved the roll.

"What a dolt that Bramwell is," Raven said, laughing at the scene. "But an adorable one."

Bramwell, Tori thought. So that was his first name. She tried to remember the day in the Rift, when the other men on the Queenshunt lifted him out. Had they called him by that name?

"I thought you said he was a brute," Jasmine said, smirking and twirling a strand of hair around her finger.

"He can be a brute as well." Raven gazed at him dreamily. "Charming at times and then cold and standoffish other times." She turned back to Tori. "Have you met such men on your travels, Lady Tori?"

"I'm afraid I cannot judge the character of the men I've met on my service."

"Oh, that's right," Raven said, her hand flying to her chest. "How disrespectful of me. I had forgotten High Priestesses are pledged to chastity."

Jasmine's brows rose. "So, no relationships at all?"

"We hold a holy station and must uphold our pledge to the Divine Mother."

"What a shame not to ever love." Raven leaned on her hand and frowned. "Have you never had the opportunity?"

"No." It wasn't a lie. She had never had any romantic feelings for any of the boys in her village. The only boy she ever found herself thinking about was from a short encounter years ago. A boy she rescued from the Rift. Her eyes went to Bramwell, convinced the more she looked at him that he was the very same boy.

"Well, on the other hand," Raven continued, picking up her fork, "you don't know what you're missing, so there's no agony in it."

"Trust me." Jasmine grabbed her goblet and took a sip. "Sometimes I think men aren't worth it. They can be more trouble than they're worth."

"I'll agree with that," Aurora said.

Raven laughed. "I can't argue, but I won't swear off men altogether just yet." Her eyes went back to Bramwell.

"I'm afraid I cannot either," Azalea added. "Logan Rathmore has me wrapped around his finger."

"I've seen you two at practice," Aurora smirked. "You can disarm him in the wink of an eye."

"Yes, but I think it pleases him," Azalea whispered.

The ladies-in-waiting laughed in unison. They sobered and went on to enjoy their meal, which Tori was extremely grateful for.

"Lady Tori," Aurora said as they were nearly finished. "We are meant to join the queen regent on a walk through the gardens later. Will you be joining us?"

"If the queen regent requests it, then I shall." Tori gave her a solemn nod. "Otherwise, I will need to tend to my prayers and studies."

"What studies must you tend to, Lady Tori?" Jasmine asked.

"The order of High Priestesses must remain educated in many subjects. Tell me, is there a library here?"

"Only the grandest library in the nine realms," Raven said. "It's not far from the chapel."

"That's perfect," Tori said. "I must ask the queen regent if I may have access to it."

TAKUMI

CHAPTER TWELVE

THE VIEW FROM HER BALCONY was breathtaking, but Tori's focus was on the high tower that stood majestically on the castle grounds. Tori held Takumi in her arms, no doubt in her mind that Takumi would be able to do what she asked; there was a reason his name meant 'clever.'

"That's our goal," she said to him, pointing to the structure. "You need to figure out how to get up there. And when you do, you'll need to show me the way."

Finja scoffed from just inside the balcony door. "You can't seriously think that animal will understand your instructions."

"He understands me." Tori stroked his head and placed a kiss between his ears. "He's followed more complicated instructions before and carried them out without fail."

Finja cast her a skeptical glance.

"You don't believe me." Tori smirked, setting down Takumi. "I guess we'll just have to prove you wrong."

Finja sighed and finished folding the sheet in her hand. "Anyway, as I was saying, the guards finish their final round of training two hours after supper. Most of them turn in after that, leaving only the night patrol around the castle and on the city streets."

Tori nodded, coming in from the balcony and sitting in one of the plush chairs in her chambers. "Right."

"The generators go out at midnight for four hours, so you'll have the darkness on your side. If you keep to the shadows, you should be able to get to the docks and back to the castle without being seen. Especially in the garb that Goran has provided you."

"The problem is finding out where Hettie is," Tori said. "At least with the book Goran needs, I have an idea of where to look. I should have access to the castle library soon."

"I doubt the books would be in such an obvious place."

"At least there's a place to start."

A knock on the door made Takumi dart under the bed.

Finja hurried to the door and opened it to find Bramwell standing there.

"Master Stormbolt," Finja nodded her head in respect.

"I was instructed to escort Lady Tori to the gardens to catch up with the queen regent's ladies for their walk."

Tori swung her cloak around her shoulders and secured it at the neck as she went to the door.

"Thank you, Master Stormbolt." Tori glanced at Finja. "That will be all, Finja."

"Of course, milady," Finja gave her a slight bow, but Tori could see that she still had a scowl on her face.

Tori adjusted her hood as she joined Bramwell in the hall. "It was kind of you to fetch me. Lady Maescia could have simply sent a page to tell me where to go."

He motioned for her to walk with him. "Lady Maescia knows the layout of the castle can take some time to get used to and didn't want you to get lost."

"It is a big castle, and the layout is not a simple one."

"I would be glad to show you around." Bramwell flashed her a small smile. "I grew up here and know the castle inside and out."

"Really? Even the secret passageways?"

His brow furrowed. "How did you know about those?"

"I didn't, until now." She laughed when his jaw dropped slightly. "Then again, don't all castles have them?"

"I suppose so."

"And you know where they are in this castle." It wasn't a question.

"Maybe you should forget that I told you that. I might miss my chance at a promotion if anyone knew I was giving out such classified information to a lady who hasn't even secured her position in the Queen's court yet."

"You have my word: I won't mention it."

"High priestesses aren't allowed to lie, are they?" His sideways glance was adorable.

"No," she answered.

"Good. Then I trust your word, Your Holiness."

He escorted her to an archway that let out to the beautiful courtyard. It wasn't the same area where the trial took place, and Tori was suddenly glad Bramwell had guided her here. She would likely have been lost if she had tried to find this expanse on her own. They followed a cobblestone path flanked by clusters of unique foliage. She had grown up in the forest, but she had never seen trees or flowers like these before. Were they native plants to Avarell, or had the King or Queen commanded laborers to travel the world and fetch them for their garden? Tori and Bramwell came to a set of stone steps that led to a lower level of the gardens. Here there was a pond full of koi fish, a fountain spouting water in the middle. The mist from the fountain cast the illusion of a rainbow over the path.

"What promotion do you speak of?" Tori asked.

"Pardon, milady?"

"You mentioned missing a chance at a promotion."

"Oh. Well, it's nothing. I've been in the Queen's Guard for a long while now and am attempting to climb the ranks to lieutenant. My closest friend Logan has achieved the position of commander, and he never lets me forget it. I know it's a foolish thing to say, but I've always been two steps behind Logan, er, Master Rathmore. It would be great to actually catch up for a change."

"Then I shall pray on it," Tori placed a hand on his arm. When he looked down at her hand on his sleeve, she pulled her hand away and ducked her head.

"Thank you," Bramwell said.

As the path rounded, the group of ladies-in-waiting and the queen regent came into view. Raven was the first to spot Tori and Bramwell, and Tori noticed she straightened her back, offering an ample view of her cleavage as she sauntered toward them.

"Lady Tori." Raven's smile was wide, and her lashes fluttered whenever her gaze landed on Bramwell. It reminded her of the way the girls back in Sukoshi would flirt with her brother Masumi. "We are so glad you could join us."

"My pleasure, Lady Raven," Tori answered.

"Bram, I hope you didn't dally when showing her here. You know Lady Maescia hates waiting."

Bram's polite smile was not as enthusiastic as Raven's. "Of course not. I brought Her Holiness straight away."

"I thought maybe your ego got the better of you," Raven continued, "and you might have taken the time to show Lady Tori what a skilled warrior you are."

"Of course not, Lady Raven. I'm sure Lady Tori has no interest in battles."

"Still, she might have been impressed with your form, as you know I am."

"If you'll forgive me," Bram said, appearing uncomfortable, "I must return to the training hall."

"Of course, Bramwell. I'm sure I'll see you later."

Bram dipped into a bow, then turned and made his way back up the path.

"And that," Raven whispered, her gaze landing on Bramwell's backside, "is the only reason I don't mind him walking away." She placed her hands on her hips and gave Tori a wink.

Tori felt heat flush her cheeks as she realized her attention had focused on what Raven was referring to. She quickly averted her gaze.

Raven laughed and linked arms with Tori. "It's a good thing you're celibate, Your Holiness. Otherwise I would have been jealous of seeing the two of you together."

Tori fought back another wave of blushing. "There would be no reason to be jealous."

Raven slapped a delicate hand to her chest. "My apologies for bringing up such a silly thing. Of course, you are right."

They strolled closer to Lady Maescia and the other ladies-in-waiting. Tori noticed that the group seemed to be missing one lady—Aurora, the one with chestnut -brown hair. Pity, she thought, as Aurora seemed to be the nicest of the bunch.

"Lady Tori," Lady Maescia said, twirling the stem of a flower between her fingers. "How long did you say you studied in Tokuna?"

"Since I was twelve, Your Grace." Tori knew these questions would come, and she found she was able to answer them easily.

"Who was your instructor?"

"I studied under the guidance of Lady Selina. If Your Grace would like her to send a letter of reference, I would be happy to contact her." Though, such a letter would be forged by one of Goran's most skilled forgery experts.

The sudden outburst of a curse word that flew from Jasmine's mouth caused them to turn their heads. Jasmine clutched her arm above the wrist, her face twisted in pain.

"What is it?" Lady Maescia asked. "What happened?"

"Something bit me!" Jasmine clenched her teeth and squirmed, the inside of her wrist already red and blistering.

"Let me see," Tori said, grabbing her hand.

She inspected the affected skin and noticed a tiny black stinger.

"It wasn't a bite. You've been stung by a velvet beetle."

"A what?" Raven asked, craning her neck from behind Tori to see Jasmine's wrist.

"It's nothing serious," Tori explained, using her fingernails to pry out the stinger, "but it will itch intensely and will swell up if not treated right away."

"Treated how?" Jasmine asked.

"Hold on." Tori released her hand and scurried around the garden. She snapped a large leaf off one of the bushes and grabbed a cone-shaped flower from another part of the garden, then rushed back to Jasmine, all the while pretending not to notice the queen regent's eyes on her.

She broke the large leaf down the center, where a transparent sap began to seep out. Tori held the broken leaf over Jasmine's injury.

"Ew," Raven said. The queen regent shushed her immediately.

Once the spot was covered, Tori took the cone-shaped flower between her hands and began rubbing. The tiny pollen-covered petals disintegrated into a powdery substance that became stuck in the sap. Tori then took the stem of the flower and mixed the sap and powder together until it turned a milky purple.

"What is that?" Raven asked.

"Varello sap and chenskit pollen. The sap will relieve the itching, and the pollen will aid in the reduction of swelling."

Lady Maescia took a closer look. "That's fascinating. How did you know what to do?"

"I was born and raised in Drothidia. Using plants and herbs for all purposes is something we all grew up learning. Not just for healing. I can also make a crushed wheat root powder that can make anyone's skin as soft as a babe's."

There was obvious interest from the ladies with that remark.

"It's a bit tingly now," Jasmine said. "Less itchy, for certain. Thank you so much, Lady Tori."

"It is an honor to serve you."

The queen regent folded her hands together in front of her skirts and regarded Tori. It was as if she was appraising a piece of art and deciding if she would purchase it or not.

"Lady Tori, a word?" She strolled a few paces away from the others and motioned for Tori to follow.

The ladies-in-waiting obediently gave the queen regent space.

"Yes, Your Grace?"

One of Lady Maescia's brow rose as her ice-blue eyes locked with Tori's. "That was quite a clever way to gain favor with my ladies."

"I wasn't trying to be manipulative, Your Grace. I apologize if it seemed so."

"Hmm." Lady Maescia's eyes flit over her face. Tori wondered if this was the same expression Lady Maescia had when she killed her former High Priestess. "Tell me. What is your understanding regarding the *sight*? What I'm particularly interested in is the tenet, which denotes that only royals are permitted to request revelations of the sight from High Priestesses. Some might say that a regent is not officially royalty and should not partake of this tradition. What do you think?"

This seemed like a trick, and Tori knew if she didn't give the correct answer, the queen regent would not hire her. Was Lady Maescia testing her nobility, or was she trying to benefit from the situation? Tori took a deep breath before she answered. "I believe, as regent, you are entitled to learning what might be in your future. After all, you are in a position of power, and any decisions you might make would greatly affect the queendom."

For a moment, Tori thought that she had answered incorrectly, for the queen regent simply stared at her with slightly narrowed eyes. But then, a slow yet small smile appeared on her face. "Yes, that is true. What a wise perspective. I would like to speak to you once more, alone, before I make my decision about your employment. But not here in the gardens, of course. Could you come to my sitting room before the evening meal so we might speak privately?"

Tori bit back a smile of triumph. "Of course, Your Grace."

CHAPTER THIRTEEN

WITH AN EDGE OF IRRITATION, Bram trudged through the courtyard on his way back to the castle's training hall. He knew Raven didn't mean to embarrass him—and it certainly wasn't the first time she had spoken to him in such an abrasive, flirtatious manner—but he wished she hadn't done so in front of Lady Tori. Logan often pushed for him to take Raven as his love interest, but something always held him back. It wasn't that Raven wasn't beautiful; she had many admirers for both her beauty and her grace. She was a nice girl, smart even. He had also spent some time alone with her, taking walks by the lake or dancing with her at a celebration feast. But he could never bring himself to offer her more than a kiss on the hand. There was no defining spark between them—at least from his side.

And now that Lady Tori had moved into the castle, his thoughts seemed to drift to her.

The sight of her on her balcony haunted him the night before, and he barely slept. But he ended up berating himself, for it was sacrilegious to think of a holy woman in a romantic way. It wasn't merely that she intrigued him; he couldn't help thinking how much she resembled the girl who rescued him in the Rift when he was sixteen.

He raked a hand through his hair, shaking his head. She couldn't be the same person. She'd been in Tokuna since the age of twelve, and the girl who had rescued him had to have been fourteen or fifteen. Perhaps he was simply projecting his long-ago feelings for that girl onto Tori because they were both from Drothidia.

He was being ridiculous, anyway. She was a priestess, committed to a life of celibacy. It was unholy to think of doing anything with her aside from praying.

Maybe he should consider courting Raven. After all, if he was really going to stay in Avarell, he would soon have to consider his future. If he wanted a family one day, he would have to find a proper wife. And Raven fit the bill. She was a lady of the court, and she would be devoted to him, without a doubt. Perhaps a spark would come later. Perhaps he would ask her to be his companion for the welcoming banquet when the court of Gadleigh visited.

As he neared the castle, the sound of whispers and soft laughter found his ears. He stopped and listened. Changing directions, he rounded a hedge of rose bushes to find Princess Wrena and Aurora sitting on a stone bench.

"I don't care," Aurora was saying to the princess. "I don't care what anybody thinks."

"Aurora?" Bram called, coming fully around the rose bushes.

Aurora straightened. "Oh, dear cousin, I did not notice you there."

"Your Highness." Bram bowed to the princess. "Aurora, the ladies-in-waiting are taking a walk with the queen regent. Perhaps you'd forgotten? Shouldn't you be with the other ladies of the court?"

"I wasn't feeling well."

"Then you should be resting."

"She needed some fresh air," the princess said with a smile. "So I took it upon myself to escort her to the gardens. It does wonders for clearing the head."

"I see." He bowed his head to her. "That is very gracious of you, Your Highness. I'm sure Aurora is extremely grateful."

"I am," Aurora said, offering the princess a small smile.

"Shall I escort you back to your room, then? I am headed that way."

Aurora glanced at the princess, and then back at Bram. "Yes, of course. If the princess does not need me anymore."

"We shall continue our conversation at a later hour, Aurora." The princess stood, and Aurora followed suit.

"Yes, of course, Wrena—I mean, Your Highness."

"Enjoy the fresh air, Your Highness," Bram added, bowing again.

Aurora joined him at his side, her face aglow. Bram couldn't help but watch her with interest. She seemed particularly happy.

"What?" she asked, catching him staring at her.

"Nothing." He blinked. "Nothing at all."

CHAPTER FOURTEEN

"HOW DID YOU MANAGE to do it?" Tori asked Finja as she tightened her corset. It had loosened during her walk and began to droop on her tiny frame.

"It cost me some gold," Finja said. "I was able to pay a handmaiden to start a small rip in queen regent's gown this morning. She had gone through a lot of trouble to get the many layers on, so she wasn't up for removing any clothing. I knew this would happen, and I was available to come in and sew up the rip while she still had it on."

"And this gave you the opportunity to put your hands on Lady Maescia?"

"Yes."

"Did you see anything?" Tori asked. Somewhere deep inside of her, she was afraid to know. She wondered if Finja would actually be able to see if Lady Maescia had killed her last High Priestess.

"It was very unclear, but I think it was enough for you to convince her that you have the *sight* when you tell her."

With her corset in place, Tori adjusted her cloak and set her mind to memorize what Finja had to tell her. Finja sat her down on the settee in her sitting area and locked eyes with her. Before she even spoke, Tori got a chill.

Her nerves were fragile as she approached the hall to the queen regent's sitting room. This act of deceit would take a lot of focus. Tori just hoped her hands would stop shaking long enough to carry out the plan.

And remember, your eyes, Finja had told her. *Your eyes have to be convincing as well or she won't believe you. Be on alert. We believe she killed the last High Priestess. She could be dangerous.*

Anxiety about being convincing was already making her feel queasy without adding Finja's daunting words to the mix. Was she walking into a killer's room? Tori still couldn't understand why Lady Maescia would have killed the last High Priestess. Finja's theory was that she had uncovered secrets about the queen regent. Secrets Lady Maescia wanted to keep hidden.

It frightened Tori to think what secrets they were.

Halfway down the hall, she spotted someone coming toward her. It wasn't until he moved into the light that she realized it was Duke Grunmire.

"Ah, Lady Tori," he said, stopping and giving her a slight bow. "I do hope Your Holiness has found our accommodations fitting."

"Duke Grunmire, how nice to see you. And yes, thank you. Everything is quite satisfactory."

"I heard you came by sea via a Khadulian ship."

Tori braced herself. The duke's eyes were full of scrutiny, despite the obviously fake grin. He was the queen regent's royal advisor, certain to be analyzing every situation even remotely attached to the queen regent. It was his job to sniff out and stop acts of treason—and to bring justice to the crown.

"Yes. I had to perform a ritual in the Crystal Islands." Tori forced herself to keep her back straight.

"That's quite dangerous territory for a young woman as yourself to be in."

"It is my duty to serve where I am called. A family needed to lay their young daughter to rest. I was called to bless the body."

"How dreadful for the family."

"It's a devastation to lose someone so young," Tori said softly, her thoughts momentarily drifting to Miki.

"I actually know someone in Tokuna."

Tori almost flinched. "Have you been there?"

"No, no." His hand went to the hilt of his sword. "My duties have kept me from visiting."

"Well, truth be told, Tokuna is bigger than everyone thinks it is. The temple where I studied was far north, far from the other temples. It wouldn't be out of the ordinary if two people who spent their whole lives in Tokuna had never even laid eyes on each other."

He looked skeptical, but Tori made sure to keep the polite smile on her face, hoping he would be convinced.

"If you'll excuse me, Lady Maescia awaits me in her sitting room."

"Yes, of course. It was a pleasure to finally meet you face to face, Lady Tori. I'm sure we'll see each other around the castle."

She dropped into a curtsy, her gaze going to the floor. "My Lord."

She turned around, her heart pounding and her hands clammy, and forced one foot in front of the other until she reached the queen regent's sitting room. She was not used to lying so much. Would she ever get used to it?

Though they didn't seem to be making eye contact, the guards at the door opened it for her as if they were expecting her arrival. She nodded in thanks despite their wayward gazes and stepped forward into the grand room.

The queen regent looked up from her lounging chair, sitting up straighter when she spotted Tori. "Ah, your Holiness."

"Your Grace," Tori curtsied. "You asked to see me."

"Yes, yes." Lady Maescia clapped her hands twice, her focus shifting temporarily to her ladies-in-waiting. "Ladies, would you mind giving us some privacy? I have important matters to discuss with Lady Tori."

Raven, Aurora, and Jasmine stood to leave, the skirts of their dresses swishing around them. The queen regent waited patiently until they cleared the room, and then she took a deep breath and flashed Tori a polite smile. "We discussed something earlier today. Do you remember?"

"Yes, milady. The *sight*."

"Might you be ready to sit with me now?"

"I am at your service, milady."

Lady Maescia gestured for Tori to sit beside her. Tori's heart sped up, her palms moist as she ran her hands over her skirt, the image of the blade strapped to her thigh clear in her mind. There was no reason for Lady Maescia to kill her. Yet. She would have to be careful with her words, mindful of what Finja had told her, and convincing that she had the *sight*. She fought off a wave of nausea and forced a pleasant smile.

"They say confession is good for the soul," Lady Maescia said, straightening the jewelry at her wrist. "Perhaps I need a High Priestess who will listen to my confessions without judgment of any kind."

Tori blanched. Was Lady Maescia about to confess to murder?

She fought to keep her voice from quivering. "Of course, your Grace."

"When it comes time for confessions, I will keep that in mind." Lady Maescia studied Tori's face. "How does this work?"

"I'm sorry, Your Grace?"

"What I mean to say is… suppose there are areas of my life that I wish to remain private for one reason or another." Tori noticed a slight tremble in Lady Maescia's voice. Her lips quivered as if she were trying to smile but couldn't quite pull it off. She blinked rapidly, awaiting Tori's reply. There was definitely something in her past she wanted to hide, and for a moment Tori wished she really did have the sight so she could see what it was.

Tori offered her a small smile. "Do not worry, milady. What you wish to conceal will remain hidden, for I can only see your open memories and—on occasion—the possibilities of your future."

Though the queen regent kept a calm face, the relieved breath she released did not go unnoticed. Tori offered her hands to her. Lady Maescia only hesitated a moment before taking them, her grip strong. Tori closed her eyes, grateful that she could keep tabs on the queen regent's hands so she wouldn't be fearful of her grabbing a weapon.

She called to mind the scenario Finja told her about, listening to the queen regent breathing heavily in anticipation.

Your eyes must be convincing, Finja had said. Tori opened her eyes and locked them with Lady Maescia's.

"Something happened in your past. Something frightening."

Lady Maescia's face went pale, and she squeezed Tori's hands tighter.

"I see a small girl. Beside her, another girl barely an inch taller. And a boy."

Lady Maescia seemed to relax a bit. "I believe what you see is my sister Callista and myself. The boy is our brother Rainer. He now reigns at Pathdown Castle in Creoca as king, wed to Queen Emiliana."

"Ah, yes. I've heard of him."

Lady Maescia blinked, the hint of a smile breaking through on her face. "What do you see?"

"You are playing on a tiny bridge over a stream. But Callista and Rainer are bigger than you. Faster and stronger. You want to prove you are just as big as they are, so you climb upon the railing. They shout at you to get down, but you are too proud. And—"

"And I fell." The look in Lady Maescia's eyes told Tori she had her interest. She believed her.

"Your brother and sister jumped in to get you out of the stream. It wasn't deep, but you hurt your ankle. Rainer carried you out of the water. They got you home safely and got your ankle wrapped, but you caught a cold. Callista took care of you, brought hot broth and tea to warm you until the shivering stopped and the fever went away."

Tori made sure to repeat every word Finja had told her. It had to be convincing. And Tori knew it was. There was no way anyone else outside of their family would have known that story. And the memory of it glowed in Lady Maescia's eyes.

Lady Maescia squeezed Tori's hands. "Yes. It's true."

"There's something else," Tori said. This was the part she and Finja made up. It was a risk to pull such a ruse, but it might prove to give Tori a hint about the Queen. "Something that happened in this very castle."

Lady Maescia trembled, the blood draining from her face.

"What do you see?"

"Something troubling you. Something dark. Something you did. But it is hidden from the *sight*, hidden in the dark recesses of your mind."

"You cannot see it?" Lady Maescia's voice was a desperate whisper.

"No. I only see a crossroads and a decision you need to be wise making."

The queen regent nodded, her mouth in a straight line. "I understand."

She released Tori's hands and stood, her eyes far away as she slowly paced the room. Unsure of what to do, Tori rose from the seat and folded her hands in front of her, waiting for the queen regent to speak. Lady Maescia wrung her hands, and then must have realized Tori was watching her, for she looked up with a start.

"I'm terribly sorry. I was so lost in thought that I… no matter. Lady Tori, you have proven yourself an asset to the throne. You truly have the gift, and you stand a true devotee to the Divine Mother. I do believe that I—that *we all* would benefit from you taking the position as royal High Priestess."

"Thank you, your Grace." Tori curtsied, relief washing through her. She straightened on wobbly knees and bowed her head in respect, despite her light-headedness. "I would be honored to stand at your side."

CHAPTER FIFTEEN

IT WAS A FEAT TO TEAR HERSELF AWAY from the breakfast feast, but Tori had a library to find. Aurora had been kind enough to give her directions, but when she offered to show Tori the way, Tori had to politely refuse. She couldn't be sure if Aurora would stick around and see the kind of books Tori was searching for. For all Aurora and the other ladies-in-waiting knew, she was furthering her holy studies.

She went over Aurora's instructions again, but she seemed to keep coming to a turn that wasn't supposed to be there or an extra hall that split off to the right. Navigating through woods and foliage had never proved to be a problem. She was easily able to recognize groupings of trees and other landmarks, but in the castle, every corridor looked the same. It was easy to end up going in circles and becoming lost. Somewhere in the beautifully decorated maze that was Capehill Castle, the grand library awaited her.

The echo of footsteps filled the hall. Although she had no reason to be afraid, her heart sped up. She continued forward, though she knew she needed to take a right soon. As she rounded the corner, she found Bramwell, along with four other Queen's Guard soldiers headed her way.

"Lady Tori," Bramwell said with a nod.

"Master Stormbolt. What a pleasant surprise."

"I don't believe you've met Logan, Eleazar, Tiberius, and Oscar."

She bowed her head, not bothering to take the time to remember their names, for fear she'd forget the directions to the library. "Are you on your way to training?"

"Yes, we are," Bramwell answered.

"You do seem to train quite often."

The tall one—Logan, she believed his name to be—seemed to smirk. "Perfection can only be attained with diligence and dedication."

"We are not brought to this world to be perfect," Tori said, squaring her shoulders. "The Divine Mother wishes to teach us something before we move on to the next plane."

Bramwell let out a chuckle and slapped Logan on the back. "Yes, true. Did you forget that, Logan? Has your mind been clouded with pride and ambition?"

"Forgive me, Your Holiness," Logan said. "What I meant to say is our discipline strengthens us. I do believe the Divine Mother encourages discipline."

"And modesty," Tori said, tilting her head.

Logan cleared his throat, visibly stumped for words. Bramwell nudged Logan with his arm, obviously fighting off a laugh.

"Where might you be headed, Lady Tori?" Bramwell asked.

"I'm quite embarrassed to say that I have been unsuccessful in finding the royal library."

"I hate to be the bearer of bad news," Bramwell said, keeping his voice low, "but you are in the wrong part of the castle."

Tori swiped a hand over her cheek as a hot blush spread over it.

"If you allow me, I can escort you there."

"But your training."

"I'm certain the men can get to the training hall without me." He turned to Logan. "Go on ahead, and if the duke asks where I am, tell him I am providing a service of charity in the name of the Divine Mother."

"Don't be too long," Eleazar—the duke's son, Tori remembered—told him.

As the other men marched away, Tori joined Bramwell at his side as he led her down the corridor. A group of three handmaids went by, each of them bowing their heads to Tori as they passed.

Tori bowed her head in return, though she was sure they hadn't seen her do it. "There are so many handmaids and servants in Avarell," she said once they were out of earshot. "Do they all live in the castle?"

"Most of them do. Though, with the size of the castle, it would be virtually impossible to account for them all. Luckily Miss Geneva keeps tabs on all household business. I swear the seneschal never sleeps."

"How could she?" Tori joked. "There's always so much going on."

"That there is."

"Tell me, do the servants and handmaids and pages take practice in communal worship?"

Bramwell seemed thrown by the question, gathering his thoughts before he answered. "I believe they worship in the city chapel or privately before their own makeshift altars, but I can't say for certain."

"I see. But the city chapel liturgy is not performed by a High Priestess, is it?"

"No. A clergyman offers prayer services to the Divine Mother there."

"It is custom, according to my training, that I hold at least one liturgy of communal worship for the help—the handmaids, servants, and pages—for a closer and holier connection to the Divine Mother. I realize they do not usually attend the liturgy in the castle chapel with the royals or the nobles, and I do not know how Lady Maescia would feel about the staff using the chapel, but I would like to offer it nonetheless."

"Perhaps I can put in a word with one of the court ladies—Lady Aurora is my cousin."

"Oh, I didn't realize."

"Yes. Her father—my uncle—took me in when my father died and my mother grew ill."

"How charitable of him."

Bram nodded once. "And when my mother passed on, he took on the role of bringing me up."

"A fine man, indeed."

"I'll have a word with Aurora and see if she might be able to persuade the queen regent to allow you the special service for the castle staff."

"I would be forever grateful. Thank you."

He flashed her a smile, and his eyes stayed on her.

"What is it?" she asked.

"Begging your pardon, but I find you extremely familiar."

Tori fought back a blush, a thrill zipping through her at the thought of him remembering her from the Rift. "I do not know how that could be possible."

"I was once saved by a Drothidian. A girl. With the same eyes as you."

"Drothidians are known for our eyes. They are all similar."

"Of course." He faced forward, his gaze far away. "She was young—so was I. I was out on my first hunt with the Queen's Guard, and I found myself in the Rift."

"How awful."

"I was injured. And the Undead soon found me. But this girl—she must have been fourteen or so—saved me. Fought off the Undead like she knew no fear and dragged me into a cave to tend to my injuries."

"A girl that young in the Rift? She sounds either extremely brave or extremely foolish."

"One is not exclusive of the other. But in my eyes, she was always brave."

"Then you were very lucky she came across you."

He studied her features again. "Are you sure it couldn't have been you?"

She feigned surprise, holding a hand to her chest. "How could it be? I've been training in Tokuna to be a High Priestess since I was twelve. And the thought of the Rift terrifies me."

"Ah, yes. Of course." He looked disappointed. "Just a strong resemblance then. Here we are."

Bram stopped at a set of oak double doors. Right before he opened them, a wave of heat flashed across Tori's skin and her stomach felt as if it were being filled with acid. She had taken her medicine for the phoenix fever that morning; she should have been fine until it grew dark. Perhaps the dosage in the capsule she took had been off. She needed to find a moment to swallow another pill.

The doors opened to the largest room she had ever seen outside of the banquet hall. Two-stories tall, it boasted of finely crafted bookshelves that stretched from corner to corner, each of them abundant with books. Tori had to catch her breath taking in the beauty of the room. It almost made her forget about how ill she was feeling, but as she took a step forward, her legs began to give out.

Bramwell was quick to catch her as she nearly collapsed. "Your Holiness, are you all right?"

She blinked rapidly, finding it hard to breathe. "I must not have had enough water today. When I am dehydrated, I get dizzy."

He led her to a couch inside the library. "I'll send for some water."

She could barely nod. As Bramwell raced back into the corridor, Tori reached for the small pouch of pills tied to the inside of her skirt. She quickly slipped one capsule out and swallowed it dry. It was rough and bitter without water, and she found herself clutching at her throat as she struggled to get the pill down.

Bramwell returned, a look of shock on his face at the sight of her. "Lady Tori!"

She couldn't answer. He ran to her side and put one hand on her back, the other on her arm. She squeezed his hand as she gasped for air. A servant girl hurried into the room with a tray. Bramwell snatched the pitcher and goblet off the tray and quickly poured water for her.

Tori drank, her throat instantly relieved by the liquid, but her body still fighting the fever until the medicine could be absorbed. Bramwell took the goblet, and Tori leaned back on the couch, concentrating on her breathing.

"Lady Tori, are you all right?"

She forced a small smile and nodded. "Yes. Thank you so much. Just a tad dizzy, but the water is helping."

"Perhaps a distraction?" He poured another gobletful of water and handed it to her. As she sipped, he continued. "That day, when I fell into the Rift, I saw my very first phoenix."

Her muscles went rigid, a fear striking though her that he knew about her disease. "Oh?"

"Well, the first one I'd seen up close, in any case. It was exquisite. The most beautiful animal I had ever seen. It swooped down toward me, and—it was probably my imagination, but I could have sworn it wanted to take my head off." He chuckled, which made Tori smile. "Or it simply wanted to show me not to mess with him. It's a shame such a fascinating creature became diseased."

"They only carry the disease," Tori said, feeling her strength returning. "The birds themselves do not fall ill or die from the sickness."

"Yes, you're right. I have misspoken. I apologize. Perhaps one day they will be free of the disease."

"Perhaps."

As he stared at her, the heat burning in her cheeks was not from the fever, but from his gaze. She quickly averted her eyes, wishing she didn't have to. She remembered sewing the cut on his leg, the way he squirmed and moaned, even in his unconscious state. She looked back at him, longing to ask him if the wound had left a scar. But to do that would be to admit she was lying.

Instead, she stood and straightened her dress. "I suppose I should start my studies now."

He stood as well and bowed his head. "Yes, of course. Are you sure you will be all right?"

"I'm sure. Thank you so much for your help, Master Stormbolt. I am in your debt."

"It was my pleasure."

He bowed once more before leaving the room, closing the doors behind him. The servant girl had disappeared sometime before that, but Tori must have been too distracted to have noticed.

She turned toward the multitude of shelves and took a deep breath, wondering how she was to begin.

"Nice of you to join us, Bramwell." Duke Grunmire's voice was like a boom in the training hall.

Bram braced himself as the duke strode toward him, the towering image of him like a dark, impending storm.

The duke clasped his hands behind his back, his shoulders squared as he looked down on Bram with judgment in his eyes. "Showing up late for practice, hardly the expected behavior of someone who only recently requested a promotion review."

"My apologies, Duke Grunmire. Lady Tori needed assistance finding the library."

"Is the position of page your desired occupation level, then? I struggle to find the difficulty in thinking to find a servant to show Her Holiness around the castle."

"I was simply being kind, my Lord. She felt faint—"

"Ah, yes." The duke pushed his tongue against an upper tooth, as if attempting to dislodge something. "Kindness. That is what I'm looking for in my guards."

As the duke turned away, Bram stepped forward without thinking and grabbed his arm. There was a wild look in the duke's eyes, his stone-cold gaze landing on Bram's hand. Bram stepped back, realizing his aggressiveness, but didn't back down on his words.

"I hardly think aiding a Lady of the court is grounds for disparagement, Duke Grunmire."

The duke breathed in deeply through his nostrils, lifting his chin. "You were tardy to practice—a clear disregard of the rules. And when confronted about such tardiness, you dare to reply with insolence. Perhaps the promotion to lieutenant is not as important to you as you had me believe it was."

Bram held back from showing the infuriation building inside him. "Of course it is, my Lord."

"There is nothing to convince me of that, Master Stormbolt," the duke said. "Perhaps I must take some time to reconsider your proposal."

"I beg your forgiveness, Captain, but I have been training twice as often as required. I head up more Queenshunt excursions than most corporals in the guard, and may I remind you that I organized the artillery transport of the specialty weapons to be allocated to Gadleigh, upon your orders and without fail."

"You mean the transport that is returning to Capehill Castle as we speak? Fully stocked, I must add."

Bram blinked in confusion. "Returning?"

"Yes." The duke flicked dust off his sleeve. "There have been some changes in the negotiation. Lady Maescia has reconsidered some aspects of the treaty, and she has decided to withdraw the artillery transport."

"But the alliance requires an equalization of armies."

"The alliance is still under negotiation."

"How can she back out of this deal on a moment's notice? Queen Callista agreed to the terms."

"Politics are not as simple as you may believe them to be." The duke glanced at Bram as if he were a dolt who knew nothing. "Royals and advisors must consider what is best for the queendom. I completely stand behind the queen regent in all her decisions. I've witnessed the political decisions she's made, and I find her method of reason a benefit to the queendom, perhaps even more strategic than Callista's tactics, in my opinion."

Bram was taken aback at the way the duke called the queen simply by her first name, and that he would criticize her so. "Forgive me, Duke Grunmire, but perhaps it is not wise to speak of the Queen in such a way. Some might call it blasphemous. Some might call it traitorous."

"I am the Captain of the Queen's Guard, Corporal Stormbolt. Believe me, I know everything there is to know about traitors."

The tap at her door quickened her heartbeat. She hurried to it, a smile surfacing on her face when she spotted Aurora in the hall. Taking a step forward to check up and down the hall, Princess Wrena felt a flutter inside her. Not a soul was to be seen in the corridor.

The princess took Aurora's hands and pulled her into her room, shutting the door behind them as a giggle escaped her lips. Though the princess was elated to see her, Aurora couldn't quite let the look of worry slip from her face.

"We were almost caught in the garden yesterday," Aurora reminded Wrena. "If Bram had showed up a moment sooner—"

Wrena placed a gentle hand on Aurora's cheek. "Sshh."

Aurora leaned into her hand, her eyes closing for a moment. "What are we doing? This is madness."

"I can't help how I feel about you."

"But you are the princess of Avarell. That doesn't come without ties. You are expected to marry Prince Liam."

"Can I not rule if I spend my days with the girl I love?"

Aurora's brows knitted together. With a frown, she paced toward the window, biting her thumbnail.

"Do you no longer wish to be with me?" Wrena asked.

"It's not that, Wrena." She turned, leaning on the windowsill. "I'm simply worried."

"About what people might think?"

"About what might happen to you."

Wrena strode toward Aurora and took her hand in both of hers, running her finger along the smoothness of her skin. "You are worth every risk."

Aurora blinked, the hint of a smile breaking through, and then she turned fully into Wrena and wrapped her arms around her. Wrena squeezed her tightly and breathed in the floral scent of her hair.

Aurora laid her head upon Wrena's shoulder. "What are we to do?"

Wrena twirled a strand of Aurora's hair around her finger. "The duke wants me to marry his son. And my aunt, for some reason, agrees with him."

Aurora pulled back, confusion plain on her face. "I don't understand. You're to marry Prince Liam. What does a marriage to Eleazar do for the queendom?"

She shook her head, letting out a soft sigh. "I do not know. I don't understand it myself."

Aurora worried her hands, her eyes trained on the floor. "Perhaps you have to."

"Have to do what exactly?"

"Marry. Marry whomever they expect you to. Just so no one suspects."

Wrena looked pensive, her eyes searching Aurora's face. "I don't want to pretend. I want you."

Aurora's shoulders fell as she moved closer and into Wrena's arms. Wrena pulled her closer, cupping her cheek until their lips met. The kiss was soft and slow, and as Aurora trailed her fingertips down the princess's neck, Wrena knew she didn't want to be with anyone else.

CHAPTER SIXTEEN

THE SHURIKEN MADE A resounding *thunk* as it pierced into the wall. Another followed, landing mere centimeters away from the first. Tori ran her fingers over the fine metal of the third shuriken in her hand, getting the feel of the weight of them and adjusting her technique.

As she released the third shuriken, Finja stumbled through the door with a small basket of fresh towels. She gasped at the sight of Tori and the blades in the wall, quickly closing the door behind her. "By the moons, what are you doing?"

Tori shrugged and chucked another throwing star into the wall. Its metal blade stuck into the hard surface with ease. "Practicing."

"You've ruined the wall."

"That wall has a tapestry that normally covers it. I simply moved it aside whilst practicing, and I'll replace it when I'm done. No one will be the wiser."

"Foolish girl," Finja mumbled, hastily putting the towels away. She peered over her shoulder, taking note of Tori's outfit. "Why are you wearing that? What if someone comes to the door?"

"I wanted to see if it fit." Tori smoothed the fine black material, the feel of it comfortable yet durable. "If someone were to come to the door, I'd put on that robe." Tori pointed to the bathrobe on the couch.

Finja looked her over. "Well, it seems to fit perfectly. Perhaps you should change before somebody sees you."

With a gekker, Takumi suddenly appeared on the balcony and ran inside. He skittered around Tori's feet, making an almost chirping noise. Tori knew this meant he wanted to show her something.

"What is it, Takumi?"

The fox zipped toward her bedchamber. Tori and Finja quickly followed. Crouching down, Tori frowned as Takumi scratched at the wall behind the bedchamber's tapestry. He ducked his head underneath it, which led Tori to lift it and push it aside. Takumi scratched at a space between two bricks. Tori felt along the edge of the bricks, and her eyes widened.

"I feel air."

Running her fingers upward, she followed the split to the top, almost to where it met the top of the tapestry. There was more space up here, so much that she could fit the tip of her finger in between. Something in the space moved, like a switch, and with a click, the wall pushed away from her.

She and Finja exchanged looks.

"Did you know this was here?" Tori asked.

"No." Finja pursed her lips. "Leave it to a fox to go and find it. Let me get you a candle."

As Finja fetched a candle to light, Tori pushed more forcefully on the wall, it pivoted further back into a dark, dank space. Takumi hopped forward into the secret passageway, stopping to look at Tori as if inviting her to follow him.

"I think he found the way to the high tower," Tori whispered to Finja, taking the candle from her.

"Be careful. Don't get caught. You haven't even accomplished one task yet. Goran will be livid if you fuck things up not even a week into your mission."

Tori nodded. "Point taken."

Squinting in the candlelight, Tori moved forward, careful about where she stepped despite the fact that Takumi was leading her. Dust floated carelessly in the air, causing Tori to cover her nose and mouth. The flickering light made cobwebs appear to move, and Takumi's shadow danced upon the wall like a macabre theater.

Up ahead, Takumi slowed, gekkering to her in warning. As she neared, she noticed the quick descent of stone stairs before her. There appeared to be no railing to grab hold of, so she reluctantly put her hand against the damp granite wall for support. They reached another corridor, this one narrower than the first, and she almost had to walk sideways to fit through it. She was grateful she didn't have her wide gown on, for she would have surely soiled it from the grimy walls.

Every few yards, they would pass the outline of a doorway, and Tori wondered how many rooms might be connected to the tunnel. Takumi stopped short in front of her, and Tori took in a long breath in anticipation. He scratched at the outline of a door, a tiny whimper escaping his snout. Tori felt the edge of the doorway and pressed her ear against it, listening for someone who might be on the other side. The crack of the door was just wide enough for her to see light, but no movement. She felt a small metal handle on her side of the door and wrapped her fingers around it. Clenching her teeth and hoping she wasn't waltzing into folly, she pulled.

She found herself in an elegant corridor much like the others in the castle, but this one had no windows and the light fixtures were a faded yellow instead of the pristine white crystal she was used to seeing. It was quiet here, and Tori wondered if this was some wing of the castle that had been abandoned.

Takumi bound forward, obviously aware of the silence of souls, and Tori had to hurry to catch up to him. He turned right and stopped in front of a tapestry. Sitting on his hind legs, he stretched upward to scratch at the fabric. The image upon it was a resemblance of the Queen, Tori noted as she pushed the material aside. She had a feeling of what to expect here. Sure enough, the wall gave way when she touched the appropriate spot. She slid through the entrance, the tapestry falling back into place before she shut the door behind her.

Candlelight illuminated another narrow passageway, this one even tighter than the last. But this one ended abruptly at the foot of stairs. Takumi scampered up them quickly, and once again, Tori was glad she wasn't wearing her heavy gown. At the top of the stairs, Takumi paced in front of a stone wall. A shaft of light illuminated the space between the wall and the secret door. Tori pressed her ear to the crack. Distant voices and footsteps could be heard. She turned her head and looked through the crack.

As the voices became louder, Tori grew tense. She knew she couldn't be seen, but she was still on edge. A guard in uniform walked by, and behind him, Lady Maescia and a man in long brown robes. They stopped in front of a door diagonal from where Tori was.

"Do you really think this will work?" Lady Maescia asked the man in the robes.

"I've had outstanding results with this potion. At least two people who were at death's door fully recovered with this treatment. I have very high hopes."

"High hopes," Lady Maescia mumbled. "Well, it's worth a try."

Judging by the tray of vials the man carried, Tori figured him to be an apothecary.

Lady Maescia lifted the end of her necklace out of her cleavage. Tori pressed her face closer to the crack to see what was at the end of it. Instead of a pendant, there was a key. It appeared forged from iron, a lot longer than a normal key. The queen regent bent and unlocked the door.

Lady Maescia instructed the guard to wait outside the room as she and the apothecary disappeared inside.

Tori let out a silent breath, not daring to leave. Glancing quickly down at Takumi, she found him curled in a ball, waiting it out with her. The guard stood, unmoving, and if he felt any trace of boredom during the long minutes that seemed to go by, Tori couldn't tell.

At long last, Lady Maescia and the apothecary emerged from the room.

"It may take some time to work," he said as Lady Maescia relocked the door.

She straightened, looking defeated. "How long did it take with the others?"

"For full recovery, it took some time. But we witnessed definite improvement the next day."

Lady Maescia nodded, tucking her key back into her dress. "Then I will check tomorrow to see if it's made a difference."

She motioned for the guard to lead them back down the corridor. Tori waited until their footfalls could no longer be heard. Takumi stood up and stretched, his nose sniffing at the crack in the wall. When he looked up at her expectedly, she knew they were in the clear.

Cracking open the door, Tori checked up and down the corridor as Takumi trotted toward the door of the room Lady

Maescia had been in. He sniffed under the door, and then let out a sneeze.

"The Queen must be in there," she whispered. First, she pressed her ear up to the door to listen, but there was no sound to be heard. Tori knew it was foolish to expect the door would open, having seen with her own eyes that Lady Maescia locked it. Still, she had to try. The handle would not turn. She bent down in attempt to look through the keyhole, but it was too dark. Perhaps the Queen was asleep. If she truly was sick, then it wasn't out of the question for her to sleep her days away. And the fact that an apothecary was called in to attempt to help made Tori think that Lady Maescia was telling the truth about the Queen's illness. Still, it was odd that she wouldn't allow anyone to see her.

Tori studied the keyhole again. Biting her lip, she reached into a small pouch hidden on her belt. She pulled out a thin metal pin with studs at the tip and slid it into the keyhole, but turning it about, she could already tell that the tool was not long enough. There was no way of getting into the room without that key.

Takumi made a short but frantic noise, and Tori backed away from the door.

"We'll have to make a copy," she said, tucking her tool pouch away. "I'll have to organize it, but when I let you know, we're going to steal that key."

CHAPTER SEVENTEEN

Bram had come through with passing Tori's wishes along to Aurora, who in turn was able to convince the queen regent to allow a communal liturgy for the castle staff. Tori made a note to thank Bram upon seeing him next. She knew it was silly of her, but having a reason to speak with him again brought a smile to her face.

The castle chapel was packed. She wasn't sure what to expect from the servants, but their need to connect with the Divine Mother was apparent in their numbers. She was just sorry that the service she was providing was a farce. Though there was no need for them to be aware of that fact.

Tori looked up to the mezzanine level of the chapel, where the princess sat with the ladies-in-waiting. Tori wondered if the princess wanted to be there or if it was meant to be a sign of support for the new royal High Priestess. The queen regent was nowhere to be seen.

All her practice paid off as she recited the prayer she painstakingly memorized. An unexpected thrill ran through her when she asked the congregation to bow their heads in prayer and they did so. She almost felt like a puppet master. Raising her hands to the ceiling and closing her eyes, she proclaimed the trust and faith they all had for the Divine Mother, giving thanks for the many blessings bestowed upon them, and then instructed everyone to fall into quiet reflection. She had memorized it all, but she had only performed it for Taeyeon before now.

She had to hold back a grin, remembering how Taeyeon would laugh at her overemphasis of the holy words.

Out of the corner of her eye, she spotted the duke watching. He wasn't sitting in prayer but lurking in the doorway. Was he keeping an eye on her because he didn't believe she was who she claimed to be?

Finja came forward to light the infinity candle which Tori then used to ignite the sage incense. As she slowly waved it in the air over her head, pacing from one side of the altar to the other, the servants and handmaids and pages bowed in respect. Tori returned the sage to the altar and then bowed in return.

"The Divine Mother is grateful for your devotion and wishes you peace." This was the congregation's signal that the liturgy was over. There was a hushed mumbling of voices as the staff left the chapel. Finja blew out the candle and began clearing the books and chalices away.

As the crowd departed, Tori kept her eye on one of the handmaids with pointed ears. Although there were a number of servants with Khadulian ears, this one had Goran's features. Tori glanced at Finja before she stepped down from the altar.

"Pardon me," Tori said to the young woman, keeping her voice low.

The girl's gaze darted to the chapel entrance as if checking for someone. She turned back to Tori with a polite smile. "Yes, Your Holiness."

"I couldn't help but notice that shawl you're wearing. That particular shade of blue is lovely."

"Thank you very much, Your Holiness. I made it myself."

"How industrious."

"Well, my wages aren't enough for much, so I have to sometimes make my own clothes. Though, it's hard to find the time to do so with my master keeping me as busy as he does."

"Your master must be someone of importance to have so much for you to do."

"Yes." Her gaze dropped to the floor for a moment. "He's the captain of the guard so he's got a lot going on."

Hettie is the duke's handmaiden, Tori realized. "Well, it is a lovely shawl, and I pray you find the time to make more lovely items."

"Thank you, Your Holiness."

"Please tell me your name so that I may ask the Divine Mother to send blessings to you."

"It's… it's Hettie, milady."

"Hettie." She smiled at the confirmation. "May the Divine Mother bless you. I hope to see you again soon."

Hettie curtsied with a humble smile, then turned to leave.

Tori watched her go, the gears in her mind reeling. Now that she'd figured out which girl was Goran's daughter, she would need to find out where her rooms were and figure out how to get her out of the castle.

Her thoughts were cut short as the princess entered the main floor of the chapel with the ladies of the court in tow. Behind them, standing guard at the entrance, was Bramwell. Tori had the urge to speak with him, to at least thank him for arranging the ceremony, but the princess and her ladies approached her with purpose.

The princess bowed her head. "It was a very moving ceremony, Lady Tori."

"It was the will of the Divine Mother, Your Highness."

"How thoughtful and generous." Jasmine remarked, waving a silk fan at her own face.

"I do what the Divine Mother would want."

"Then I am pleased that Lady Aurora brought your proposal to my attention."

"Oh, I didn't realize that it was you who approved the ceremony. I am eternally grateful, Your Highness." She wondered if the queen regent had any say in the matter.

"The pleasure was mine." Princess Wrena offered a smile. "Good day."

"Good day, Your Highness. And thank you, Lady Aurora."

Aurora gave Tori a smile as she bowed her head, and then turned to join the princess as she left the chapel.

"Lady Tori." Raven looked over her shoulder at the group leaving. Tori was sure she was meant to follow, but Raven obviously had something to discuss with her. Her palms were pressed together as if she's still praying, and she cleared her throat before she continued to speak. "I found the service extraordinarily interesting."

"Surely you've attended prayer assemblies before, Lady Raven."

"With the royals, yes. But there was something different in the air tonight. Perhaps it was the energy of the servants. It was so pure and… full of hope."

"The Divine Mother wishes hope and peace for all of us."

"Yes, yes." She wrung her hands, looking over her shoulder again. "I do have a question regarding one of the gifts the Divine Mother bestows upon High Priestesses."

"Yes?"

"I was just wondering… do you really have the *sight*?"

Tori blinked, unsure of why Raven was asking. "The Divine Mother is generous with her gift to the High Priestesses who carry her message. But, Lady Raven, the gift is to be shared strictly with royalty to ensure the peace of the nine realms."

A blush covered Raven's cheeks. "Yes, of course. Forgive me."

"What is it that troubles you?" Tori asked. "I am not only here for my visions. I am here for counsel as well. Perhaps I can help."

"It's silly, really. It's about my future. Particularly, *who* will be in my future." Raven glanced at the doorway. Bramwell was no longer there, but Tori knew that she meant to ask about him.

"You have a suitor, and you want to know if you should marry him?" Tori asked.

Raven's blush grew darker, and she clasped her hands together so hard her fingers grew white. "Yes."

Confliction stewed in Tori's gut. Something inside her wanted to say that Raven was mad to think Bramwell would marry her, but that feeling had manifested from a place Tori was afraid to address. Could she really be jealous of Raven's relationship with Bramwell? Internally berating herself, Tori kept a passive expression. "Even if it were permittable for me to share the *sight* with you, nothing is written in stone. There is a saying in Tokuna: If you hold it in your heart and believe it to be true, it will be."

Raven's face lit up, her eyes and smile wide. She took Tori's hands and bowed low. "I do believe it to be true, Lady Tori. Thank you." Still holding her hands, she kissed them, then curtsied before she hurried out of the chapel.

She knew she shouldn't be concerned with whether or not Bramwell preferred Raven. It was out of the question, in any case. Not only could they never be together while she was under the guise of being a High Priestess, but she wasn't in Avarell to secure a relationship. She had a mission to carry out.

As if reading her thoughts, Finja stared at her from behind the altar, brows drawn down and her mouth in a straight line.

Tori almost flinched at the look she was giving her. "What is it? Is something wrong?"

"Lest you forget," Finja said, "the ship comes in two days."

CHAPTER EIGHTEEN

WRENA SUPPRESSED A GIGGLE as the shrimp Theo had been attempting to fork flew across the table. Her aunt, the queen regent, was too busy conversing with the duke to pay any mind. Theo let out a snicker behind his hand, and Wrena stealthily returned the fugitive shrimp to his snack plate, giving her brother a secretive wink.

The duke lifted his wine, standing by the window of the lounge where Lady Maescia, Princess Wrena, and Prince Theo partook in a private meal.

"But is it necessary to have the welcoming banquet?" Maescia asked him. "I don't think the Gadleigh court will feel very welcome once we lay out the amended terms of the negotiation."

"Welcoming banquets are tradition," Duke Grunmire said after sipping his wine. "And the negotiations won't take place until the following day. I would highly advise that, as queen regent, you adhere to the traditions that are already in place in Avarell. It sends a message otherwise."

"Amended terms?" Wrena asked, suddenly interested in their conversation. Normally she would not interfere, but her engagement to Prince Liam was of particular interest to her.

"Yes, my dear," Maescia said, turning to her. There was a tiredness in her eyes, and she didn't hold her shoulders as high as she did when she was in public. The stress her aunt felt was almost tangible. "The terms of the alliance were never a solid agreement. Up until the final documents are signed, alterations can take place from both sides."

"We're talking about the engagement." Wrena rose from the small table and approached her aunt and the duke. "My engagement. If you've changed those terms, I would like to be notified."

Maescia stepped forward and took her hands. "My dear niece, do you *want* to marry Prince Liam of Gadleigh? Be honest."

Wrena's gaze went to the duke and then Theo. Her brother looked up at her and tilted his head. She went inward for a second, thinking about how she felt when she was with Aurora. "No, I do not."

"Then this amendment is to your benefit. The union between you and Prince Liam is unnecessary for the negotiations to continue. And this way, you are free to marry Eleazar."

She gently pulled her hands from Maescia's. "Why Eleazar?" She knew that her aunt and duke were pushing for them to marry, but she still couldn't understand why.

"Eleazar is titled, and he is the next in line to command the Queen's Guard. A union between the two of you would show solidarity, guaranteeing the loyalty of the soldiers who pledged their allegiance to your mother, so that you will have a strong sovereignty over the army."

"Shouldn't I anyway, when I become Queen?"

"Yes, of course. But this union would reinforce it. Besides, you love Eleazar. You've been close friends for ages." Maescia took a sip of her wine, her gaze elsewhere. "What we need to discuss is how to pragmatically handle the arrival of the Gadleigh court. They are traveling far and not expecting bad news. It will not only be a shock, but a great disappointment."

"I am quite puzzled at the turn of events myself," Wrena said.

It was moments like these that she wished she could see and speak to her mother. It wasn't that she was ungrateful for her aunt stepping in, not only to take reign but also to watch over her and Theo. But she missed her talks with her mother, who always seemed to know the right things to say, who provided comfort when she needed it the most. And deep in her heart, she felt that her mother would understand about her feelings for Aurora.

But she'd only seen her mother a rare few times, and never alone. Her aunt was always with her, and her mother was never awake. Her mother stayed in a quarantined room in the high tower, always in bed, covered with heavy quilts. The lights were kept blocked out of the room because the illness left her mother's eyes sensitive. Though the lack of light prohibited Wrena from properly seeing her mother's face, she didn't look the same. Like she was withering away, her cheekbones sticking far too much out of her pallid face, her breath raspy and full of liquid.

She didn't know if her mother would ever really get better, but her aunt promised she was working with the best apothecaries to find a cure for her illness.

"The Gadleigh court will likely be furious with the new terms," Wrena said, taking a seat in the chair beside her aunt's. "They will likely withdraw their part of the bargain, not stand with us in allegiance against the threat of forces from the Nostidour Kingdom."

"I have no doubt they will not be happy with the terms," the duke said, "but a union of armies with Gadleigh is not necessarily needed against the Nostidour forces."

"What makes you so sure?" Wrena asked the duke.

"It is not for you to worry about."

"As the Princess, I think it is."

A knock on the door interrupted them. The duke swirled the wine in his goblet, his face stoic.

The door opened, and Aurora stepped inside. Behind her one of the castle nursemaids bustled in.

"All right, Prince Theo, time to wash up and get ready for bed, Your Highness." The nursemaid snatched up a few of his toys and waved him over to her. "We've prepared your bath and oils. And I do believe Mazie found the bubbling soap you like."

Theo quickly gobbled up the last of his snack and stood from the table.

"Come give your aunt a kiss first," Maescia called to him.

Theo switched directions and ran over to kiss his aunt on the cheek. "Goodnight," he said as he grabbed his toys and left the room.

Aurora smiled at him as he ran past her, and then her eyes met Wrena's. "I thought you might need an escort to your rooms, Your Highness."

Wrena stood, relieved to no longer discuss the alliance with Gadleigh. "How thoughtful, Lady Aurora. Thank you."

"Princess Wrena," the duke called out. "Would you mind waiting a moment. I promise it won't take long."

She froze in place. Had the duke caught the tender look she and Aurora shared? She wanted nothing more in that moment than to flee with Aurora, but she flashed him a fake smile. "Yes, of course."

"I believe Eleazar is looking forward to you accompanying him to the ball the night of the welcoming banquet. I do hope you will do him the honor of being by his side for the event."

Maescia raised a brow, waiting for Wrena to answer.

"It would be a pleasure," Wrena said.

"Oh, there's one more thing I wanted to ask you." The duke sauntered closer, studying the wine in his goblet. "Do you know the stable hand, I think his name is Rudy."

At first, she was taken aback. But then realization dawned on her. Wrena knew exactly of whom the duke spoke. And the reason he might bring Rudy's name up made Wrena nervous. "I believe so. He tends to my horse."

"Do you also know of the rumor that he's been seen in an intimate situation with one of the servants?"

Wrena fought not to shiver. "I do not know of any such rumors, but I also wasn't aware that stable hands were forbidden from engaging in relationships?"

"The servant he was seen with was male."

Wrena wanted to scream. She wanted to push the duke and ask him why that made a difference. But the way her aunt watched her made her rethink. She couldn't respond, so she simply looked up at the duke, her lips pressed tightly together so as to hold her tongue.

"As you know, men lying with men—and such relations—are frowned upon by the queendom."

"I know that centuries ago it was frowned upon, yes."

"Centuries of good standards are the backbone of a strong queendom. But this boy and his disregard for morals, his lack of ethics... It makes me question the reliability of such a character—one who sneaks around to do questionable things that are frowned upon in the queendom, an immoral individual who has no sense of tradition or principals."

Her gaze hit the floor for a second, but she forced herself to face him again. Inside she was screaming. She would love nothing more than to claw the duke's eyes out. She could feel Aurora's stare from behind her at the door. Still she did not speak. She feared the duke might do something terrible to Aurora.

"Wrena," Maescia said, straightening the skirts of her gown, "these are acts against the authority of the crown. Impure. Unclean."

The duke stepped forward. "If you are aware of any such appalling activities, you'll be sure to tell me, won't you, Your Highness?"

Wrena swallowed hard, but kept her chin up. "Yes, of course," she barely managed to get out.

"Thank you. I bid you a good night."

She turned to go, taking in Aurora's pale, horror-stricken face that must have matched her own.

TORI

CHAPTER NINETEEN

TAKUMI WAS CURLED UP by the fireplace as Tori adjusted her black mask. It was well past midnight, and she needed to make sure no one would recognize her as the High Priestess. The black outfit Goran provided for her was snug against her body, and the black, waist-length cloak swayed behind her. There was a section of her trousers to tuck her shuriken into and another section for her kunai.

She studied the leaf-shaped blades, each with a ring on the pommel. With her weapons hidden in their appropriate spots, she pulled the hood of her cloak over her head and studied herself in the mirror. The sturdy but soft mask covered the upper portion of her face, an intricate design of curving stitch-work marking the material. Since it would be easy to identify her if anyone saw her eyes, she checked that the eyeholes were small enough to hide the slant of her eyes but big enough to see through. She had to hand it to the Khadulians: they were experts at design.

Slipping out onto her balcony, she lowered the rope Goran had also provided over her railing. It was tied tightly so not to slip. Her experience climbing trees gave her the strength and the know-how to lower herself down to the castle courtyard. At this hour, the main generator for electricity was off, leaving only the watermills to keep the outside lights on. Here in the courtyard, it was dark.

Finja had been helpful in singling out which building Hettie lived in, and she had also gone to the trouble of locating her room and tying a thin, dark ribbon to her door handle for Tori to find. As long as no one had removed the ribbon, she would be able to find Hettie. It was easy enough to make her way through the maze of bushes and columns and pavilions in the courtyard, but when she arrived at Hettie's building, she needed to be more resourceful. As one of the duke's personal handmaids, Hettie's rooms were nearby the part of the castle the duke occupied, and there was bound to be at least one guard keeping watch in that section of the castle.

She kept silent as she approached, crouching low behind some bushes, and watched as the guard on duty made his rounds. The guard paced down the arched walkway, and Tori waited until he was out of sight to leave her hiding spot. She made her way to the door of the building and slipped out her tiny tool pouch. This lock was manageable, and Tori quickly snuck inside the building, quietly and undetected.

Her next challenge was to find the servants' rooms. She worked her way up the stairs, careful with each step she took, and found herself at the end of a hall of doors. She passed each door, studying their knobs, as silent as the night. Halfway down the hall, she found Finja's ribbon. Her hand wrapped around the doorknob, and she turned it.

Quickly slipping inside the room, she found three beds arranged in a tight space. Tori recognized the shawl on the foot of one of the beds and presumed it was Hettie's. Upon further inspection, she found she was right. Tori reached out and put a hand on Hettie's shoulder.

Hettie shot up straight and grasped her sheets. The other occupants in the room were roused, one of them moaning in fear. Hettie was quick to grab her knitting needles and aim them at Tori's face. Tori ducked out of the way swiftly and then snatched Hettie's arm to stop her from striking her.

One of her roommates leaped from the bed, but Tori was quick to pull out a shuriken and whip it in the girl's direction, catching her night dress so she was anchored to the wooden frame of her bed. Hettie opened her mouth as if she were going to scream. Tori clasped her hand over Hettie's mouth, not wanting to hurt her, but needing her to keep quiet.

"Quiet," Tori whispered. "I'm here to help."

"Let me go," Hettie said through Tori's fingers.

"I was hired by your father."

Hettie stopped squirming, and her roommates regarded each other, the timid one pulling her covers to her chin.

"She's lying," the girl trapped by the shuriken said. She ripped at her night dress to free herself and ran to the door. Tori grabbed a kunai and flung it at the door, piercing it into the wood with a *thunk*. The handmaid stopped dead in her tracks, petrified.

Hettie's eyes were wide, and she shook with fear. "Who are you?"

"I've been sent to help." Tori was grateful for the concealment of darkness. She also made sure to keep her voice at a whisper so it was harder to recognize. "Your father, Goran, has employed me to find you and free you from your services here."

Hettie blinked. "I… I haven't seen my father for years."

Tori could tell Hettie wasn't convinced. "He told me to give you this." She retrieved the necklace Goran had given her, handing it to Hettie.

Hettie studied the piece of jewelry by the light of the moon. "How do I know you are not simply a thief who stole this?"

"Your father told me to tell you it once belonged to your grandmother Delores, who cared for you for a month when your mother was ill."

Hettie studied what she could see of her face, swallowing visibly.

Tori took a step back and waited for Hettie to accept the truth.

"What is your plan?"

"It is your father's plan. His ship is set to arrive in two days' time. You should gather your personal effects, and I will come fetch you on that eve to bring you to him."

Hettie looked at the necklace again, and then back at Tori. "Just leave?"

"Without a trace."

"It would be going against the law. I would be a fugitive. A criminal."

"Your father has arranged to hide you at home, for you to be back with your family. Surely the risk is worth it?"

Hettie's shoulders slumped as she nodded, a look of relief washing over her features. "Aye. Aye, it is worth it. My father truly sent you to rescue me?"

"He did."

Hettie held the necklace to her chest, and though it was difficult to see, Tori swore there were tears in her eyes.

"The ship comes in two days. I will return for you then."

CHAPTER TWENTY

WRENA SMOOTHED HER HAND over the fine muslin of the wedding dress. It was originally her mother's dress, altered for Wrena to appear more modern and fit her properly. It was presented to her during the first talks of the engagement to Prince Liam, but now Wrena wondered if she would ever wear it. Her fingertips brushed over the delicate lace and beads, and she wondered if there would be a High Priestess somewhere in the world who would give their blessing and marry two women.

Theo flew his wooden toy bird over his toy horse and made a cawing sound. "Wrena, you said you'd play with me."

"Yes, I know. But I want to be the phoenix."

"You can be the phoenix next time. Be the horse."

Wrena set herself down on the floor and took the horse. "Why is everyone forcing me to be someone I'm not."

Theo narrowed one eye and gawked at her. "I'm not forcing you. We can take turns."

Wrena laughed. "That's not really what I meant. Sorry, Theo."

Wrena went through the motions, playing Theo's game. As Theo held his wooden phoenix up in the air, his focus went beyond it. Lowering his phoenix, he wrinkled his brow, his eyes still fixed on the dress hanging on the hook in the wall.

"Why is that wedding dress there?"

"I wanted to look at it." Wrena glanced at Theo under lowered lids. She knew she couldn't get away with such a simple answer, so she raised her chin. "It used to belong to Mother."

"Oh." Theo's mouth twitched. It was like he was fighting not to frown. "I heard she could die."

"We shouldn't think of such things, Theo."

"But what if she does?"

She let out a slow breath and cupped his chin. "You'll always have me, no matter what."

He gave her a smile, but then his expression sobered. "What was father like?"

"He was a very stubborn man. Liked to take what he wanted."

Theo shrugged. "He was the King. Isn't that what kings do?"

"Unfortunately, yes. But sometimes people—even kings—need to think about those around them. The citizens of the realm serve royalty, but royalty should do what's right and what's good to serve the people. Without the people, we are nothing. She stroked his hair. Maybe you'll remember that when you're King."

They were interrupted by a knock at the door. Wrena stood, abandoning the wooden horse, and opened the door to find Raven. The look on Raven's face was troubling, as if something urgent was worrying her.

"Your highness." Raven curtsied, then wrung her hands.

"Raven, what is it?"

"I've been asked to fetch you. You are needed for judgement in a trial that is taking place."

"When?"

"Now."

Wrena furrowed her brow and turned to her brother. "Theo, why don't you take the game back to your room. We'll continue it later."

"All right," he answered, disappointed.

Raven curtsied as the prince left the room. Wrena stepped into the hall to join Raven and closed the door behind her. She was never in the right mindset for emergency trials, and she didn't even understand why she needed to attend. She suspected it was mostly for show, so that the citizens of Avarell saw unity in the royals, deeming whatever judgement Lady Maescia declared a unanimous verdict.

"Do you know what this is about?" Wrena asked Raven as they made their way to the courtyard.

"I do not, your highness. The trial was called so suddenly, and I was asked to fetch you immediately, with no delay."

"I understand. Thank you, Raven."

They made it to the courtyard right before Lady Maescia was about to march outside. Wrena hurried to her and took her by the arm. "What has happened?" she asked her aunt.

Lady Maescia motioned for her to follow as she headed outside and climbed the stairs to the scaffold outside the tower where prisoners were held. Upon the scaffold were their two thrones.

"A crime that needs urgent attention."

"What kind of crime?"

Lady Maescia gestured at the princess's chair. "You shall see, my dear."

Wrena took her seat, keeping her back straight for the sake of the crowd gathered in the courtyard. The duke strode past her and took his place beside Lady Maescia's throne. The chopping blocks in the middle of the courtyard did not go unnoticed. Nor did the baskets meant to catch any rolling heads. Not too far away, Tiberius, the head executioner of the Queen's Guard, stood sentry.

The yard filled up quickly, the nobles of the house as well as the castle staff shuffling in with looks of confusion. Apparently, no one knew why the trial was called or what was about to happen.

Her eyes went immediately to the row of chairs where the ladies-in-waiting usually sat. Jasmine and Raven sat whispering to one another. Sitting beside the High Priestess was Aurora. She looked just as perplexed as everyone else, and when their eyes met, Wrena could only offer her a subtle shrug.

Soldiers of the Queen's Guard escorted in a young man with a bruise on his cheek. Wrena held back a gasp, realizing it was Rudy, the stable hand. Her heart nearly stopped. Her mind spun. Could this really be about what she thought it was? Could the duke—could her aunt—really have a vendetta against this man?

As two more guards—one of them being Aurora's cousin Bramwell—brought out a second man, Wrena fought the urge to stand up and protest. She nearly did. What was stopping her? When the guards holding Rudy roughly forced him to his knees, she knew the reason. Rudy screamed as his arm was bent back at an impossible angle, and the guards responded by knocking him in the back with the hilt of their swords. Wrena couldn't let that happen to Aurora. She wouldn't let them lay a hand on her. Her fear of what might happen to her lover kept her silent.

The magistrate stepped onto the stage, bowing to the queen regent and Wrena before he faced the two accused men. "Good day, citizens of Avarell. We are here to call forward the case of Rudy Blackwell and Patrick Oakheart, standing accused of offences against the dignity of the crown." He stared pointedly at Rudy. "For the record, please state your name."

Rudy held his fists tight, his chin quivering as he answered. "Rudy Blackwell, sire."

"And you work at the stables, is that correct, Mr. Blackwell?"

Rudy nodded, frowning.

"And for the record," the magistrate said, turning to the other man, "please state your name."

"Patrick Oakheart, sire. But I did nothing wrong!"

"Please do not speak unless answering a question, Mr. Oakheart." The magistrate paced along the stage. "Mr. Blackwell, we have more than one witness who claim that you and Mr. Oakheart have been spotted in intimate relations. Do you deny it?"

The crowd murmured. Whispers were exchanged. Rudy opened his mouth, sweat pouring from his temples, but could not produce any sound. Wrena squirmed in her chair, feeling sorry for the man. Patrick Oakheart's head dropped, his shoulders shaking as he began to sob.

"Have you nothing to say, Mr. Blackwell?"

"I… I—"

"Do you deny it?" The magistrate's eyes bulged as he shouted the question at Rudy. "Did you have intimate relations with Mr. Oakheart, yes or no?"

"It's not a crime!" Rudy shouted. "It's not."

Wrena fought to keep still, the same sentence buzzing in her head, urgent to get out.

"Perhaps we need to look at all the facts before we can decide if it is a crime or not, Mr. Blackwell." The magistrate ignored Rudy's blubbering and turned to Patrick. "Mr. Oakheart, could you please tell the citizens of the court if you are, in fact, married."

Patrick let out a horrendous sob. Rudy's face fell. Wrena's gaze drifted to a woman in the crowd who had tears streaming down her face. Could that have been his wife? Wrena's gut twisted. Perhaps accusing men of lying with men was not a strong enough argument to pass sentence. Perhaps it was frowned upon in the court's eyes, but it was not a crime. Someone had found a way—a technicality—to condemn them anyway.

"Mr Oakheart, please answer the question."

"Yes." It took a lot of effort for Patrick to speak through his sniffling. "I am."

The crowd let out gasps and mutters. Rudy bit his trembling lip.

"Then you are both guilty of adultery, which is a crime, both in the eyes of the queendom and in the eyes of the Divine Mother." The magistrate turned to Lady Maescia. "Your Grace. We await your verdict."

Wrena turned her face toward her aunt, but her eyes were far away. She felt as if she were dreaming—having a nightmare. They were setting an example. Wrena felt, in the hopeless pit of despair in her mind, that her aunt knew about her and Aurora.

Lady Maescia placed her hands gently upon the armrests of her throne. "I would like to know which one of you is willing to die."

Her demand was met with silence, save for the murmuring of the crowd.

The queen regent clicked her tongue. "Very well. If neither of you can decide, I have no choice but to send both of the accused into the Rift."

"No!" Patrick yelled. "No, please. It was my fault. I wasn't honest with Rudy. He didn't know I was married. Spare him. I will die. Let him go!"

Rudy's eyes were wide. "No, Patrick," Rudy blubbered. "You can't take all the blame. I… I can't let them kill you. Let them send us to the Rift. We could make it."

Lady Maescia tapped her chin. "Oh, did I mention that we'd be keeping your arms?"

The two men gawked at her in horror.

"You are both free to fight your way through the Rift—where you will undoubtedly perish—but because you have affronted the queendom, I will need some sort of payment for your crimes. Your arms should do."

Wrena glanced at her advisor, the duke, who looked pleased with her sentence.

"Should we take your arms, then?" Lady Maescia asked, her head slightly tilted.

"No, please, don't!" Rudy cried. "Take my life. Leave Patrick be. He… he has a wife to care for. I have no one."

"Rudy, don't." Patrick sobbed some more.

"A head it is then," Lady Maescia said. "But whose? I believe I will need a moment to decide."

She motioned for her guards to move the accused men to the chopping blocks. Their moans and cries of mercy were almost unintelligible. Most of the women in the crowd cowered behind their hands, unwilling to watch. Rudy's neck was forced down upon one chopping block, and Patrick's on the other. Tiberius marched over with his battle axe, stood between Patrick and Rudy, and awaited the queen regent's word.

Wrena couldn't breathe. As much as she wanted to close her eyes and shut out the world, she couldn't take her eyes off the executioner. Lady Maescia drummed her fingertips against her chin again, leaving the whole courtyard rife with anticipation, until finally she glanced at Tiberius and raised two fingers.

The axe swung.

Gasps and whimpers echoed in the courtyard as blood splattered and spilled onto the ground at Tiberius's feet. Wrena covered her mouth, fighting with all she had inside her not to scream.

Patrick let out a long moan, his sobs causing him to shudder as Rudy's blood slipped between tiny pebbles and was soaked up by sand.

Wrena's gaze went to Aurora, who had lost all color in her face. Beside her, the High Priestess had her head bent in prayer. Wrena moved her trembling hand away from her mouth and pressed in onto her lap, straining to keep control.

The next few moments were a blur. The world seemed to fade from her view, the sounds and sights of the courtyard emptying like a dream as she followed her aunt off the raised platform and into the castle.

Once they were inside, Wrena stopped short and backed up against the wall, her breaths coming in curt, shallow puffs.

"Wrena, dear." Lady Maescia put a hand on her shoulder. "Are you all right?"

"I… I don't know." She pressed her hands against her chest in an effort to slow her pounding heart. After taking a deep breath in and letting it out, she locked eyes with her aunt. "Why didn't you talk to me before the trial began? You could have warned me."

"I followed protocol. A crime was committed, and an execution followed."

"But you didn't discuss the punishment with me."

"I wasn't aware that it would make a difference."

"Death? Was the love they shared so horrible that it should end in death?"

"Love." Lady Maescia scoffed. "The fact is an offence was committed. I didn't make the rules, Wrena. That was written in stone generations before us."

"Exactly. Things are not the same now as they were then. The only thing that has remained the same is that no one is bold enough to speak about it."

"You might care to hold back your boldness yourself, child. You do not know whom it might affect."

Wrena narrowed her eyes. "That sounds like a threat."

The queen regent sighed as she closed her eyes, then reached out and put a hand on her shoulder. "My dear, sweet, niece. No one is threatening you."

"Then what are you saying?"

"I'm saying be careful. When you are in a position of power, there are eyes everywhere." Lady Maescia's expression was intense. Then suddenly, her featured softened and she patted Wrena's shoulder. "Now, go on and get ready for supper, dear."

CHAPTER TWENTY-ONE

TORI COULDN'T GET TO HER ROOM fast enough. The second her door closed, tears escaped and flowed down her face. It took everything she had not to retch onto the floor. As she reached for a cloth to wipe her cheeks, Takumi made a whimpering noise and circled around her feet.

What did she just witness? The events of the last half hour left her stomach sour and her head spinning. She didn't know how much longer she could go on pretending to serve a Queen who would allow such a travesty to happen.

Tori collapsed into the chair by the fireplace, pressing her palms into her eyes. The door opened, but she didn't look up to see who it was. Her gut told her it was Finja, and since Takumi wasn't panicking, she knew she wasn't in danger.

"Get up, girl," Finja said, her voice stern.

"What?" Tori glanced at her, her stomach still roiling with acid.

"You must get ready."

"For what?"

"You're the official High Priestess of the castle now. When there is a death in the castle, the High Priestess must be present for his burial in order to prevent the bad spirit of the corpse to come back from the ethereal plane and haunt the castle."

Tori stared after her in disbelief. Was she really expected to perform a *job* after witnessing something so horrific?

Finja hurried to Tori's trunk and threw it open. Tori almost objected, but she had no energy. The gold cloak Finja pulled out reflected sunlight coming in through the window.

"Get up and put this on," Finja said, her mouth twisted into an agitated frown.

"I am *not* a High Priestess. I cannot prevent a spirit from haunting the castle. And I could only wish that that man's ghost would come back and hound the queen regent for what she did."

"You cannot afford to blow your cover. You haven't even carried out any of your tasks. Do you really want to throw it all away now? What would your family think?"

Tori clenched her teeth. She pulled the small throw pillow up off the chair and screamed into it. After releasing her anguish, she stared at Finja, her breath bated.

"Feel better?" Finja asked, one brow raised.

"Not really," Tori answered.

"Too bad. Now put this on."

Bram paced the meeting hall of the barracks, appalled by what happened. He was close enough to almost have blood splattered on him when Tiberius lowered his axe, and all he could do was stand sentry and stare. There was nothing he could have done; the queen regent gave the order, and it wasn't his station to disagree.

A small cough caught his attention. Bram stopped pacing and stepped forward to investigate the noise. His eyes widened when he found Prince Theo hiding behind one of the large chairs at the back of the room.

"Your Highness, what are you doing here?"

Prince Theo tentatively took a step out from behind the chair. "They said I wasn't to come outside. I didn't want to be alone in my rooms."

"What about your nursemaids?"

"They all left to see what was happening outside."

"They left you alone?"

Prince Theo narrowed his eyes. "What is everyone so excited about? What did I miss?"

Bram approached him, unsure of how to answer. Taking in a deep breath, he put a hand on Prince Theo's shoulder. "Do not worry, Your Highness. It doesn't affect you. And to tell you the truth, I wish I had missed the event myself."

The prince appeared confused, dropping his chin and pursing his lips.

Logan appeared at the doorway, clearing his throat. Bram signaled for him to mind his actions around the prince. Logan stepped into the room, and Azalea came in to stand by his side. They both seemed as jaded as Bram felt.

"I'm always missing out on things," Prince Theo said, kicking at the chair. "They think I'm too young. Or too stupid."

"I'm sure that's not true."

Logan stepped closer. "Perhaps they think you should only be bothered with the very important things."

"So why won't they let me see my mother?"

Logan and Azalea exchanged looks. It was Azalea who squatted down so that she was more eye-level with the prince. She took his hand gently. "Your mother is very sick, Your Highness. They do not want you to become sick as well. Because you are too important for that to happen."

He stared at her for a moment before a tiny smile broke out on his face. "Fine. But one day I will grow weary of being left out. One day I'll be a king."

"Yes," Bram said. "You are right about that. And we will be at your service."

Azalea stood, flanked by Bram and Logan. The prince seemed to beam up at them.

"Your Highness." The voice came from the doorway. One of his nursemaids stood there, wringing her hands. Bram gathered she must have been embarrassed for having left the prince and then was unable to find him. "Her Grace, Lady Maescia, would like for you to ready yourself for supper."

Prince Theo glanced up at Bram, who gave him an encouraging wink. "We'll see you at supper, Your Highness."

Prince Theo bowed his head. Bram, Logan, and Azalea returned the gesture and watched as the prince left the room.

Logan patted Bram on the back, the frown returning to his face.

Footsteps sounded in the hall. Bram turned to see Tiberius pass by the door only to double back and enter the room.

"What are you all doing in here?" Tiberius asked.

"Nothing. We were just speaking with the prince."

"Oh." Tiberius smirked. "Glad he didn't see me, then. There's enough blood on me to make the river run red."

Bram wasn't sure, but Tiberius actually looked pleased with himself. "You might want to hurry and change before you stain the floors."

"Right." He stretched out his shoulder.

"You all right?"

"All in a day's work." He rubbed at the shoulder and stretched his neck from side to side. "Sucker's neck was thick. Might have to ice the arm. By the way, the duke announced we're to go out on a Queenshunt in preparation for the guests from Gadleigh. Said we'd be needing some game for the feast."

Bram nodded solemnly. "When are we heading out?"

"Soon. He said no dinner tonight until we return. It will improve the hunt, he reckons."

Azalea squeezed Logan's hand before she departed for her rooms.

"You all right?" Logan asked Bram once they were alone.

Bram twisted his mouth into a half frown and gave him a nod. As Logan left, Bram's eyes focused on a small red spot on the floor where Tiberius had been standing. He wasn't sure he understood a world where life could be taken away so swiftly, so carelessly. Shaking his head to clear the thoughts, he headed to his rooms to change for the hunt. The Queenshunt always took them close to the Rift. It made him think about how much had changed since he'd fallen in the Rift and was rescued by the young Drothidian girl.

CHAPTER TWENTY-TWO

WRENA COULD BARELY LOOK at her dinner, let alone eat it. Her stomach still roiled with disgust from witnessing Rudy's death. She pushed her food around her plate, her mind screaming for her to get up and leave the banquet hall. She felt as if the walls were closing in on her, suffocating her and fogging up her mind.

The entire hall was silent save for the tinny din of silverware upon plates. The ladies of the court kept their eyes focused on the food they solemnly ate, and the soldiers were absent due to the Queenshunt. The sorrow was stifling, and Wrena wished nothing more than to have the ground swallow her up.

"Dear Aunt, may I please be excused?" Nausea burned like acid in her throat.

"But you've barely eaten."

"I'm not feeling well. I doubt I'd be able to keep anything down if I did eat."

Lady Maescia pursed her lips, obviously not thrilled with Wrena's desire to leave. "Very well. Do rest. I bid you a good night."

"Good night, Aunt Maescia."

The second she stood, servants rushed over and tended to her plate and goblet. But she barely noticed, for her gaze went directly to Aurora. Aurora's glance was fleeting, but Wrena knew she received her message. Though it would appear too suspicious if Aurora were to leave right away, Wrena knew she wouldn't keep her waiting too long. She needed to see her, and she suspected Aurora felt the same.

Wrena's handmaids scampered to lay out her night clothes, a bit hasty in their efforts as they hadn't expected her to turn in so soon. One of her servants snatched up the hair brush, ready to work out Wrena's tangled locks, but Wrena politely dismissed her and the rest of the crew. She needed to be alone. She needed silence to process.

As soon as her chamber door was closed, she went over to her wash room to splash water on her face. The feeling of suffocation hadn't subsided yet, so she undid her corset, which only helped a little. She slipped into her night clothes and paced the room, absently brushing through her hair. Her whole body was trembling and her skin felt cold. It felt like forever, waiting there in her quiet room, until finally there was a light knock at the door.

Seeing Aurora was like instant relief, the weight on her shoulders immediately falling. She took her by the hand and led her into the room, closing the door to lock out the rest of the world.

"Did anyone see you?" Wrena asked, her voice low with grief.

"No, of course not."

Wrena walked over and sat on the edge of her bed, her eyes stinging. Chills washed over her body for the tenth time since Rudy's beheading

"What just happened?" Aurora asked, raking her hair back away from her cheeks. "I feel like it was a dream. How can they enforce a law like that?"

"They said it was adultery." Wrena shook her head. "It *was* adultery, but they made a display of the fact that it was two men together."

"How can they be so crass?"

"I don't know. I don't assume to understand anything anymore. I don't believe anyone has been accused of having relations with the same gender before."

Aurora shook her head. "Or no one was ever punished for it."

Wrena joined her hands in front of her stomach and dropped her gaze. It was clear to her that Aurora being with her was dangerous. For both of them. "Where does that leave us?"

Aurora was quiet for a moment, her eyes searching Wrena's face. "We have to be careful," she said, determination in her voice.

"I'm afraid for you, Aurora." There was a vise on her heart, squeezing it into numbness. "I don't want to lose you. I don't want you to die."

Aurora took her hands. "I don't want either of us to die. But I don't want this to end, either. I won't let it. How can I live if I can't be by your side?"

CHAPTER TWENTY-THREE

TORI PUSHED BACK the feeling of dread as she returned from performing the blessing of the dead. It was the worst hour she had ever spent in her life, pretending to be a dignified High Priestess while inside she wanted to scream at the queen regent. The worst was enduring the sobs of Rudy's family. Finja told her that Patrick was being held prisoner in the dungeon. She couldn't imagine what he was going through.

She was just grateful that the duke and his men were out on a hunt. That no one from the court aside from Finja and the footmen who carried Rudy's body were there to watch her. She didn't know if she could have looked Bram in the eye.

Full understanding finally hit her. She knew now why Goran wanted so desperately for her to intervene. The queen regent was dangerous. Dangerous to the citizens of Avarell, and perhaps, if she couldn't be put in her place, dangerous to the nine realms.

Tori was more determined than ever to help stop the madness. Not only for her own family, but for the people of Avarell and Khadulan. Lady Maescia was turning Avarell into a fearful place, and the people were bound to feel repressed soon. It was only a matter of time before blood would be spilled and a rebellion would emerge. The question was if she would be at the head of that rebellion.

She could barely sleep, though Finja had insisted she get some sleep before Goran's ship came in. She wandered out to her balcony, looking out onto the few lights that were still lit in the city before retreating to her room to change into her black outfit.

Though her heartbeat was fast and loud in her ears, she felt as if she were moving in slow motion, going through the movements as she slipped on her black cloak and mask. Taking the extra dark cloak Goran had stored in her trunk, she slipped down the rope off her balcony, hoping that Hettie would be ready to go.

When she reached the courtyard, Takumi stuck his head out from under some bushes, his tiny feet padding along the ground as he joined her. Takumi scampered beneath another bush when they reached Hettie's building, and Tori crouched low behind a bench as she waited for the patrolling soldier to continue his rounds.

Once he was out of sight, Tori rose. Hettie emerged, as if from nowhere, and crept toward her. Tori gestured for her to get behind the bench and out of sight.

"Are you ready?" Her whisper sounded harsher than she had intended.

"Yes." She looked nervously back at the building that housed her room, then adjusted the strap of the bag secured over her shoulder and followed Tori.

"Have your roommates agreed to keep silent?"

"Yes. They won't say a word."

They reached a high hedge, and Tori stopped to turn to Hettie. "I have a cloak for you. It's from your father. It should help to keep you hidden on our journey to the docks."

Hettie nodded, dropping her bag on the ground and putting on the cloak. Tori noticed that the bag she carried was not very big. She supposed Hettie had little to take with her because she never had much, never acquired much. But if she were in Hettie's place, there wouldn't be need for much else if she'd been promised to see her family again.

She led Hettie through the gardens of Capehill Castle toward the stables, where the rear walls of the castle grounds met the woods. They passed the shed where the workers kept their gardening equipment. Behind it was a locked gate, meant to be used by the gardeners to dispose of overgrown shrubs and plant clippings. Tori pulled out her tool pouch and picked the lock, which gave way easily. The gate let out a small creak as they opened it, and Tori held her breath, wishing the sound away. Once they were through, they hurried into the cloak of the woods.

Like a darting shadow, Takumi ran toward them, then circled around Tori's legs. His whiskers wiggled as he smelled the air around Hettie. Hettie let out a shriek and backed away.

Tori held her hands up, signaling for Hettie to keep quiet. "It's okay. This is Takumi."

"You… you own a fox?"

Tori gave her a half smile. "I don't own him. He's my friend."

Hettie shook her head. "How I ended up following a masked woman with a fox for a friend is a mystery I may never solve."

Tori smirked for a second, but then they reached the edge of the woods, which opened up to an alley behind a pub. From here, they would have to travel through the back streets of Avarell City. Luckily, only a few of the street lights were kept lit by the watermill. The main generator would be out for a few hours, leaving the remainder of the city in darkness.

The way in which Hettie followed her through the shadows of the cobblestone streets reminded her of Miki. If ever there was someone who could silence her footsteps, it was her. There were times when their mother would bake apple muffins and leave them out to cool. Miki had been able to sneak past their mother and snatch up a few for the three sisters and older brother to share. No one had ever heard her navigate to the kitchen and back.

Though Tori's heart beat quickly from sneaking through the dark city streets, it also ached for her dearly departed sister. Even now, years later, she missed her terribly.

They kept to the shadows, but closer to the outskirts of the city, the buildings were sparse, leaving them little to hide behind. As they passed the deserted stands of the marketplace, they heard heavy footsteps. Tori pulled Hettie behind a fisherman's stand and yanked her down to a crouch. Peeking through the leg of the stand, Tori spotted a guard headed past the market. She and Hettie locked gazes, a silent agreement between them to keep quiet. Takumi sniffed at the air, and just then, a cat rounded the stand. As the cat caught sight of Takumi, who hissed at the feline, the cat let out an awful shriek and bolted from the stand, knocking down a small stack of empty crates at the next stand. Tori clenched her teeth, noticing the guard stop at the noise.

The guard unsheathed his sword, his eyes searching for the source of the commotion. Tori hoped he would see the cat run off and leave it at that, but the guard did no such thing. He approached their hiding spot, his brows lowered.

Thinking quickly, Tori slipped a shuriken from her supply and hurled it low across the street. It knocked into a jug which sat on a windowsill of a shop, toppling it over. The guard swiftly pivoted to face the shop, his sword raised. It was a good distraction, but it wasn't enough to get him to leave. Tori bent down and whispered to Takumi, "Distract him."

Takumi took off, trotting by the guard at first to get his attention, and then sprinting between stands and buildings. The guard let out a curse word and chased the fox, undoubtedly thinking the animal was there to steal food from the citizens of Avarell. As Takumi led him up the road and away from the market, Tori took Hettie's hand and hurried toward the towering archway of the city entrance. She hurried through and then began their trek toward the docks.

She finally managed to get her to their destination. The winds were stronger as they got closer to the bay, and the waves on the sea were aggressive. At the sight of the bay, Hettie's eyes seemed to light up. The ship was there, waiting, and Hettie's pace became hurried.

The docks were occupied by workers unloading supplies from the ship which needed to be brought to the castle at first light. Standing on the docks, overlooking his men, was Goran.

Hettie took off at a run, and he turned toward her. Goran's jaw nearly dropped at the sight of Hettie. Tori kept back to give them room, but she could still clearly see tears forming in his eyes as his daughter approached.

He wrapped his arms around Hettie, swinging her off the ground as he buried his face in her hair. When he set her down, he held her by the shoulders and looked her up and down, as if surveying her condition and checking if she was well.

"Oh, my Hettie! I can't believe how much you've changed."

"I'm still the same girl, Papa, if a bit more worn for the wear."

He ran a gentle hand down her cheek. "Did they hurt you?"

"I'm fine, Papa. I just want to go home."

"Very soon, my darling. At the first light, as soon as the delivery is handed over. Until then there is a nice, comfortable room for you on the ship."

"Will you be there?"

"I will join you as soon as business is conducted, and then I will never let you out of my sight again." He squeezed her to his chest.

Tori stood watching the scene, the wind kicking up her cloak around her. Goran's teary eyes met with Tori's, and he gave her a nod. "Thank you," he said.

Once Goran got Hettie settled inside the ship, he came out to talk to Tori alone. The men were almost done unloading, and once the shipment was handed over, Goran and Hettie would set sail.

"You did as well as I expected," Goran said. "I'm extremely pleased with your progress. But do not forget about the rest."

Though Tori knew he was happy to have his daughter back, she understood that her job was not over. Having witnessed what the queen regent was capable of, she stood with Goran in solidarity to carry out the remaining tasks. Besides, Goran's wife was still out there somewhere, and Tori herself would not be satisfied if only one member of her family was saved and not the others. Goran wanted his wife back just as much as Tori wanted her family and the villagers of Sukoshi to be cured of the phoenix fever.

And the bigger task was to assure that the queen regent didn't push her power over the nine realms in the future. She had to be stopped.

"I think I found where the Queen is being kept," Tori told Goran. "But there is a key to the room she is locked in, and the Lady Maescia wears it on a chain that hangs around her neck at all times. I've tried to pick the lock but it is impossible. I will somehow need to steal the key, but I fear she will notice if it is gone."

"Perhaps you can copy the key."

"How would I do that?"

"I have a way. If you get the key, even for a few minutes, you should be able to make a mold of it." Goran turned to one of his workers and asked him to fetch a molding box. His worker hurried off to do what he asked.

"What happens after I get the mold?"

"I have an iron worker under my service in Avarell. Give the mold to Finja and instruct her to take it to him. He'll make you the key you need."

It didn't escape Tori how much time this would take. She would have to find the opportunity to steal the key, place it in the mold, return the key, then get the mold to Finja. And then she would have to wait until the iron worker delivered the copy of the key without the Queen's Guard or Lady Maescia finding out. The understanding of the stretch of time it would take to accomplish all this made her realize how long it would be until she could see her family again.

"Do you know how my family is faring? Have any of your people gone to check on them?"

"Yes. I've had one of my men sent to survey the situation. They are well."

She wished she could have more details, but she knew she was unlikely to get any.

He took a pouch out of his coat and handed it to her. "More medicine for you," he said. "I will be back in a week's time. I hope you'll have the books by then."

She took the pouch and stuffed it away. "I hope so too."

CHAPTER TWENTY-FOUR

ORDINARILY, HE WOULD HAVE been asleep in his rooms at the castle, but tonight Bram couldn't sleep. Even the pints of ale he and Logan downed after the Queenshunt didn't dull his senses enough to allow him to fall into slumber.

It had been Logan's suggestion, after coming back from the hunt, to relax with a drink. But it was a short night, and after getting a very drunk Logan back to his rooms, Bram found himself walking the streets of Avarell. He hoped no one would mistake him for a thief or a vagrant, since he wasn't in uniform.

His mind reeled with frustration. Not only was he still upset about the beheading of the stable hand, but after the Queenshunt, the duke informed him that his promotion review would have to be postponed. He then went on to assign Bram sentry duty on the castle ramparts for the following day. This assignment felt like a demotion, and it didn't leave a hopeful feeling in Bram's heart. In fact, he'd spent the past hour giving the offer from the Gadleigh commander serious consideration.

The Gadleigh court would be arriving in a few days' time. The commander would most likely want a private audience with him. He needed to consider what he would say.

If it weren't for Aurora, he might have already accepted. Aside from that, he'd miss Logan's taunts if he were to go. Until the forces were joined through the alliance, that is. Still, it could take some time before the two armies melded into one.

The hint of sunrise broke free on the horizon, casting a pink glow in the lower part of the sky. In the corner of his eye, a figure in black streaking through the streets caught his attention. He froze, his adrenaline rising, and shouted, "Hey! Hey you!"

The figure only spared him a glance from behind a black mask before the person took off behind a building. Bram was quick to make chase. He rounded the shop, but the figure was gone. He stopped short, searching his surroundings for a sign of the suspicious character. Suddenly dust and dirt rained down on him from the shop's overhang. Moving farther away from the building, he caught a glimpse of the figure in black skittering from rooftop to rooftop.

He could tell by the tight-fitting outfit that it was a woman, which heightened his curiosity. He took off, running along the buildings and tracking her, but she suddenly shifted directions. He grumbled as he lost sight of her, but then the noise of a terracotta tile breaking gave away her location. He bolted in the direction of the noise and began climbing the drain pipe. An almost whistling whoosh sound was heard, and before he could climb any higher, a metal weather vane fell atop him, catching him on the head and causing him to fall. He landed on the side of his body, and though pain shot through him, he didn't think that any bones were broken.

Beside him on the ground was the weather vane and a strange metal instrument. Upon closer inspection, he realized it was a weapon—and it appeared very familiar. Not willing to allow the masked figure to get away, Bram snatched up the weapon and tucked it into his coat.

Guessing the woman's getaway course, he cut through two buildings, taking alleyways he was familiar with and checking above him for signs of the woman. Skillfully, he managed to get in front of her. It was pure luck that she chose that moment to jump down from the roof.

Face to face with the figure, he could see the intricately stitched pattern on her mask. The mask covered the upper portion of the woman's face. Between that, the low light of dawn, and the shadow cast over her face from the hood of her cloak, he couldn't make out her features.

Then it hit him. The weapon was the same shape as the one the Drothidian girl used in the Rift. Excitement bubbled up in him as he stared at her with bated breath. She didn't move, though her stance told him she was about to run.

"Who are you?"

She didn't answer.

A loud clanging from the bakery echoed in the streets, as if someone had dropped a tray and knocked some things over. Bram turned his head toward the noise, hearing a man yelling at a boy to be careful. He turned his head back to the mysterious woman, but she was gone.

He stood dumbfounded for a moment, trying to piece together something that hovered at the edge of his mind. Could it really be a coincidence that this mystery woman used shuriken as her weapon? The same weapon as the Drothidian girl from the Rift. And wasn't it odd that this woman would appear only a week after the Drothidian High Priestess arrived—a woman he could swear was the doppelganger of the that same girl from the Rift?

Perhaps… perhaps Lady Tori hadn't been completely honest with him.

He took off at a run, heading back to the castle. If his theory was correct, he would find Lady Tori in the black costume, undoubtedly out of breath from their chase. The excitement of the possibility that he was right fueled his run, his adrenaline helping him to run faster than he'd ever run before.

By the time he breached the castle walls, he was barely able to catch his breath. Heading past the great hall, he didn't even bother to greet Eleazar and Tiberius as he rushed by them. His first instinct was to go to her rooms, but as he rounded the corner, he noticed the lights on in the chapel. He stopped short, breathing labored as he charged into the mezzanine looking over the ground floor of the chapel. His brow wrinkled as he took in the sight of Tori, wearing her blue cloak, kneeling at the altar, praying. He couldn't see her face for her head was bowed in prayer, the hood cascading over her head.

She didn't seem to be breathing hard. In fact, she seemed at peace. And he couldn't bring himself to disturb her just to check his theory. Disrupting a sacred thing such as prayer was frowned upon. The realization that he might be wrong pushed disappointment through his veins. The thought of Lady Tori being the girl from the Rift had somehow lifted his spirits. But it couldn't have been her if she'd been here the whole time.

A servant girl cleaned the floors of the mezzanine, her bucket of soapy water nearly empty.

"You there," he whispered. "Can you tell me how long Lady Tori has been in prayer?"

"At least an hour, sire," the servant girl whispered, a wrinkle in her brow. "That's 'ow long I've been 'ere cleanin', and Lady Tori was sat there prayin' when I got 'ere."

He felt a frown pull his mouth down. "Thank you."

He watched a moment longer, utterly upset that he'd been wrong, and then Tori rose from the alter and walked calmly into the small room adjacent the chapel where the chapel materials were kept. He rushed down the stairs, darting through the chapel, hope beyond hope that somehow his theory was correct.

Without thinking, Bram threw open the door to the chamber.

Lady Tori, who was replacing a book on one of the shelves, gasped, her blue cloak swinging around her as she turned toward him. Again, his face fell.

"Oh. Good morning, Master Stormbolt. Can I help you with something?"

He studied her. He couldn't have been wrong, could he? She wore a simple yet elegant lavender dress, not a tight-fitting black outfit. He glanced around the room, in case she somehow disposed of the black outfit in her hurry to change clothes, but everything was in order. Finja knelt in the corner of the room, sorting candles in a wooden container.

He was wrong. The mysterious masked woman was not Tori. The servant girl said Lady Tori had been in prayer for at least an hour, so how could she have been in two places at once? He rubbed at the collar of his tunic, his heart feeling as though it were shrinking inside him.

"No. No. I was just… Nothing. I thought I saw something, but I was mistaken."

"Of course. If you'll excuse me, now that my morning prayers are done, I'll need to get ready for breakfast."

"Yes, yes. Of course. I'm sorry to have disturbed you. I'll see you in the banquet hall."

"We'll see each other then. And May the Divine Mother bless you." She bowed her head.

He returned the bow, then left the room, his head spinning with confusion.

CHAPTER TWENTY-FIVE

"STUPID GIRL!" FINJA TOSSED the wooden box of candles aside.

"Stupid?"

"You were almost caught!"

"No, I wasn't." Tori flung the hood of the blue cloak off her head, revealing hair streaked in sweat. "It was fine. Our plan worked. The girl who cleans the mezzanine must have told him that I—well, you—had been praying for some time."

"I don't know how anyone could pray for that long," Finja grumbled, wiping the dust off her trousers. "My knees were in pain after the first five minutes."

"Well, it worked. She thought it was me. And Bramwell was detained long enough, watching you at the altar and thinking it was me, that I was able to change."

While Bramwell's eyes were fixed on Finja, Tori had been able to slip into her dress. And when Finja had come into the room, she merely handed the cloak over to Tori, who donned it and pretended to be putting the liturgy books away.

"Bramwell? Since when did you start calling Master Stormbolt by his given name?"

Tori fought off a blush. "I didn't mean to. It must be because of Raven; she never stops talking about him."

"Hmph." Finja crossed her arms over her chest. "Well, it was a good thing you got back when you did."

Tori pulled one of her capsules out of the pouch that Goran gave her. Finja poured her water from the carafe on the chapel office desk. Exhaustion pushed down on Tori as she swallowed her pill, but she had no time to rest until after breakfast. She had to make an appearance in the banquet hall so as not to arise suspicion. It was only a matter of time before someone discovered that Hettie was missing.

"I'll have one of the kitchen staff bring you a black tea," Finja said. She must have noticed the way Tori was rubbing at her eyes. "It will wake you."

Tori gave her a small smile that was not returned. "Thank you."

"Was the ship there when you arrived at the docks?"

"Yes. Hettie arrived safely, and Goran was pleased."

"Good. Do you know what you need to do next?"

"Yes. Find the books. In the meantime, I have a job for you."

"For me?"

"I need to create a situation in which to steal the key which hangs around the queen regent's neck."

Finja scoffed. "Good luck, child."

"I already have a plan, but I need your help, since you know the kitchen staff better than I do."

"What is this plan?"

"Have you ever heard of Devil's Fang?"

Finja's eyes narrowed. "No. But from the sound of it, I'm afraid of what you have in mind. Poison won't work on the queen regent. She has tasters for everything she eats and drinks."

"Not to worry, it won't kill her. But mixed with the right amount of palmetto seeds and neutralizing the taste by means of her daily tea, she will suffer mild headaches. Not enough to render her ill, but enough to be annoying. Her tasters won't ingest enough, and if they do, their only symptom will be a headache that goes away within a few hours."

"And what is the reason behind this?"

"How else am I to offer Lady Maescia a cure?"

Finja smiled.

"I have some in a pouch in my chamber. I'll get it to you after breakfast if you can get someone on the kitchen staff to put it in her tea for the next few days."

"Consider it done."

Bram stood by his chamber window and ran his finger along the metal shuriken he found in the street. The mystery woman must have been the Drothidian girl. And even if he was wrong about Lady Tori being that girl, that girl—woman—was in Avarell.

The sharp bite of metal roused him from his thoughts. Wincing, he sucked at the drop of blood that welled up on his finger.

A quick rap at the door sounded before Logan let himself in. "Aren't you hungry, dear friend? The kitchen's famous raspberry tarts are the perfect cure for a hangover."

"My head is fine," Bram said, smirking as he tucked the shuriken away. "It's *your* head that's always been the problem."

Together they ventured down to the banquet room, all the while Logan describing the peculiar dream he had about a fox walking on his balcony.

"I swear it was laughing at me," Logan said.

"Do foxes laugh?" Bram asked.

"This one did."

They rounded the corner, and Bram spotted Lady Tori about to enter the banquet hall. "Lady Tori," he called without thinking through what he wanted to say.

She paused and gave him a smile. "Master Stormbolt. How nice to see you again."

"I wanted to ask you about your morning prayers."

She joined her hands in front of her and waited for him to continue.

"How often do you usually do them? Every morning?"

Logan raised a brow at him, probably thinking it a strange question. But Bram couldn't help wanting to speak with her, even if it was about something as mundane as morning prayers.

"I do try to," Lady Tori answered.

"I just—" He rubbed at his chin. "—I find it odd because that was the first I've seen of such a ritual. By you, that is. Since you've been here."

Logan leaned closer to Bram. "Are you sure you're not still drunk?"

Bram pushed him away, making sure to keep the smile on his face for Lady Tori.

"What happened to your finger?" she asked.

He blinked in confusion. "What?"

She took his hand. "You have a cut. It looks a little swollen."

"It's nothing." Inside, he enjoyed the feel of her soft hand on his.

"Was it on metal?"

"Why would you ask that?" He wondered if she knew he'd cut himself on the shuriken.

"You're in the Queen's Guard. You handle swords on a daily basis. Odds are you've cut yourself on one."

"Oh. Um, yes, it was metal. Why?"

"It could become infected." Still holding his hand, she pulled him along. "Come with me. Please excuse us, Master Rathmore."

"Of course, Lady Tori," Logan said, nodding his farewell to Bram.

She continued down the hall, tugging him along until they reached the doors that led out to the courtyard. They made their way out toward a section of the gardens that had a million different kinds of plants.

"What are you doing?" he asked.

"Stop fussing. I'm helping you."

She scanned the plants, stopping at one and bending down to pick a leaf. She took a small pouch out of the belt lining of her skirt, retrieving a tiny vial. From the vial, she dabbed some kind of ointment on the leaf.

"What is that?"

"Are you afraid?" She smirked.

He narrowed his eyes, but a small smile broke out on his face.

She wrapped the oily leaf around his finger and then retrieved a small strip of cloth from an inner pocket of her blue cloak. Their eyes met as she tied the cloth around the leaf. "There. Now you won't get an infection."

"Thank you," he said, his eyes still on her. The subtle curves of her face were mesmerizing. He remembered looking at the Drothidian girl like this when she tended to his wounds.

Lady Tori cleared her throat and took a step back. "To answer your questions, I suppose my travels have thrown me off schedule," she said, interrupting his thoughts. "But with the recent… deaths, I've been reminded about the importance of communicating with the Divine Mother. I should be back on track now. Would you like to attend a service?"

He was thrown off guard by her question. He stammered for a moment before he answered. "I'm not a very religious man."

"That's okay. You can simply come to reflect. To ponder the questions you have inside of you. You'd be surprised what answers you may find if you simply remain quiet enough to listen."

He smiled at her again. "Thank you, Lady Tori. I may take you up on that offer."

Tori was grateful that nothing hindered her nap, for she needed it desperately. But now that she'd gotten some rest, she needed some fresh air. As she strolled out into the gardens, she happened upon Prince Theo crouching and playing a game with small rocks and a tiny ball on the pathway.

"Oh, I know this game," she said.

"You do?"

"Yes. I played it when I was your age. With my sister."

He held out the ball to her. "You have a sister."

She wanted to explain that she had two, but she didn't want to sadden him with more talk of death. "Yes. Her name is Taeyeon."

He looked surprised when she settled down on the pathway in her big dress. She bounced the ball and snatched up a couple rocks before catching the ball in the same hand.

"You're good," he proclaimed.

"Thank you."

"Can you do three rocks?"

"I can do five," she boasted. She then bounced the ball again and snatched up five rocks to prove her point.

He laughed. "I will have to get better then, so I can beat you."

"I'm sure you will master it in no time."

"Then you must promise to play with me again tomorrow."

"Tomorrow after breakfast," Tori said. "I promise."

There was a raucous from the arched walkways. Tori stood to see members of the Queen's Guard rushing toward the main part of the castle. She then spotted the duke marching behind them, a look of infuriation on his face

"What's going on?" Prince Theo asked.

Tori let out a slow breath. "I'm not sure," she lied. The fact was, she knew exactly what was happening.

CHAPTER TWENTY-SIX

BRAM FELT AS IF THEY'D been searching for days, but it had only been a few hours. He and Logan had been assigned with the group covering the castle and surrounding grounds to search for the duke's missing handmaiden Hettie. Eleazar, Tiberius, and Azalea were sent into the city with another group to scour the buildings and alleyways of Avarell, in case the girl was hiding somewhere nearby. The duke had been furious to find out his servant was missing, realizing when she didn't come to clean his boots that she had probably run off. Abandoning your service was not something taken lightly, especially if one was the servant of a titled nobleman.

"Why would she run away?" Bram asked.

"Perhaps she was sick of smelling his filthy laundry," Logan joked.

"Well, whatever the reason, she's gone. She's not in any of the rooms, and there is no sign of her in the tunnels."

"Maybe we should check the local pubs." He gave Bram a wink.

"I don't see what the big deal is, honestly. Can't he get another handmaiden?"

"He could have a hundred. But if he wants the one who ran away, then who are we to question him?"

"Soldiers with better things to do?"

"Bram, what's gotten into you? You seem so rebellious lately."

Bram shook his head. "Nothing."

Bram thought of the mysterious lady in black. Could she have had anything to do with the duke's servant disappearing? Why would someone help a servant leave the castle? Leave their duty? What did the woman in black have to gain for such an act?

Aurora appeared at the end of the hall, hurrying toward them. "The other soldiers have returned from the city. No one has found the girl. Lady Maescia wants us to meet in the throne room."

Logan and Bram exchanged a look, and then followed Aurora to the throne room. The queen regent sat upon her massive throne, the princess beside her. The duke, who was red-faced and fuming at this point, paced before the thrones, his hand on the hilt of his sword as if he would unsheathe it at any moment and start slashing.

They waited while the rest of the troops came into the room, gathering around to hear what Lady Maescia had to say.

"As you know," the queen regent finally said once the room was full, "one of Duke Grunmire's handmaidens has disappeared. We believe she has abandoned her assignment without giving notice. However, we also believe that someone knows about her disappearance and has lied when questioned about it."

The duke shifted his weight from his toes to his heels and back, his eyes roaming over the crowd as he clenched his jaw.

"If information regarding the handmaiden's disappearance is not made known, I have no choice but to enforce a punishment upon her roommates."

Tori's hands were balled into fists. She watched as Hettie's roommates were hauled in front of the queen regent and the princess, the guards forcing them down upon their knees. She recognized them from the night she snuck into Hettie's room. They had kept their word. They hadn't said anything about a masked woman helping Hettie escape. But now their loyalty to Hettie would cost them. Tori's muscles tensed at the thought of what might happen to them. And whatever it was, she was at fault.

"I'll ask once again," Lady Maescia said to the young women before her. "Do you know anything about Hettie's disappearance?"

Both young women shook their heads, mumbling that they didn't know.

"If that is to be your ultimate response, then I have no choice but to punish you both for lying to the royal court."

The roommates clung to one another. One of them was crying, the other held her chin up.

"Being dishonest to your Queen, queen regent, or the princess, is a crime, and will not be tolerated. Consequently, you will be sentenced to a punishment of my choosing."

The duke lifted his chin, awaiting Lady Maescia's verdict. The princess wrung her hands together, but kept a stoic face.

"Guards," Lady Maescia called. "Come midnight, please escort these two women outside the city walls and drop them both into the Rift."

Tori held back a growl of protest. Her blood boiled with frustration. These girls had done nothing wrong save keep a promise to their friend. She couldn't let this happen to them. She wasn't about to let innocent people suffer the consequences at the hand of an unfit ruler. No. Tonight at midnight, she was going to the Rift.

CHAPTER TWENTY-SEVEN

TORI ADJUSTED THE BLACK CLOAK at the clasp, the length of it cascading over her black outfit. She took a deep breath, going over her supplies in her head.

"I don't know why you insist on going out there," Finja said.

"I just sat there when Rudy was beheaded. Sat there! Like a lump. I couldn't do anything about it. But I can do something about this."

Finja scoffed. "There are always casualties where there is war."

"I wasn't aware this was a war yet." She tucked her shuriken in their place. "Lady Maescia repulses me. How can I serve such a queen?"

"You are not here to serve her. You are here to complete your tasks. When we are able to get you into the tower to find the real Queen, then we can have Lady Maescia excommunicated from the throne."

"That day can't come too soon," Tori mumbled, throwing her hood over her head.

With narrowed eyes and a frown, Finja watched as Tori grappled off her balcony, disappearing into the night. What she had planned was more complicated than breaking into a servant's room or sneaking someone to the docks. She couldn't be sure which part of the Rift the guards would bring the two young women. She would either have to follow them—which would prove difficult on foot—or somehow sneak onto the carriage transporting them to the Rift.

Tori opted for the latter.

The two roommates sat securely in the carriage guarded by two soldiers, the duke perched on the seat on the front of the carriage beside the coachman. Sure that no one could see her, she hopped onto the back of the carriage just as it left the castle. Holding on was a feat, but once she stabbed into the wooden frame of the carriage with her kunai and held tight, it made things much easier. It helped that the city was bathed in darkness. The ride over cobblestone streets still jostled her, and she let out a sigh of relief when they finally exited the city and slowed down by the woods.

Tori hopped off the carriage before they came to a full stop, running low to the ground and finding a tree to hide behind. From her hiding spot, she could see the duke step down from the carriage, ordering the soldiers to escort the women toward the woods.

Tori moved closer, scrutinizing a way to climb down into the Rift and also checking for any Undead that might be near. Her foot connected with a rock, sending it toppling down into the Rift. The duke turned his head toward the noise. Thinking quickly, Tori pulled herself up onto the tree's branches and shimmied into the cover of leaves, pulling her feet up just before the duke walked by. She held her breath, grateful she was wearing black, and waited until he moved away. But the duke was obstinate, scanning the surrounding with a sharp eye.

"What is it, Duke Grunmire?" one of the soldiers asked.

"I thought I heard something."

"Could be the Undead," the soldier said. "They're out there, ready to catch what we throw in. It's like feeding hungry dogs."

The duke turned away from the trees. "Then let's not have them wait any longer."

Tori hovered above him. If it weren't for the soldiers and the coachman, it would have been a perfect opportunity to drop-jump him and slit his throat. Surely she could take out the soldiers and coachman too. She had enough weapons with her. But she dwelled on it too long, and the duke moved back toward the carriage.

She lowered her head to see what had become of the two young women, and caught sight of them just in time to see the two guards haul them toward the precipice of the Rift. The women squirmed and thrashed, their arms tied with rope behind their backs. On the duke's command, the two women were shoved over the edge by the boots of the soldiers.

Tori clenched her jaw, wincing as the thumps and thuds and screams of the roommates falling found her ears. She wasn't even sure they would still be alive once she found them.

The duke, looking satisfied, climbed into the carriage with the soldiers, and as soon as they got the carriage turned around, they were on their way back to the castle.

Tori dropped down from the tree and searched frantically for an incline that wasn't too steep. Her hands stung with a few cuts as she made her way down into the gully to find the women.

Their moans are what helped her locate them, but the noise was also a dangerous thing in the Rift. If they didn't keep quiet, there were sure to be Undead headed their way.

The braver of the women, having somehow gotten free of her binds, helped the other one to stand. She reached for the rope on the woman's wrists, pulling and yanking to get them off of her. She was so focused on the task that she did not see an Undead approaching her from behind.

Tori flung a shuriken at the creature, catching it in the eye. The Undead staggered, arms flailing before it toppled to the ground. The women gasped in horror at the sight of him, and then their eyes went to Tori.

"You!" the braver one said.

"Quiet," Tori urged. "They'll hear you."

Tori took her kunai and cut the rope off the frightened girl's wrists.

"There!" the braver one shouted. "Behind you!"

Tori turned to find an Undead coming in for a kill. She flipped her kunai around in her hand and flung it at the creature. The blade went straight through his gray, decaying forehead. He fell backward immediately, rasps of air expelling from his mouth until he finally stilled. Tori placed her boot on his neck, just in case, as she retrieved her kunai and wiped it off on her trousers.

When she turned around, the two women were gaping at her.

"Who are you?" one of them asked.

"No one of importance."

"I beg to differ. You saved our lives."

"Yes. But I'm afraid your lives will be different from now on. You cannot return to Avarell. If you are caught, you will be executed for sure."

The more frightened woman wrapped her arms around herself. "Where are we to go?"

"Come. I'll take you to the western border of the Rift. From there you can travel into Drothidia. It has many small villages. Perhaps you can find shelter, convince someone to help you. You at least stand a chance out there."

The fearful girl let out a shuddered breath, and then suddenly hugged Tori.

"Thank you. Thank you from the bottom of my heart."

Tori nodded as the girl let her go. "Don't thank me yet; I still have to get you out of the Rift. Let's go."

WRENA

CHAPTER TWENTY-EIGHT

WRENA APPLIED A SMEAR of pink tint to her lips. It was a gift from Lady Tori, who delivered on her promise to make some simple supplies for her and the ladies-in-waiting.

She could almost tell by the sound of the footsteps in the corridor that Aurora was near. With a small grin, she jumped from her chair and ran to the door to open it. Just as she had suspected, Aurora ran toward her. But taking in the expression on Aurora's face, Wrena's grin disappeared.

"What is it?" Wrena asked, pulling Aurora into her room and closing the door.

Aurora's eyes were wide, the color drained from her face. "It's Patrick. Rudy's lover. He was found hung in the dungeon."

Wrena dropped Aurora's wrists, her hands flying to her face. "Someone killed him?"

"No. He was alone in his cell. It appears he hung himself."

They stared at each other, the news and its connection to them sinking in. Aurora closed the space between them and wrapped her arms around Wrena. Wrena squeezed her tightly against her, not wanting to let go. How could this feeling between them lead to something as sinister as death? How could such sadness and grief come from something so wonderful and uplifting as love?

Slowly, they parted, sorrow still apparent on both of their faces.

"Your lips look pink," Aurora said.

Wrena placed her fingertips on her bottom lip. "It was a tint from Lady Tori. Does it make me look foolish?"

The hint of a smile appeared on Aurora's face. "No. You look lovely, as always."

"Do we really have to attend the Solstice feast?"

"There will be talk if we don't." Aurora shrugged. "Besides, according to legend, if you don't show the Divine Mother your appreciation for the Solstice, ruin shall follow."

"Stupid legend."

"You don't believe it's true?"

Wrena let out a breath of defeat. "I believe ruin has already begun."

Aurora let her weight fall into a chair, her brows knitted. "What is happening with your aunt?"

"I do not know. She has changed."

"Beheading people for minor crimes? Dropping people into the Rift? That's beyond cruel."

"I can't even imagine how she came up with the punishment. It's inhumane."

"Not to mention punishing innocent people. Those girls did nothing wrong."

"I know." Wrena closed her eyes and shook her head. "It's horrible."

"Can't you speak to her?"

"And say what?"

Aurora stood and stepped toward her, joining their hands. "Fight for us, Wrena. Fight for the people."

"I'm afraid my pleas would fall on deaf ears. She won't hear me out. I can't even talk to her about the real reason I don't want to marry Prince Liam."

They were quiet for a moment, each of them pondering their fate.

"Perhaps we should run away," Wrena suggested. "We could go to stay with my uncle, Prince Rainer, in Creoca. He would take us in, give us sanctuary."

Aurora blinked, letting out a laugh of disbelief. "Creoca? It's always cold there."

"Aurora." Wrena knew she was simply trying to avoid the subject of escaping Avarell.

"I don't know if I could." She turned and toyed with the ends of her hair. "I can't leave Father. And Bram. Besides, you are to rule here. What happens if you go to Creoca? Will you lose your claim to the throne?"

Wrena took Aurora's hands from her hair. "Alliances change. But my heart hasn't. It is with you."

"Leaving wouldn't change things, though, Wrena. Things will keep getting worse here. You are the only one who has even a hope of talking some sense into your aunt. If only your mother—"

Silence filled the room. They knew better than to rely on the possibility that the Queen would recover from her illness.

Still, Wrena didn't have it in her to give up. "My aunt says she's doing everything she can to find a cure for her. She's employed the very best apothecaries from around the world."

"I've seen them. Once in a while. But not very often. They're in and out of the castle so quickly no one would realize they'd been here."

"They travel from great distances. I pray one of them will be able to cure her. She might be our only hope." She moved her hand to stroke Aurora's cheek, but then stopped short, a troubling thought suddenly coming to her. "Wait. You said Patrick hung himself?"

"Yes."

"Where did he get the rope?"

Aurora shook her head, her brows lowered. "I do not know. I can't imagine anyone would have given it to him. Only the guards had access to the cell."

"Not only guards. So did Duke Grunmire."

As Bramwell suspected, a letter arrived for him from the commander of the Gadleigh army. Their arrival was approaching fast, and a private meeting was requested. More than ever, Bram felt the pressure of considering their offer. Perhaps, this time, he could accept it. There was no doubt his father would have smiled upon his alliance with them. The Gadleigh and Avarell armies would eventually be joined as one after the union of Prince Liam and Princess Wrena, so did it matter that he might be skipping steps to a higher position?

The wrap on the door was to a beat that could only mean Logan was there. Bram tucked the letter from Gadleigh away.

"Ready to go to the feast?" Logan asked when Bram opened the door.

"Yes. I'm ravished."

They walked side by side down the corridor, Logan whistling.

"What's got you in such high spirits?" Bram asked.

"I don't know." Logan looked over his shoulder as if checking if anyone was near. He then leaned closer to Bram. "Azalea said she overheard some of the others talking. Word is the negotiations are supposed to name Avarell's soldiers as higher in rank than Gadleigh's soldiers. Aren't we lucky?"

"Have you confirmed this rumor?"

Logan shrugged. "No. But it's feasible."

"What makes you say that?"

"Avarell is greater in size than Gadleigh and we have more men… and a woman. Plus, we house the Princess. Everyone knows that is the deciding factor. She is the prize, and if Gadleigh wants her, they should abide by our rules."

"She's not an object, Logan. She's a person."

Logan scratched at his head. "Yes. Yes. Of course. I didn't mean it like that. I just meant, she's more important."

Bram smirked. "I'm sure that's what you meant."

"So, are you planning on taking a stroll with Raven after the meal?"

Bram's brow furrowed. "Why would you ask that?"

"The ladies have been a whirlwind of excitement ever since Lady Tori gave them little trinkets as gifts."

The mention of Lady Tori brought Bram to fuller attention. "Trinkets?"

"Little pots of perfumes and salves and such. I don't know about the others, but Ace seemed pretty excited. She was given some kind of cream to make her skin soft, and it's given her so much confidence that she's become rather… forward with me."

"I see."

"I think I might need to approach Lady Tori this evening and thank her."

Bram laughed as they entered the banquet hall. Gathered in a small circle, the ladies of the court laughed and whispered together. Although, Aurora's expression was more subdued. Bram wondered if she wasn't pleased with her gift as much as the others were.

When the queen regent and princess entered the room, the crowd quieted and took their places at their tables. Lady Tori then appeared, looking tall and elegant in her blue robe. She called for everyone's attention and began the blessing of the Solstice meal, all in the name of the Divine Mother. But Bram couldn't focus on her words. He watched her graceful movements and soft expression as she spoke, somehow finding peace and comfort just from looking at her.

She had said he should come to the chapel to reflect on any questions that might be troubling him. Perhaps he should go to the chapel the next time she was there and reflect on whether or not to accept Gadleigh's offer. Could the rumor Logan told him be true? What if he accepted Gadleigh's offer and was consequently lowered in rank? Perhaps he would have to speak to the commander about it and find out the truth.

Was that what had suddenly sparked the impulse to go to the chapel? Or was it the urge to speak with Lady Tori alone?

CHAPTER TWENTY-NINE

THE COOL WIND THAT SWEPT over Tori's balcony did little to calm the sick feeling that burned inside her. It wasn't just a symptom of the phoenix fever; her skin still crawled with revulsion from the manner of which Lady Maescia punished her subjects. And the news of Patrick's hanging in the dungeon turned her stomach sour. If she hadn't been there on a mission, if she hadn't *needed* to stay in Avarell to save her family, she would have already resigned her position and left the queendom.

Feeling stifled, she withdrew from her balcony and fetched her cloak. She needed to go outside. Takumi gave her a questioning look as she headed for her chamber door.

"I just need some air." She narrowed her eyes at him. "Stay out of trouble."

As she reached the downstairs corridor and pushed open the doors to the courtyard, the tight muscles in her shoulders seemed to relax somewhat. Perhaps because it felt as if she were about to run away. She couldn't go so far as to do that, but if she just kept walking as far as her legs could carry her without actually leaving the castle grounds, then maybe she could feel a bit of respite.

The day had turned gloomy and gray, matching the feeling in her heart. When the sound of a horse's neigh caught her ears, she realized she had been heading in the direction of the stables. It was as if she was subconsciously paying homage to Rudy.

Hearing the whinnying of the horses, she moved closer, the urge to pet one growing. Being close to nature always made her feel better. Perhaps all she needed was some animal interaction.

As she entered the stables, she spotted a figure brushing one of the horses. She almost backed out of the stable, not wanting to interrupt or intrude on anyone, but then she realized it was Bramwell. As if sensing she was there, he turned around.

"Oh," she said, feeling awkward. "Sorry. I didn't know you would be here."

He let out a small laugh. "That's all right. Come closer if you'd like. This is my horse. Her name is Uma."

Tori stretched out her hand, longing to touch the horse. She stroked her hair, a smile lighting up her face. "She's lovely."

"Do you ride?"

"No."

"I suppose you didn't have much occasion to while you were studying in Tokuna."

"No. I can't say there are many horses there." It wasn't a lie; she couldn't say if there were or not.

"I heard what you did for the ladies of the court." He flashed her a charming smile. "That was very kind of you."

She let out a deep breath, her gaze going back to the horse. "I thought they needed a little cheering up. So many sad things have happened recently."

"Yes, that's true." He nodded solemnly, as if reflecting on it. Tori wondered if he would be out of line to discuss the decisions of the queen regent. Perhaps it would be considered treason if he spoke up against her. "Since they haven't replaced the stable hand, I figured I should come out and take care of Uma. Give her a little attention."

"I think she appreciates it. Look how happy she is."

He laughed again, and the sound of it sent a thrill through Tori.

"We should go for a ride," Bram said.

"What? No. I can't."

"Come on. I can show you. You can take Aurora's horse Daisy." He gestured toward the white horse in the next stall. "I'm sure she won't mind."

As soon as Tori lay her eyes upon Daisy, she couldn't resist. She bit her lip and looked back at Bram. "Are you sure?"

"Of course. We'll go slow, don't worry. And Daisy's quite gentle."

"All right."

His face lit up, and he instructed her on what to do. After both horses were brushed down and their hooves were checked, Bram fitted them with saddle blankets and tacks.

"Ready?" he asked, offering to help her onto Daisy.

Instead of answering him, she put a hand on his shoulder and climbed up onto the saddle. Bram mounted Uma, and they left the stables together. Bram led her through the back gate, which a servant opened for them, and they trotted toward a path that went through the woods.

"Are you sure it's safe?" Tori asked. "What about the Undead?"

"They only dwell in the Rift. There's a bit of land between these woods and those. If we stick to the path, we should be fine."

Just to be sure, she felt for her weapon supply without him noticing.

As they rode into the thicker part of the woods, Tori felt more at home. This was what she needed: nature and fresh air. And the company of someone pleasant. She watched Bram as they galloped through a patch of ash trees, his chin held high to watch the path, his grip firm on the reigns. Yet he was gentle as well, patting Uma lovingly when she obeyed his commands. His form was strong, and Tori had to force herself to look away when she caught herself staring.

A good while into their ride, Bram slowed down, holding his hand out to catch Daisy's bridal. He clicked his tongue, trying to get the horses to stop.

"What?" Tori asked. "What is it?" Fear spread through her as she imagined the worst. Could they have wandered into the Rift by mistake? She didn't notice riding down an incline, but she was unfamiliar with the territory, so it wasn't out of the question.

"Look there," he whispered, pulling her horse closer to his. His leg brushed up against hers, and heat blossomed in her face. "Just there, halfway up the tree."

She adjusted her gaze to where he was pointing. There, a flash of color caught her eye. She gasped. "A phoenix."

It wasn't that the bird itself impressed her, but seeing the phoenix after not catching sight of one for so long made her think of home.

Bram was captivated at how Tori's eyes filled with wonder. He wondered if she'd never seen one before. He wasn't aware if phoenixes were common in Tokuna, but surely she'd seen them when she was a child in Drothidia. Perhaps she was simply mesmerized because she hadn't seen one in so long.

"Isn't it glorious?" he asked, keeping his voice low so as not to scare the bird away.

"Yes. Have you ever seen one breathe fire?" she asked, still staring at the phoenix.

"No, never. Have you?"

"Once," she said. "I was very young, so it was extremely frightening. But I came across one who got into a squabble with a weasel who was trying to get the eggs in the phoenix's nest. She didn't like that very much, so she torched him. It was an amazing thing to see, but the smell of the burnt weasel still haunts me."

"Sounds wretched."

"It was."

"I think it's a shame they've gotten an unsavory reputation from the disease they carry. You would think now that everyone is immune, they would be seen for the beautiful creatures they are."

Tori's gaze dropped, and Bram wished he knew what she was thinking.

"I was thinking about what you said about coming to the chapel," Bram said, "to reflect on questions that are on my mind."

The corner of her mouth lifted. It was the most beautiful thing he'd ever seen. "What are you hoping to find out?" she asked.

As he took in her features, the soft curve of her face and the elegant slant of her eyes, there were suddenly more questions filling his head other than his loyalty to the Avarell army. He shook his head, smiling. "Never mind."

She watched him, and he felt as if she could see right through him.

"How was your review?" she asked. "You must have gotten your promotion by now."

His smile turned to a frown, the feeling of disappointment weighing down his bones. "It's been postponed."

"Oh. I'm sorry."

"The duke is all in a huff about his handmaiden running away, so much that he has put a dead stop to anything other than enforcing stricter curfews and concentrating on the visit from the Gadleigh court. The only other thing he will even think of talking about is the upcoming festivities for the Queen's birthday."

"I didn't realize it would be celebrated—with her being ill and all."

"It's tradition. Lady Maescia insists that we throw her a party. That it would be unjust not to."

Thunder rumbled above them. Bram looked up to see the sky had darkened considerably. Drops of rain hit their skin. The horses shifted.

"We'd better head back," Bram said.

"All right."

"Think you can keep up if we picked up a little speed?"

"I can certainly try."

Rain began to pelt them as they turned the horses around and raced back to the castle. Bram deliberately kept a slower pace than his norm so that Tori wouldn't get left behind. Lightning lit up the sky, and thunder boomed, shaking the ground. The sky grew eerily dark, and the torrents of rain left them drenched.

A servant spotted them as they neared the back gate of the castle and let them in. Bram immediately jumped off his horse and took Daisy's reigns. He told Tori to run into the stables for shelter, and then he handed the reigns to the servant to cool the horses down.

His hair dripped into his eyes as he trudged into the stables to find Tori. She was shivering, her cloak soaked and her skin damp. He grabbed a clean blanket from the stable supplies and offered it to her.

"You'll need to remove your cloak, Lady Tori."

She nodded, her teeth chattering. She unhooked the cloak and let it fall to the ground. He wrapped the blanket around her, pushing her wet hair off her cheeks. Her skin felt hot.

"There's a small room in the back. We can wait there until the storm dies down."

"Yes," she said, her voice void of power. "Okay."

The rain became heavier, the sound of it hitting the stable roof like a horde of charging elephants. Bram led Tori to the back room, where a few stacks of hay sat, as well as a table with a small lantern. Bram brought Tori to sit on a stack of hay while he lit the lantern and checked out the window. He couldn't see anything. The rain came down like a gray curtain, blocking everything out.

When he turned back to Tori, her eyes were glassed over, and she was panting. She pulled at the neckline of her dress, as if she weren't getting any air.

"Lady Tori! Are you all right?"

"Feverish," was all she was able to say, barely able to keep her eyes open.

He placed his hand upon her forehead and confirmed that she was burning up with fever. Still, she pulled and tugged at her clothes.

"Lady Tori, forgive me, but may I help you?"

"Too tight," she said, her cheeks turning red. She swallowed hard.

"I'll just loosen it a bit, all right?"

She nodded and turned away from him. He untied the upper portion of her dress, resisting the urge to run his fingers along the smooth skin of her back. Tori yanked on the dress, which now hung loose around her shoulders. Her eyes were almost all the way closed now, and she swayed, finally leaning against him, no strength left in her body.

She moaned, and Bram slipped his arm around her. Though worry spread through him like ice, the feeling of being this close to her filled him with fire.

Her head was on his chest, and the floral smell of her hair filled his nostrils. He closed his eyes and set his cheek upon the top of her head. She shivered, pushing herself into him. He stroked her hair and shushed her, hoping the fever—and the storm—would soon pass. Until it did, he would hold her and keep her safe.

CHAPTER THIRTY

THE WINDS BLEW HARD against the castle walls and rattled the flag poles that sat perched upon the towers.

Wrena wandered the corridors, feeling forlorn. She would have gone to see Aurora, but she was exhausted and had gone to bed early. Wrena found herself heading to the lounge, where her aunt was sure to be.

Before her aunt Maescia had become queen regent, she had spent a lot of time with Wrena, telling her tales about when she and Wrena's mother were young, giving her advice only a cherished aunt could give, and going out of her way to please her. But ever since she'd taken the position on the throne, she had become more distant and less accessible. It broke Wrena's heart, because now, more than ever, she needed a mother figure. Now, when her own mother was not able to be there for her, Wrena needed a shoulder to lean on.

Wrena approached the lounge, wondering if she could find a small sign of the Aunt Maescia she used to be. Maybe, if she could find that version of her aunt underneath the dictator Maescia had become, she could find out why she had become so cruel, so heartless, so void of hope.

"Backing out of the treaty could mean war."

It was her aunt's voice Wrena heard, just as the guards opened the lounge door for her. Wrena entered the room, suddenly unsure of what she should say.

"War?" It was the first thing that came to her mind.

The duke turned to face her, his expression stern. "Your Highness, we weren't expecting you."

"I wasn't aware we were backing out of the treaty altogether," Wrena said. "I thought it was simply the engagement we were cancelling."

Maescia blinked, seemingly flabbergasted. She cleared her throat, then plastered a small smile upon her face, approaching Wrena and taking her hands in hers. "We mustn't bore you with all the details, my dear. It's just politics. Or rather, it's business."

"What kind of business leads to war?"

"It was an exaggeration," Maescia said.

"Was it?" Wrena asked. "It sounded rather serious from your tone."

Maescia was about to respond, when the duke raised his hand to interrupt her. "Perhaps it's wise to inform the princess of the offer we received. After all, it will be her queendom one day."

Maescia pressed her lips together in a thin line and nodded. "The promises of Gadleigh's alliance, as well as their army, has been matched by another realm."

"Which realm?"

"That's a matter for the queen regent," the duke said.

"If it has to do with whom I am to marry, then I need to know. Have you promised me off to another prince?"

"Do not worry," her aunt said, her features softening. "We will not be sealing this deal with a marriage. It's strictly a monetary exchange. However, the citizens of Avarell *will* be expecting me to announce an engagement at your mother's birthday celebration. The people need to know that your reign will include a strong bond."

For a moment, Wrena's voice stuck in her throat. She had to fight to get the words out. "Whom do you propose I marry?"

When the duke showed the hint of a smile, Wrena knew the answer.

"Eleazar?"

"As the son of a duke, he is an earl. He has a title. He will inherit land."

"He will get Avarell if he marries me."

"And be prince. Eventually King."

Wrena felt flushed. Her heart picked up pace and her head spun. She took her aunt's hands and lowered her voice. "Aunt Maescia, I hope you're not letting the duke sway you into agreeing with his idea."

Her aunt squeezed her hands, her eyes darting to the duke for a split second before going back to Wrena. She raised her chin. "It was my idea."

A wrinkle formed between Wrena's brows. "It was?"

"It's a good match." Maescia released Wrena's hands and adjusted her crown. "You and Eleazar have been friends since childhood. He fancies you. And he will be head of a great army."

"As King."

"With you at his side, as is your destiny." Maescia placed her fingers under Wrena's chin, their eyes locking. Her gaze was so intense, Wrena wondered if her aunt was trying to convey some unspoken message to her. "You should be grateful we are offering you this union. It could be legions worse."

"Worse?" Wrena narrowed her eyes. "Wait. What realm are you negotiating with?"

Maescia straightened her back, her mouth set in a straight line. "Nostidour."

CHAPTER THIRTY-ONE

A ROOSTER CROWED somewhere nearby. Tori kept her eyes closed. She didn't want to move; it was too comfortable where she was—wherever it was. All she knew is her head was nestled somewhere safe, somewhere that smelled musky and wonderful. And her body was wrapped in a relaxed cocoon of warmth.

And arms and hands. Her eyes shot open.

Slowly stretching her neck, she saw that her suspicions were correct. Bram held her against his torso, his strong arms around her like a protective shield, as his soft breathing expanded and contracted his chest. He was asleep, and logic told her they had both fallen asleep in exactly this position.

Before she dared to move, she took in the firm shape of his jaw, the dark wisps of lashes, the shadow of stubble upon his chin. She found herself staring at his mouth, and then the rooster crowed again, like a warning. She shouldn't get lost in such thoughts; she wasn't here to fall for anyone. She was here to try to prevent a mad woman from starting a war between the nine realms.

Regaining her composure, she pushed herself off Bram and adjusted her sleeves, which hung a bit too low off her shoulders.

Bram stirred, opening his eyes and looking around as if he, too, had forgotten they had been in the stables.

"Lady Tori," he said, clearing his throat and raking his hands through his disheveled hair. "Are you well?"

She hadn't even thought of her well-being until he had asked. As a reflex, she put the back of her hand upon her forehead, checking to see if she was still feverish or perhaps clammy with sweat. "I'm faring better," she said. "Though I should get back to my rooms. My handmaid can help me; she makes a wonderful tea that cures all."

"Yes, of course." He attempted to stand, but the skirt of Tori's dress had somehow gotten tangled in his legs, and he nearly fell on top of her. Their eyes locked as he caught himself, his face mere inches from hers. He swallowed hard before he spoke. "Your… Your Holiness, forgive me."

Tori fought off the harsh blush that spread over her face. "It wasn't your fault. I'm the one who…" She felt flustered, remembering how she practically fell into his arms the night before. She let out a deep breath. "It wasn't your fault."

Bram averted his eyes as they both stood, and then he went to the nearest window to check outside. "The weather has cleared. It's actually a beautiful morning."

She reached behind herself, attempting to adjust the clasps of her corset, but to no avail. It wouldn't do to head back to the castle looking like she did. Even with her cloak wrapped around her, her dress would sag noticeably. She had no choice but to ask Bram for help. "I'm sorry, Master Stormbolt, but would you mind helping me tighten my corset?"

"Oh." He seemed to be staring at her shoulders. "Yes, of course. If you would, um, just turn around?"

She turned, a shiver running through her as his hands touched her back. She almost gasped as he pulled the corset tight.

"Is that all right?" he asked, his hands falling away.

"Yes, perfect," she said, realizing only seconds later how breathy she must have sounded. "Thank you. Though, I'm sure I still look a fright. I'd hate to think what people might think if they see me coming back in this state."

"It would appear questionable," Bram agreed, "the two of us stumbling back to the castle at this hour in the morning." He rubbed his chin, glancing around. "Luckily, I know the way through the secret passageways."

She almost laughed. "That would be extremely convenient."

"Come with me. There's an entrance in the gardener's shed."

Quietly, they made their way out of the stables and strode across the lawn to the gardener's shed. No one was around, which Tori was grateful for, and she hoped that no one happened to be gazing out the castle windows in their direction. Bram led her to a closet, where one wall pushed out into a dark staircase leading downward.

She nearly tripped as she followed him, and when he stopped to take her hand, she didn't pull away. His hand was strong and warm, and she felt as if her hand was meant to be in his.

"We used to use these passageways to get everywhere when we were kids," Bram whispered in the darkness as they reached the bottom of the stairs. She couldn't see his face, but she could tell he was smiling. "They connect to everything in the castle. I haven't been down here in a while, but it's as if the map of the tunnels is embedded in my mind."

"A fact I'm extremely thankful for," she said.

They came to where the passageway split. A cold wind seemed to come from the corridor to the left. Tori paused. "What's down there?"

It took a moment for Bram to answer. "We shouldn't go that way. It's actually supposed to be blocked off, but that wind tells me some boards must have come loose."

"Why is it blocked off?"

"It goes out under the castle lands toward the Rift. Not that it was meant to go into the Rift, but rather a stretch of woods that eventually became taken over by the Undead. Logan and I used to dare each other to go down that tunnel. The bravest would go the farthest. Eventually, we both made it out to the woods. But we turned around and ran back the minute we were out there."

"Do you think the Undead could come up through the tunnel?"

"No, they shouldn't be able to unless they are good climbers, which they have proven not to be. There is a steep embankment at the end of the tunnel, difficult for us to climb down into the Rift without falling, and practically impossible for the Undead to climb up."

"But still possible?"

He smiled. "Do not worry, Lady Tori. I won't let anything happen to you."

She smiled, thinking about how it was she who saved him in the Rift.

He still held her hand as he traveled with her through the maze of passageways. Eventually, they arrived at a secret door that opened to the corridor outside her room. Bram craned his neck to make sure no one was around before he pulled her gently into the corridor.

"We made it," he said.

She couldn't help the playful laugh that escaped her throat. "We did, thanks to you."

"Of course, Your Holiness. It was my pleasure." They exchanged a long look, and then Bram looked down at their hands, realizing their fingers were still entwined. He released her hand, shifting his weight from his toes to the balls of his feet. "Yes, well, I hope you feel better soon."

She nodded. "I'm sure I will. Thank you, Master Stormbolt."

He bowed his head as she turned toward her door.

Once inside her room, she pressed her cheek against her door, feeling exhilarated despite the ache in her body. She wasn't able to suppress the smile that felt plastered to her face until she turned around and met with Finja's cold stare.

"Where were you?"

"We got caught in the storm and had to sleep in the stables," Tori said.

"We?"

Tori patted her hair down, walking past Finja toward her bedchamber. Takumi flitted out from under a chair and sniffed the air around her. "Master Stormbolt was with me."

Finja narrowed her eyes. "What are you doing out chasing that boy when you should be looking for the books?"

"He's not a boy," Tori said. She realized that wasn't how she meant to answer Finja and cleared her throat. "I don't chase boys. I got trapped by the storm."

Finja practically stomped toward her and put a hand against her forehead. "You're feverish. Have you taken your medicine?"

"I didn't have any with me." Tori made a point of taking out a pill and showing it to Finja before she popped it in her mouth and swallowed it. "I've taken it now."

Finja scurried to fetch a wet cloth. After wringing it out she went over to wipe Tori's brow. "I'm surprised you even survived."

"I barely did. My head throbs and my stomach is in knots."

"Then why are you smiling?"

Tori covered her mouth, as if to hide the smile Finja knew was there. She sat on the edge of her bed, and Takumi snuggled into her lap, nudging his head underneath her hand to be pet. "I don't know."

"Foolish girl," Finja mumbled, patting the wet cloth onto the back of Tori's neck. "Lie down, then child. Rest for one day. Tomorrow, your mission continues."

CHAPTER THIRTY-TWO

WITH HER CLOAK BILLOWING around her in the cool, late-afternoon wind, Tori stood beside Lady Maescia, a symbol of the queen regent's connection with the Divine Mother, as the royal court of Gadleigh approached the castle. The visiting royals had arrived at the northern border and were escorted to Capehill Castle by the Queen's Guard, the Avarell banners flying at their approach.

Tori noticed that Lady Maescia held her hands tight against her stomach, letting out a deep breath, before forcing a smile and lifting her chin for the visiting king and queen. Princess Wrena wore no such smile, her eyes far away, even as Prince Liam exited his carriage.

Lady Maescia's smile faltered for a moment, her hand pressing quickly to her temple before lowering it.

"Are you all right, Your Grace?" Tori asked her.

"Just a slight headache," Lady Maescia said. "I've been getting them recently. Probably stress."

"I can make something that can help you. It would be no trouble at all."

Lady Maescia nodded once. "That would be most helpful. Thank you." Her smile reappeared as she looked out to the approaching royals.

King Adam held his hand high at chest level, Queen Layla's delicate hand resting atop it, as they strode toward the waiting queen regent and the princess. The King was considerably taller than the Queen, and the prince's height practically matched his father's. They each wore the silver colors of Gadleigh, which contrasted nicely with their dark hair and olive skin. The King's bushy beard made Tori think of her father.

As soon as they were near enough, Queen Layla and Lady Maescia exchanged air kisses on the sides of their cheeks, and then the King kissed the royal ring that Lady Maescia wore for her sister. The handsome Prince Liam then bowed his head to Lady Maescia and took Princess Wrena's hand to kiss. The princess merely blinked and nodded her head once in acknowledgement.

Tori followed suit when the duke bowed to the royals, placing her hands together before bowing her head.

"We apologize for the late hour," Queen Layla said. "The northern towns of Avarell are more mountainous than we remembered."

"No apologies necessary," Lady Maescia said. "You've arrived in plenty of time to partake in the feast we've prepared."

"That sounds perfect," King Adam announced. "I'm famished."

"As is to be expected after such a long journey." Lady Maescia ended her statement with a laugh and gestured for her guests to enter the castle ahead of her and the princess. The guards and servants bowed and curtsied as they passed. An entourage of Gadleigh court lords and ladies followed in their stead, and Tori recognized a cloak similar to her own. Finja had warned her that the Gadleigh royals would bring their High Priestess, and Tori had spent extra time studying to make sure her act would remain perfect.

Everyone gathered in the grand banquet hall, and the Gadleigh royals joined Lady Maescia and Princess Wrena at the head table. The captain of the Gadleigh army sat at the duke's table with their highest officers, most certainly discussing war strategies. Once the wine was poured, Lady Maescia signaled to Tori that she could begin the blessing of the meal.

Tori stood and tried to ignore the fact that all eyes were on her. She pushed down the fear that she would say the wrong words during the blessing of the meal, even with the High Priestess of Gadleigh watching her. And she fought to control the stability of her voice despite the look in Bramwell's eyes when their gazes locked.

When she was done with the blessing, Lady Maescia took her hand and thanked her, loud enough for King Adam and Queen Layla to hear, and Tori couldn't help but think the queen regent was putting her on display.

"What a blessing," Queen Layla said, observing Lady Maescia's adulation of Tori. "I heard about the loss of your last High Priestess, and it caused much worry in my heart for your queendom. How wonderful it is that you were able to find a new one so quickly. Such terrors entered my mind at the thought of our Liam's betrothed housed in an unsanctified castle, but now I see there is no need to worry."

"The Divine Mother has blessed us with Lady Tori," Lady Maescia said, flashing Tori a smile she had never seen before. "We are grateful to once again be protected from the evils that dare burden Avarell."

"Lady Tori, please do come and sit with our High Priestess. Lady Gabrielle, do you know Lady Tori?"

Lady Gabrielle motioned for Tori to take the seat beside her. "No, I don't, but I left Tokuna some time ago, and Lady Tori appears to be quite young. Perhaps you arrived there after I left, sister."

Tori gracefully slid into her chair and kept a polite smile on her face. "Perhaps."

"Who did you study with?" Lady Gabrielle asked.

The rest of the royals kept their attention on Tori, and she begged her body not to sweat. "I was taught by Lady Selina," she answered, glad that she had memorized the name.

"Ah, yes. She's a wonderful teacher," Lady Gabrielle said. "So you must have been housed in the Oracle temple."

"Yes, I was." Tori fumbled with the clasp at her throat, fearing that Lady Gabrielle would find a question that Tori could not answer.

"It's a lovely temple. I was housed in the Felicity temple. I miss it still. It had a lovely view of the mountains. Do you know of it?"

"Yes, and you're right. A lovely view."

Relief washed over Tori when the first course was served. She was sure Lady Gabrielle wouldn't be able to interrogate her too much if she was chewing. Before Gadleigh's High Priestess was even finished with her plate, Tori stood and excused herself.

"I shall return shortly," Tori explained to the table. "I just remembered the request from one of the soldiers about more information about reflection in the chapel. I'd hate to let it go before he strays too far from the faith."

"Oh?" Lady Maescia asked. "Which of our fine soldiers do you speak of?"

"Master Stormbolt, Your Grace."

"Ah, yes. A fine guard. Don't be too long, Your Holiness. I know the King and Queen are desperate to hear of your travels to the Crystal Islands."

King Adam and Queen Layla perked up at the mention of it, and through her frustration, Tori forced a polite small and a bow of the head. "Of course, Your Highnesses."

Though she was tempted, Tori made sure not to run from the table.

As if sensing she was coming toward him, Bramwell turned his head in her direction, his back straightening at the sight of her. Tori noticed right away that he had shaved, his jaw clean and smooth. There seemed to be a light in his eyes as he stood to greet her.

"Lady Tori," he said. "To what do I owe the pleasure?"

"I remembered I wanted to have a word with you, Master Stormbolt." She bowed her head to the other members of his table and then took a few paces away. Bramwell followed her without question, which caused a tingling sensation in her stomach.

When she turned around, Bramwell was standing so close to her she could feel the warmth coming off him, accompanied by a pleasant aroma of sage and musk.

"I haven't had a chance to ask how you are faring." Bramwell said. He moved his hand as if he were about to touch her arm, but he retracted it at the last moment.

"Much better. Thank you for asking."

"I'm glad to hear it. What was it you wanted to speak to me about?"

"If I'm to be perfectly honest, I was seeking refuge from the heavy stares and questions at the royal's table."

A smirk broke out on Bramwell's lips. "Yes, I can imagine the pressure that must put you under."

"But I did want to remind you to come to morning prayer for reflection. If you are still seeking it, that is."

His eyes seemed to be searching hers. "Yes, of course. I will come."

"I look forward to it."

They stayed silent for a moment, their eyes locked and their breathing audible. Tori sobered, tearing herself from his gaze, and cleared her throat. "I was also hoping to learn more about the city and the history of Avarell. I don't know if there are any such books in the grand library that might help me in these studies."

"Not in the grand library," he said. "All the books kept on anything important that has happened in Avarell would be located in the city hall. If you'd like, I can ask to have a book keeper give you access to the ledgers that might interest you, as they're in a restricted section."

A vibrant energy suddenly filled Tori's veins. She had no intention of waiting for permission to see the books. She would sneak out tonight, while everyone was busy at the welcoming banquet. "Yes, that would be lovely. Thank you."

"You're welcome."

The lilt of Raven's voice carried its way to them. "Bram. Bram, there you are."

Though the thought of Raven taking Bramwell's attention bothered her, Tori had sense enough to prioritize her actions. "If you'll excuse me," she said to Bram, quickly escaping before Raven could draw near.

Tori put on a troubled face, her mouth nearly pulled into a frown as she approached Lady Maescia at her table. The royals were engaged in a talk about the season's changing when Tori drew near to the queen regent and spoke in soft tones. "Your Grace, I'm terribly sorry to disturb you."

Lady Maescia had the flash of a scowl twist her lips before it returned to the fake smile she'd been showing all evening. "Of course, Your Holiness. What is it?"

She placed a hand on her stomach. "I do believe the quail did not agree with me. Or perhaps it was the plum sauce. I do apologize, but I must excuse myself to my rooms."

Lady Maescia placed a hand upon Tori's. "Oh dear. Do you have a tincture you can take to ease the pain? Or perhaps one of your herbal remedies?"

"I do, Your Grace. Thank you."

"I'm pleased you were able to bless the meal. Do feel better. Should I send someone to check on you?" It didn't go unnoticed that Lady Maescia spoke loud enough for the visiting royals to witness her devotion to her High Priestess.

"That won't be necessary. I will have Finja help me."

"Very well. I hope to see you at breakfast tomorrow, Your Holiness."

"Yes, thank you for your kindness, Your Grace. I bid you good night." She turned to the Gadleigh royals and curtsied. "My apologies, Your Highnesses. Perhaps we can speak some more tomorrow."

"Yes, of course," Queen Layla said. "I do hope you feel better soon."

Flashing a gracious smile, Tori swiftly made her way out of the banquet hall. But she only made it as far as the corridor before someone called her name.

"Lady Tori, a word, if you please." It was Lady Gabrielle, her eyes narrowed and her head tilted.

They were alone in the hall save for a handful of servants who would scurry by with trays of food. "Yes, Lady Gabrielle?"

Lady Gabrielle closed the distance between them and lowered her voice. "I was just wondering what possible scheme you might have in mind."

"Begging your pardon, I don't know what you mean."

"Why have you lied about studying in Tokuna?"

Tori's heart hammered in her chest. "You must be mistaken, sister. I have not lied."

"There is no view of the Mountains from the Felicity Temple. The enormous pines practically darken all the windows."

Tori ignored the sweat forming on the back of her neck. "Lady Gabrielle, you have been away from Tokuna for some time now. The trees became infected and had to be cut down. Patrons of Felicity Temple now enjoy a stunning view of the mountains."

Lady Gabrielle blinked, her jaw slowly dropping for a moment before she got her wits about her.

Before she could speak again, Tori took her hand and patted it. "Do not let it worry you, sister. But take heart. You know the scriptures; we must not condemn others for no reason."

"Yes, of course," Lady Gabrielle said, grimacing in apology.

"Now, if you'll excuse me, I'm not feeling well and need to lie down."

"I hope you recover so that we may chat properly tomorrow, Lady Tori. Good night."

Wrena could not conjure up any more small talk to pacify the Gadleigh royals. She particularly found it hard to keep eye contact with Prince Liam when he gazed at her so admiringly. Especially tonight, when Aurora looked so lovely in her blue dress, her hair swept up to expose her neck.

When the prince stepped away to fetch more wine, Wrena took the opportunity to escape onto the terrace. The cool night air felt refreshing, the tiny blast of cold wind caressing her skin. But when she caught sight of Aurora coming out onto the terrace to join her, a warmth deep inside of her grew and cast away the cold.

"Are you surviving?" Aurora asked cheekily. They stood side-by-side, their hands on the terrace railing, and looked out over the Avarell city lights.

"Barely. Though you've given me a second wind." Wrena glanced over her shoulder quickly before continuing. "I love it when you wear your hair up."

Aurora smiled and dropped her gaze. "I love it when you flatter me."

"The only thing getting me through this dreadful evening is the thought of you coming to visit me tonight. Please say you will."

Aurora only turned her head slightly, but her eyes met Wrena's with a passion to match her own. She slid her hand along the top of the railing until her pinky entangled with Wrena's. Wrena let out a slow, deep breath, wishing she could move closer to Aurora. Wishing the entire party would disappear so they could be alone.

"I'm sorry," Prince Liam said, suddenly appearing behind them. "What… what is going on?"

Aurora swung around, immediately clutching her hands together in front of her and curtsying. "Your Highness, I did not hear you come outside."

"I should say not," he said, question in his eyes.

"Forgive me," Wrena said, her tone calm and her movements ever graceful. "I don't believe you've met Aurora, one of my ladies-in-waiting. She will be helping me with all aspects of the wedding."

"All aspects. I wonder, besides the usual, what that might include."

Wrena could tell that Aurora was about to panic. She wanted to take her hand and tell her everything would be fine. She hated that this prince from another land was causing Aurora such distress.

"Ah, there you are."

All eyes went to the figure who stepped outside onto the terrace to join them. The prince eyed Eleazar skeptically, and Wrena wasn't sure what turn of events his appearance would bring. Wrena blinked in surprise when Eleazar waltzed over to Aurora and put a hand on her waist.

"Lady Aurora," Eleazar said, "you go above and beyond your duties to make sure the princess's bridal needs are met. Perhaps the princess will give you the night off so that you may dance with me, and so that she can entertain her betrothed."

Eleazar began to escort Aurora off the terrace. Aurora, finally catching on, took his arm. "Yes, that would be nice. Thank you, dear Eleazar, for saving me from my own undoing."

Prince Liam lifted his chin. "I'm terribly sorry, but I thought…"

"You thought what, Prince Liam?" Wrena asked, batting her lashes.

Prince Liam chewed his lip. "Nothing." He nodded his head to Eleazar. "Enjoy your evening."

Eleazar bowed and led Aurora into the grand ballroom.

"Forgive me," Prince Liam said to Wrena.

"Think nothing of it." She forced the biggest smile she could muster, knowing she would not have to compensate for what the prince had witnessed. "How about that dance, then?"

CHAPTER THIRTY-THREE

THE BLACK MATERIAL DID WONDERS with keeping Tori warm during such a cold night. It helped that the lining of her mask was velvety smooth, like a blanket for her cheeks. She managed to make it out of the castle and into the city center unnoticed, but she wasn't sure which building was city hall.

Takumi skittered ahead of her as if he did know where city hall was located. He had a gift for finding places, so she had no qualms about following him. Still, she kept her eyes peeled for signs that might lead her to the right building.

City hall was smaller than she thought it would be, it's square stature small enough to fit into the banquet hall of the castle. Takumi gekkered, padding along in a circle in front of the door until Tori could catch up to him. She was grateful for the shadow that concealed them as she used her tiny tools to manipulate the lock. With a click, the door opened, and the duo slipped inside.

After the foyer came a room with a long wooden table in the center, surrounded by leather chairs. Tori assumed this is where the important townspeople held their meetings and made decisions that were not already handled by the Queen. Beyond the table were iron bars that separated the meeting room from shelves of hardbound books.

“It must be in there,” Tori whispered.

Takumi ran and perched himself on one of the high windows of the building, staring out the window, keeping watch. Tori studied the lock on the iron gate and picked out the correct tools from her kit. The lock was easy enough to manipulate, but the loud creaking the gate made as she swung it open gave her pause. Even when she slowed down her movements, the gate continued to let out an ear-shattering groan. How did the people work here with such a sound?

Pulling open the gate only wide enough to slip her body in sideways, Tori slunk into the records room and attempted to adjust her eyes to the lack of light. She inspected the shelves, pulling out various books, maps, and folders with tedious paperwork. The documents and ledgers named various treaties and sales, but she needed to find the one documenting the year Goran’s wife went missing.

Takumi suddenly made a clicking noise, signaling to Tori that someone was coming near. Tori stopped searching, ducking instantly in case someone was to see movement through the windows. Keeping still, she heard footsteps and voices. At this late hour, they must have been either drunken patrons of the nearby pub or Queen’s Guard soldiers. She held her breath until the footsteps and the voices faded, but didn’t dare move until Takumi made a noise to let her know the coast was clear.

It took Tori ten more minutes to find the books marking the year she was searching for and five more minutes before she narrowed the ledgers down to the sale of slaves. A peek inside revealed lists of money amounts, names, and realms. Though she questioned why any realm would enter such a business, she forced back her questions and tucked the heavy book against her chest as she left the records room.

Tori and Takumi left the way they came in, listening in case more guards wandered by. Once they were safely out of the city hall, they kept to the shadows and made their way back to the castle, the ledger concealed under Tori's cloak. It was a heavy book, which slowed her pace, but Tori reminded herself that it was one step closer to getting the cure for her family. And for herself.

The sun breached the city's horizon as Tori picked the precise herbs and seeds for the tonic she needed to make for the queen regent. As she tucked the ingredients into a silken satchel, she looked up to find Bram approaching. She straightened, smoothing down the skirts of her gown, and smiled through the warmth that blossomed in her cheeks.

"Master Stormbolt," she said. "How very nice to see you."

"Good morning." He bowed his head, one side of his mouth twisted into a smile. "I didn't expect to see you before breakfast. Outside of the chapel, that is."

"I needed to gather some supplies," she said, gesturing to the plants behind her.

"You disappeared after we spoke at the welcoming banquet last night. I was told you weren't feeling well and had to depart."

Tori's heart swelled, her skin tingly at the thought that he had asked after her. "Yes, well, I think it might have been something I ate."

"Well, the main thing is that you're fine now."

"Yes, I'm feeling much better. Thank you."

He glanced behind her. "Is that lavender?"

She followed his gaze, and then smiled. "Yes, it is."

"My mother used to use it for teas and in cooking," he said. "Especially in the evenings, when she claimed I was full of too much energy to be able to get a proper rest."

"Your mother was right to use it. It's very relaxing." She studied him. He had a faraway look in his eyes that told her his thoughts were elsewhere. "You miss her."

"Yes, well, it's been years. But lavender does remind me of my childhood, mostly of growing up in Gadleigh."

"Oh, I didn't realize you weren't an Avarell-born citizen. I recall that you said your uncle took you in when your parents passed on, but I hadn't gathered you had completely moved continents. This visit from Gadleigh must bring up memories for you."

"Yes, it has." Bram nodded.

Tori couldn't help but think there was something more behind his unreadable expression. Was it more than just the memory of losing his parents? She could understand his pain, having lost her sister, but there seemed to be something else bothering him. Though she wasn't spiritual at her core, she figured that playing her role might help him work through his troubles. "Perhaps whatever is troubling you can be reflected upon at the chapel. Though it matters not *where* you pray, there is something magical about a house of the Divine Mother."

His shoulders seemed to drop slightly, as if letting a heavy weight slip off them. "I think I will take you up on that offer."

She felt the satchel in her hands. "I will be there shortly. I first have to deliver something to Lady Maescia."

"Of course. I will see you soon."

"This is for your bath," Tori said as she handed Lady Maescia the mixture of herbs. "It will relax both your mind and your body."

Lady Maesica took the satchel and smelled it. "It's a lovely mixture of scents. And if you say it will work, then I believe you."

"And these should alleviate your headaches." Tori handed her a small gold tray with two medium-sized leaves on it, which appeared covered in pollen.

"Oh," Lady Maescia grimaced. "I can't look at another tea."

"No, these aren't for tea. You must place them over your eyes while you are in the bath. They are guaranteed to make your headaches go away."

Lady Maescia eyed the leaves skeptically. "Over my eyes?"

"Yes." Tori studied Lady Maescia's face. "Your Grace, they say confession is good for the soul. Perhaps your worries are weighing you down. You *can* confide in me."

Lady Maescia's eyes were locked on Tori, and she seemed to be holding her breath. Was she weighing her options? Would she confess to Tori about killing the last High Priestess?

She took a step closer to Tori and her mouth opened, but at the last second, something changed her expression. She held up the herbs. "Will these really work?"

Tori suppressed her disappointment. "Along with a prayer to the Divine Mother from your very own High Priestess, yes, they will work." And they would give Tori the perfect opportunity to steal Lady Maescia's key.

CHAPTER THIRTY-FOUR

BRAM DID HIS BEST to avoid direct eye contact with Captain Thornwood during the proceedings in the royal negotiation room, but it wasn't entirely possible. He had managed to dodge him during the welcoming banquet, but he knew he wouldn't be able to escape him during—or after—the negotiation meeting. The duke sat across from Captain Thornwood, his face as stoic as ever, with a number of each company's soldiers lining opposite walls as they awaited the arrival of the royals. Logan waited patiently beside Bram, and Azalea stood by Logan. Tiberius, the executioner, had a strange smug smirk on his face that made Bram question his interest in the meeting.

The tall double doors opened. First, King Adam and Queen Layla entered the room. All the guards in the room bowed to them respectfully until they were seated. They bowed once again when Prince Liam entered the room, and lastly when Princess Wrena and Lady Maescia arrived.

Queen Layla looked around, concern on her face. "I'm not quite sure we need such a large crowd to discuss the matters of the wedding."

"Queen Layla, we are not here to discuss the wedding. We are here to renegotiate the treaty my sister drew up with you."

"Renegotiate?" King Adam asked.

"I was under the impression the treaty was a done deal," Captain Thornwood said, his words slow and careful. "What more is there to negotiate?"

"It's quite simple, really," the duke said. "The deals that were made with Queen Callista have been reviewed, and we need to reassess our interest in the treaty."

"Your interest?" King Liam asked with a scoff. "I would think your interest would include an alliance that would hold strong against the Nostidour forces."

"While a strong army is, of course, a viable goal, it has come to Lady Maescia's attention that a union between Prince Liam and Princess Wrena is not in our best interest."

The room erupted in grumbles from the Gadleigh court and the high officials of their army. Prince Liam's face fell, his mouth in a straight line. Princess Wrena would not look at him, her chin high, but her eyes trained on her delicate hand that sat on the table top.

Queen Layla leaned forward on the table. "Queen Callista signed the agreement."

"Queen Callista is incapacitated," Lady Maescia retorted. "And there is question as to whether she was in the right frame of mind to have signed the agreement in the first place."

"This is absurd," King Liam said, his jaw clenched.

"We have drawn up a new treaty," Duke Grunmire announced, sliding parchment across the table to Captain Thornwood.

The captain looked over the paper with a scowl on his face. "This is unacceptable. You call off the engagement but still expect the Gadleigh army to answer to you?"

"It's a matter of numbers," Duke Grunmire said. "We have the larger army, we have fought more battles, and we have more experience. Joining our army would only benefit yours, Captain Thornwood."

"This treaty states that Gadleigh's division would rank below Avarell's. Putting you in charge of both armies." The captain shook his head. "This is not only preposterous; it's insulting!"

"I disagree." Duke Grunmire leaned back in his chair. "Politically and strategically, it makes sense. Without our army's support, it will only be a matter of time before Nostidour attacks Gadleigh."

"I cannot believe this," King Adam mumbled.

"I am not without reason," Lady Maescia said. "I will give you a month after you return to Gadleigh to accept the new terms of the treaty."

The King scowled. "I can tell you right now, that the terms will not be accepted."

"Then we have nothing further to discuss." Lady Maescia rose from her chair. "Duke?"

The duke appeared smug as he followed Lady Maescia out of the room.

The next few moments were silent. At last, the Gadleigh royals stood and attempted to keep their heads high as they departed, Prince Liam casting a glance at Wrena before he charged out the door. Wrena held a hand to her stomach, her face pale and drawn into a frown.

Eleazar, who had been watching her the entire time, walked up to her and placed a hand on her arm. "Wrena, are you all right?"

She simply nodded, patting his arm, before leaving the room. The rest of the guards followed her out.

"That was unexpected" Logan said.

"I don't know," Bram put in. "I had a feeling something was afoot."

"But calling off the wedding?" Logan shook his head. "Bold."

"Foolish," Azalea added.

"Yes." Bram rubbed at his chin. "I wonder what will become of this."

The trio made their way out of the negotiation room, and Logan and Azalea parted with Bram, heading in the opposite direction.

Though Bram braced himself for the confrontation with Captain Thornwood, it wasn't until he rounded the corner and found the good captain standing there, waiting for him, that he tensed.

"I would think that you've had ample time to think about my offer." Captain Thornwood took poised strides toward Bram, closing the distance between them. "It's not an offer I make lightly. Or often. And you should take heart when considering it."

"Captain Thornwood, please understand." Bram glanced over his shoulder quickly before continuing. "I have a lot of stock in Avarell—friends and family, my station—and I can't simply decide to leave."

"Master Stormbolt, do be cautious." Captain Thornwood placed a heavy hand on Bramwell's shoulder. "An impetuous move like what they've pulled in there could lead to war, and you should decide which side you want to be on if that happens."

Tori kept the crack in the secret passageway door miniscule as she waited for Lady Maescia to get into her bath. She could smell the lavender and other herbs she'd given Lady Maescia to cure her headaches—headaches she and Finja manipulated her into having—and even spotted the golden tray that held the special leaves Lady Maescia was to place over her eyes.

She hadn't lied to the queen regent; the herbs and leaves would indeed sooth Lady Maescia's headaches, but that was not the reason Tori gave them to her. With her body and mind relaxed and her eyes covered, Lady Maescia would be less likely to detect Takumi's entrance to the washroom.

Lady Maescia disrobed behind a partition, and Tori caught sight of the necklace being placed on a dresser beside a mirror, hairbrushes, and other accessories. The handmaids were then dismissed, leaving candles burning for soothing lighting in the room, and Lady Maescia let out a soft sigh, entering and sinking deep into the bath. Tori watched as the queen regent studied and smelled the leaves she gave her before placing them on her eyes. Tori waited a few moments more, just to give Lady Maescia time to relax, before cracking the passage door wider open.

Takumi padded out on silent paws, making his way behind the partition. Tori's eyes darted between Takumi in his efforts and Lady Maescia, her teeth clenched together until her fox friend darted back to her unnoticed. She quickly let him into the passageway and took the key from him, which was still attached to the necklace. Tori then pressed the key into the clay in the box Goran had given her. Goran had told her to press firmly for one minute. Tori counted in her head. The minute seemed to last forever. She hoped the clay would actually work.

After the minute was up, Tori carefully removed the key from the box and rubbed the remnants of clay away. She returned it to Takumi, who directly scampered off to bring the necklace back to Lady Maescia's dresser. Tori almost let out a sigh of relief, but her eyes widened as Takumi swung around atop the dresser, his bushy tail knocking down a hairbrush.

The queen regent shifted in the bath, and Tori held her breath. Takumi jumped down and hid under the dresser, waiting. Lady Maescia slowly sat up and removed the leaves from her eyes.

"Is someone there?" she asked, brows drawn down as she waited for a response. Tori didn't dare move, and she knew Takumi would hold his ground as well. As Lady Maescia's eyes swept across the room, Tori begged the Divine Mother herself to keep the crack in the wall concealed from Lady Maescia's vision.

Just then, the door opened, and a handmaid entered. "Begging your pardon, Your Grace, but here are the lotions you requested."

"Ah, yes. Very good."

With their attention elsewhere, Takumi took the opportunity to run back to Tori. She opened the secret door and let him in without being detected. Wiping the sweat from her palms, she stowed the box into one of the pockets of her cloak, then headed back to her rooms, her heart practically slamming through her chest.

AURORA

CHAPTER THIRTY-FIVE

AURORA ORGANIZED THE ITEMS on Princess Wrena's dresser as the handmaids finished drawing the princess's bath. Wrena picked up various bottles of bath oils, smelling each of them as if taking her time picking just the right one. Once the bath was full and steam began to fill the room, Wrena dismissed the handmaids, and Aurora remained.

Wrena submerged herself in the wonderfully hot and soapy water, allowing the heat to tend to her tense muscles. The day had taken a toll on her nerves, and she couldn't get the disappointed look Prince Liam gave her out of her head.

The soft feel of a sponge snapped her out of her stupor. Aurora ran the soapy sponge along Wrena's arms and shoulders, and when Wrena glanced at her, Aurora had a look of uncertainty on her face.

"What's the matter?" Wrena asked.

"I'm just worried."

"About what?"

"About the consequences of calling off the wedding. About what will happen to us. About our safety. I actually thought I would die of fear when Prince Liam caught us on the terrace. If Eleazar hadn't come out and rescued us…"

Wrena shifted in the bath and took Aurora's hand. "We don't need a man to rescue us, Aurora. I should have told Prince Liam the truth, then and there. The only thing stopping me was the thought of something awful happening to you."

Aurora was quiet. Wrena turned again and leaned her back against the tub.

"I don't understand how people can lack understanding. The duke, for one, is atrocious. Did you know I actually heard him joke with Tiberius that if Gadleigh doesn't accept their terms, they should lead them out to the Rift?"

Aurora sighed and shook her head. "Maybe *we* should run away to the Rift. Can't be any worse than here."

"You might be right," Wrena said with a laugh.

"Sure, the Undead want to consume you, but at least you can love whomever you want."

Wrena opened her eyes and turned her head toward Aurora. "The duke wants to smooth over the news about the broken engagement by giving the citizens of Avarell hope for a new union. I have to attend my mother's birthday celebration with Eleazar as my companion."

Aurora dropped her gaze. "I know."

"But I promise not to have a good time."

"Perhaps you shouldn't promise that. You saw what they did to Rudy. I don't want that to happen to you."

"They wouldn't. My aunt? She wouldn't dare betray my mother like that."

"She might not have a choice. If the queendom finds out and the queen regent doesn't enforce the same rules unto her own kin, there will be an uprising."

"Maybe there should be."

"Don't say that. This is your queendom. You will inherit it all. And once you do, you can lead the way the queendom is meant to be led."

Wrena sat up, water dripping off her skin. "But where does that leave me? With a man I don't love by my side."

"Perhaps. But I will also be by your side. And I vow to stay there, no matter what."

"Perhaps we should consider fleeing to Creoca. My uncle would never turn us away."

"And be fugitives? That sounds rather dangerous."

Wrena reached out and touched Aurora's cheek. "You mean exciting, do you not?"

A slow smile crept onto Aurora's mouth as a soft kiss closed the distance between them.

"Duke Grunmire," Bram said. "May I have a word?"

He knew he should have simply left the training hall, but his recent conversation with Captain Thornwood swayed him into action. He needed to know where he stood in order to make the decision he'd been putting off.

"Master Stormbolt, I do hope this is important. The Gadleigh court has left in an uproar and we must prepare ourselves for what they might do."

"It is." At least, it was to him. "I understand this may not seem the appropriate time to breach the subject, but in light of the negotiations with Gadleigh, I need to be certain of my station."

The duke eyed Bram skeptically, sucking air from between his top teeth. "Would this happen to be about your promotion review?"

"Yes, my lord."

"In light of the fact that you have not been showing focus during training—and showing up late to training altogether—I can only conclude that you, yourself, do not see any flaws in your dedication to the guard."

Bram was about to defend himself, but the duke cut him off.

"I tell you what: let us have a match. Right here and now. If you win, you can have your promotion."

Bram narrowed his eyes. "You're willing to judge my worthiness on one fight? Haven't I proven to you how much I'm willing to work for this by my efforts?"

"You win, you get the promotion. Right away."

Bram's hand fidgeted on the hilt of his sword. "Agreed."

The duke turned and paced a few steps away while drawing his sword. Bram slid his sword from his sheath and brought it to position, readying his body for the challenge. As the duke turned to face him, there was a mysterious smirk on his face.

The duke charged, but Bram was quick to deflect, his muscles cooperating with him despite the small voice of doubt in his head. The duke was not a young man, but he proved to hold on to the stamina and strength of his youth.

The training hall filled with the echo of steel striking steel. Bram, filled with determination, grunted as he surged forward, striking again and again, barely allowing the duke time to parry. Slowly, Bram's mouth twisted into a smile. He gained momentum. He could win this.

Suddenly, the duke spun to the side, dodging Bram's lunge, and as he ducked low, his boot came out to connect with Bram's knee. Caught off guard, Bram fell to the ground, barely catching himself with his arm. In the next moment, he looked up to find the duke's sword pointed at his throat.

Duke Grunmire snickered.

Bram clenched his jaw, his breaths coming out in pants, waiting for the duke to back away and claim his win. But the cold expression on the duke's face sent tremors of fear through Bram's body. Unsure of what the duke might do, Bram threw down his sword.

"You win, then," Bram said, bracing himself.

The duke glared at him a moment more before pulling back his sword and sheathing it. "Yes," the duke said. "I always do."

CHAPTER THIRTY-SIX

TORI WAS GRATEFUL to see the ship at the dock, exhausted from carrying the heavy book. She ignored the cold wind harshly whipping at her face and the drizzle of rain as she marched directly to Goran, who watched her approach. The workers behind her unloaded more cargo than usual, and Tori suspected it was because of the Queen's birthday festival. Goran's men struggled to get the crates and boxes covered with tarps so as not to have their delivery destroyed by the rain.

"You found it," Goran said. It wasn't a question.

She dropped the heavy book onto his waiting hands, glad to be rid of it. "I can't promise you'll find your wife's name in there."

He nodded solemnly, tucking the book under his cape. "I know. But I have to believe I will."

"I've also given the molding box to Finja. She's not sure how long it will take for your iron worker to produce the key."

"It shouldn't take too long. Keep an eye out for it."

She nodded, reflecting on how soon this could all be over. She just hoped it would all end well.

He tapped the book under his cape, studying her. "How are you faring?"

"In all honestly, the only thing on my mind is how desperately I want to go home."

"You've been doing extremely well in your tasks. There is only one left."

Exhaustion pulled on her nerves. "Why do you need to find out about the Queen? Haven't I done enough for you?"

"This isn't for me. It's for the nine realms."

She knew he was right, and she knew she wouldn't be mollified until she found the Queen. "I don't know if I can give you the answer you want."

His gaze went to the castle, and a deep breath escaped his nose. "Find the Queen. Rescue her if she's alive. And if she is dead, strategies will be altered. Either way, we need to get Lady Maescia off the throne."

They were quiet for a while, the only sound around them the grunts and shouts of the men unloading the cargo from the ship.

"How is Hettie?" Tori asked.

Goran let a small smile slip. "She is adjusting to being back home. But she is nervous. Keeps thinking the Queen's Guard are coming to get her."

"I wish her well."

He nodded. "If all goes well, you'll see your family soon."

She couldn't respond. As much as she wanted to promise she could carry out the last task, and as much as she desperately wanted to see her family, she was afraid to hold on to the hope. She was afraid that their goal might never be achieved.

Goran handed her a pouch. "I'm assuming you need to replenish your supply of pills."

Tori took the pouch and tucked it into her cloak pocket. "Yes. I'm almost out."

"Perfect timing, then." His gaze went over her shoulder. "Speaking of timing, it looks like the soldiers are here to assure the delivery has arrived safely. You best go."

Pulling her hood more securely over her head, she swiftly left Goran's side, taking the route behind the crates of supplies to conceal her exit. She slipped on her mask and sprinted silently through the rain toward the city.

Halfway back to the castle, she rounded the corner and came face to face with a soldier. Her mouth fell open and her heart stuck in her throat. She froze, as did he. Her head swam. A ringing in her ears drowned out the sound of pouring rain. How could she have been so careless? The guard assessed her, his hand on his sword. She recognized him as Tiberius, the queen regent's executioner.

Coming to her senses, she shifted and ran. Tiberius was quick to follow her, keeping up with her pace as she zigzagged through buildings. When she was sure he couldn't see, she quickly jumped upon some wooden crates beside the bakery and climbed up onto the roof, flattening herself upon the roof tiles so that he couldn't spot her. But in that moment, her cloak caught the wind. A flash of movement caught her eye just as Tiberius rounded the corner.

She fought to suppress the curse that almost flew from her lips. The flash of movement was the pouch of pills Goran had given her. She watched in horror as the pouch fell into the gutter, which ran with a constant stream of rainwater. She heard Tiberius's approach, so she curled back from the side of the roof and kept still. She bit down on her fist, wanting to scream, but keeping silent as Tiberius rushed past the bakery, searching for her.

The sound of his heavy footsteps diminished, and she carefully rolled back to the edge of the roof. She checked the gutter, searching for her pouch, but it was gone.

The sun had barely broken through the morning sky when Bram found Aurora alone in the courtyard, throwing bread toward the ducks in the pond.

"Good morning, cousin."

She turned and smiled at him. "Good morning, Bram. Why are you up so early?"

"I've actually been up most of the night, thinking."

"Oh?" She tilted her head, giving him a concerned look. "Thinking about what?"

"Come sit with me," he suggested, gesturing to the nearby bench.

She followed him, and they both took a seat. The ducks swam about, nipping at the remnants of breadcrumbs, and the mourning doves flew overhead.

"Aurora, are you happy?"

She blinked at him. "I'm as well as to be expected. Why?"

He took her hand. "Aurora, I know."

"What do you know?"

"I know—" He took a deep breath and let it out before he continued. "—about your feelings for the princess."

Aurora slammed a hand down on his knee, her head swiveling left and right in search of someone who might have heard. "Bram, keep your voice down. If someone were to hear…"

"Aurora, it's okay." He squeezed her hand.

She looked frightened, her lip beginning to quiver. "What do you mean?"

He released her hand and placed his palms on her cheeks, leaning closer and locking eyes with her. "You needn't worry about what I think. You are my cousin, and I love you no matter what."

A shuddered breath escaped her lips, and tears welled in her eyes. He stroked her cheek, then pulled her into an embrace, wrapping her in his arms, shushing her quiet sobs.

"But it will never be the way we want it to be. It's a doomed love."

He pulled back and wiped her tears away. "I'm sorry. I, too, know of doomed love."

Her brow furrowed. She sniffled. "What do we do about it?"

"I don't know. But I, for one, have to move on."

She wiped at her face, looking confused. "Move on? What do you mean?"

"I'm leaving Avarell."

"Leaving? Where will you go?"

"I've been offered a position in the Queen's Guard of Gadleigh."

Her eyes widened and she grabbed his wrists. "And you've accepted?"

"I'm sending a letter in response tomorrow."

She studied him for a moment, and then finally she nodded. "It's where your father served."

"Yes. And apparently, they consider me his legacy. They want me to fill his shoes, so to speak."

"Does the duke know? Or the queen regent?"

"Not yet. I'll turn in my resignation after the Queen's birthday banquet. I don't want to intrude upon the festivities. Plus, I don't expect them to take the news too well."

She let out a small laugh and then pulled him into a hug. They stayed like that for a while, silent and reflective.

"Thank you for telling me," Aurora finally said. "I love you, Bram."

"I love you, too, Aurora. Always."

CHAPTER THIRTY-SEVEN

BRAM WATCHED TORI as she knelt at the alter in the castle's chapel. Though he knew leaving Avarell was for the best, he would miss the sight of this intriguing woman, High Priestess or not.

When she stood, she looked over at him and flashed him a small smile. "Master Stormbolt. It's pleasing to see you have kept your word about coming to prayer."

"I've done a lot of reflecting, Your Holiness. And you were right; it helped tremendously."

"The Divine Mother is surely content."

"I was wondering if you might be attending the Queen's birthday celebrations."

"Of course, I'm obligated to be there to bless the meal."

"Then perhaps I will see you there."

"Of course."

"And perhaps you might do me the favor of saving me a dance."

She seemed surprised, and Bram swore she had a little more color in her cheeks. "I do not know if it is my place to dance at the Queen's celebration."

He smirked at her. "You owe me, you know?"

She looked as if she held back a laugh. "What do you mean?"

"I practically saved your life. The night of the storm."

She smirked, nodding. "Perhaps you did."

"So, you'll save me a dance?"

She studied his face. He was afraid to move and break the spell he seemed to be under. "I'll think about it."

"I'm certain the Divine Mother is content about that as well." He bowed his head and quickly left the chapel, his head dizzy from his forwardness. Perhaps it was the fact that he was leaving that gave him the courage to speak to her in such a manner. But he didn't care. He was determined to at least enjoy one dance with Lady Tori before he departed. Who knew if he would ever see her again?

With a skip in his step, he ventured toward the banquet hall for breakfast. He spotted Logan and Azalea entering the hall ahead of him, and just as he was about to call out to his friend, a gentle voice called his name.

"Bramwell. Good morning." Raven smiled at him as she approached. "Were you coming from the chapel?"

"Yes. I was observing the enchantment of morning prayer."

"Ah, yes." Raven eyed him up and down. "Lady Tori is quite fascinating. She's so devout."

"Was there something you wanted to see me about?"

"Might we take a quick walk in the gardens before breakfast?" Raven gestured toward the doors.

Bram knew he would have to have a talk with Raven at one point or another, and decided this was the perfect opportunity. "Yes, that would be fine."

As they made their way out to the gardens, Bram came up with a million different ways to let Raven down, but nothing he thought of sounded true. He knew that no matter what he said, she would be upset, so he might as well stick to the basic truth without elaborating on anything.

"I can't wait for you to see my dress for the festivities," Raven said, wrapping her arm through his.

"Raven, about that—"

She stopped short and tilted her head, a coy smile playing on her lips. "I do hope you aren't planning on being a scoundrel this time. I would hope that by now you'd have the decency to escort me as my companion at the party instead of playing your silly games. I've grown weary of chasing you."

"You shouldn't have to chase anyone, Raven."

"Exactly! Oh, I'm so glad you finally admit it. And why stop at parties. We should be together all the time."

"Raven," he said, his hands placed gently on her arms. "I need to be honest with you."

Her smile slowly faded into a frown full of uncertainty.

"I'm afraid that what you feel for me… Please don't take this the wrong way, but I do not feel in my heart what you do."

Her mouth dropped open slightly, her bottom lip quivering and her eyes glassy. "I don't understand. Is there someone else?"

His mouth opened, and something inside of him almost prompted him to tell her how he felt about Tori, but as he got his wits about him, he decided against it. There would be no sense in mentioning Tori when it wasn't possible for her to feel the same way for him. "There is no one else, Raven. But it would be a lie to pretend I love you."

"What is wrong with me?"

He squeezed her hand. "There is nothing wrong. I promise you."

She turned away from him. Her shoulders shook as she began to sob quietly.

His heart hurt for her, but it wouldn't be right to lead her on. "The truth is I'm leaving Avarell."

She sniffled and turned around, a furrow in her brow. "Leaving? Where would you go?"

He let out a sigh. He didn't want to tell too many people before he gave his official notice. But he figured he owed Raven a full explanation. "I've been offered a position in the Queen's Guard of Gadleigh."

"Gadleigh?"

"Yes. My father served there, and they would like to take me on."

"Right." She nodded slowly, and then suddenly shook her head. "But what about Aurora?"

"I admit, at first I found the prospect of leaving my family difficult. But Aurora is a grown woman now. She doesn't need me. She can't stop me from living my life any more than I can stop her from living hers."

She tugged at her lip with her teeth, dropping her gaze. "I understand. No ties, then."

"I do hope that we can remain friends."

She lifted her chin, her frown transforming into a scowl. "Friends?" She scoffed. "I couldn't bear it. I won't!"

Before he could stop her, she turned on her heels and ran back into the castle.

CHAPTER THIRTY-EIGHT

WHEN FINJA ENTERED THE ROOM, Tori straightened, forcing a relaxed expression on her face, and turned to her. She didn't want Finja to know about her fever or the weakness in her joints. She just hoped Finja wouldn't notice the sweat at her temples or the dark circles under her eyes.

Of course, Finja was as observant as ever. "What's wrong with you?"

"Nothing. I'm just a little tired. It's a strange effect that the change in seasons has on me."

Finja narrowed her eyes. "Are you sure? We can't risk you falling under now; there's too much at risk. Have you been taking your medicine?"

"Yes, of course. Why wouldn't I?" Tori quickly turned away from her, focusing instead on Takumi, who was curled up by the fire. The truth was she had skipped a few doses, spreading out the remainder of her supply so that it would last her until Goran came back into Avarell.

"And what's the matter with him?" Finja asked, jutting her chin at Takumi. "He usually scampers away when I come into a room."

"Perhaps he's gotten used to you." Tori smirked. "Or maybe he's grown fond of you."

Finja scoffed. "I have no time to worry about whether a wild animal is fond of me or not. Here, take this."

Tori reached for the object Finja handed her. It was a folded blanket, but when Tori took it, she felt the surface of something hard inside. "What is this?"

"It's the key. The iron worker finally finished."

Tori unwrapped the blanket and found a thin, long, wooden box. Inside, resting on sawdust, was a black key identical to the one hanging around Lady Maescia's neck.

This was it. This was all she needed to perform the last of her tasks. A shudder went through her, but she couldn't be sure if it was from her fever or from the fear of what would happen after she found the Queen. She guessed it all depended on whether or not the Queen was alive when she found her.

"What will happen?" Tori asked. "After I find the Queen?"

"If she is alive, under duress, and you rescue her, Lady Maescia will no longer rule Avarell. If she is not alive, Princess Wrena will become the rightful ruler, the new Queen."

"And Lady Maescia?"

Finja crossed her arms. "If it was your mother? If you just found out she'd been dead all these years? What would you do to the woman who lied to you? Aunt or not."

Tori didn't have to answer. A lie like that would fill her with rage unlike anything she'd ever known. Deceit like that might even stir a madness powerful enough to lead her to kill.

"Find her. Tonight, during the celebration. Find a moment to sneak away and use that key. Goran only awaits your word. He's ready to lead his army here to take down the queen regent."

"What will happen to us?"

"We will have to fight. We will have to fight for what's right."

Tori shivered. She wrapped her arms around herself and forced away the chills. "Is Khadulan's army strong enough to do that?"

"Perhaps not, if they are to fight alone. But as of recent there has been correspondence between Khadulan and Gadleigh."

"Gadleigh? How do you know this?"

"I have my spies." Finja didn't smile, but she looked proud of herself. "The breaking of Princess Wrena's engagement to Prince Liam has caused ill feelings in the Gadleigh royals. We've managed to get word to them about our discontent with the way Lady Maescia is ruling, how we seek change. They are considering our offer to join forces."

"That means war."

"To the core, there is no peace in Avarell. And where there is lack of peace, war is inevitable."

CHAPTER THIRTY-NINE

THE BIRTHDAY BANQUET for Queen Callista was in full swing. Even throughout the years that she was ill, Lady Maescia threw the celebration for her sister in her honor. And from what Tori learned, every year the celebration seemed to get bigger. From what she took in of the decorations and the entertainment, it was certainly a mammoth display of commemoration.

Enormous seven-layer cakes and trays of sweets lined the banquet hall. Imported meats and delicacies from around the globe were displayed on every table. Everywhere she looked there were musicians, fire-breathers, court jesters, and dancers with masks. She'd never seen anything like it.

After Tori blessed the meal, Lady Maescia stood from her table.

"Citizens of Avarell, I have wonderful news. The physicians have told me that Queen Callista may be well enough to leave her sickbed and join us for tonight's festivities."

The princess's jaw dropped, her eyes wide with shock. The murmurs in the banquet hall grew, the crowd looking pleased, and there were even some shouts of joy and praise to the Divine Mother.

Tori, however, was confused. If the Queen had really been ill and was now expected to join the party, perhaps become well enough one day to take back the throne, what did that mean for her plans? For the alliance between Gadleigh and Khadulan? If Queen Callista returned to rule, perhaps peace would be restored in Avarell and the nine realms.

But something in Tori's gut wouldn't let her be hopeful.

Prince Theo jumped from his seat and ran to Tori, pulling on her arm. "Did you hear? My mother is coming!"

Tori bent down and took his hands, smiling at the sight of his delighted face. "Yes, I heard. How wonderful."

"I can't wait to show her all the toys I made. And my games."

"She'll be very delighted to see them."

The prince jumped up and down a couple times before running to his sister and wrapping his arms around her. "Wrena, Mama is coming!"

Princess Wrena smiled and hugged him, but when his head was buried in her hair, she turned her head toward her aunt, question in her eyes. Did she doubt Lady Maescia as much as Tori's gut told her to?

Merriment filled the room as the food was served, the musicians playing joyful tunes and the fire-breather turning the ice sculpture of the phoenix into one of a bear. The festivities carried on through dessert, but there was no sign of the Queen. Tori watched woefully as the prince and princess's expressions grew more doubtful with each passing hour.

The queen regent, who had disappeared for a while, returned to the head table and clapped her hands to call for silence. The musicians stopped playing and everyone kept still and quiet.

"Friends, I'm afraid the Queen needs more time. She asks that you continue with the celebration, and she will join us as soon as she's capable."

This time the murmurs and mumbles were less enthusiastic. And this time, Tori knew Lady Maescia had to be lying. It was a ruse to trick the citizens into forgetting about all the injustices that had taken place. It was a deception to make the people of Avarell think that Lady Maescia was doing everything she could to support her sister. But Tori saw right through her.

Tori pushed away her dessert and stood, heading for the terrace. She needed some air. If she couldn't run away, then she would at least step outside and breathe in what little nature she could get. When she stepped out onto the terrace, she noticed Lady Raven sitting by herself near the fountain.

"Lady Raven?"

Lady Raven wiped at her face. Though she pushed out a smile, Tori could see that she had been crying.

Tori made her way to her side. "Lady Raven, what has you so distraught?"

"I believed, you know? You said if I held it in my heart to be true…" Lady Raven broke down in tears before she could continue.

Tori put an arm around her. "Dear Lady Raven, I'm very sorry."

"He doesn't love me," she said through her blubbering. "He said there was no one else, but I don't know if I can believe him."

Tori rubbed at Lady Raven's back, wondering if Bramwell had told her the truth. Did he discontinue his relationship with Lady Raven simply because he wasn't interested, or was there another reason? Some deep, secret part of Tori wanted her to be the reason. Her heart fluttered at the thought.

"Lady Raven, the Divine Mother always holds our best interests at heart. If it was not meant to be, then there is another fate in store for you. Sometimes, though our hearts do not agree, we must let things go. To hold a caged bird will not make it sing for you."

Lady Raven nodded, sniffling back her tears. "Yes, I know. You're right. I know, logically, that you are right. But I can't fathom how I will get over him."

"It will take some time, I'm sure, but you are a lovely girl, and I know there are plenty of men in Avarell who would love to be the one escorting you to festivals and balls. And they would be lucky to."

Lady Raven smiled through her tears, nodding. "Thank you, Lady Tori. You are truly a blessing."

With the remnants of the feast cleared away, the crowd adjourned to the dance hall. Wrena stood by her aunt, and though she doubted her mother would truly make an appearance, she couldn't help but constantly look at the doors. She hated to stomp down the hope in her heart, but she would have thought that if her mother were awake enough to agree to come to the party, she would have sent for her daughter. Would her mother not have wanted to see her after all this time? Would she not want to see how she'd grown, to hear how her voice had changed, to praise her for the woman she turned out to be?

The music was lovely, and Wrena loved to dance, but she could not bring herself to dance with Eleazar, no matter how many times he asked. Luckily, he was a good enough friend to understand that she wasn't feeling quite up to it yet.

When she wasn't checking the door, she was searching for Aurora. They were going to decide this night what their fate would be. Wrena had already ordered a boat to wait at the shore. But Aurora hadn't given her a definite answer yet. Additionally,

Wrena wanted to find out if her mother was truly getting better before she made the decision herself.

She looked over when the duke entered the dance hall. He marched over to Maescia and whispered something in her ear. Maescia's face fell, and she nodded. The next moment, Maescia clapped her hands together, and the room grew still.

"Dear friends, I'm afraid I have more disheartening news. My dear sister, the beloved Queen, is too ill after all and will not be joining the festivities tonight, but her wish is for everyone to enjoy themselves in her honor. And so that you do have some happy news to fill your hearts with joy, I am proud and honored to announce that my niece, your princess, Wrena Elizabeth Bracken, Her Royal Highness of Avarell, is now engaged to Earl Eleazar Grunmire."

The crowd went from disappointment to joyous again, the music picking up and the partygoers dancing and declaring their joy. Wrena swallowed hard, unprepared for the announcement but unable to do anything about it. Eleazar came over to join her at her side, holding his hand out for her to place her hand upon as a symbol of their newly found engagement. Wrena did her best to smile for the crowd, but she was sure everyone could see right through her. She now had two reasons to be disappointed.

As soon as the crowd settled and the citizens had all congratulated her, she excused herself from Eleazar and went to find her aunt. Focused on her goblet of wine, Maescia hardly looked up when Wrena approached her.

"Aunt Maescia, I would like to see my mother. If she was well enough to begin getting dressed, then I can at least go and talk with her. Besides, she deserves to hear about my engagement, and I would like to be the one who tells her. Or have you taken that away from me as well?"

"My dear, I haven't taken anything away from you. And as for seeing your mother, it's simply not a good idea."

"But I haven't heard her voice in years. I just want to talk to her."

"She is very ill, Wrena. You have to understand."

She shrugged obstinately. "I don't."

"She feels terrible for not being able to see you, but she insists that it's for the best. She does not want you to see her in this condition."

"I don't care how she looks, I want to see my mother." Her voice was louder than she intended it to be.

Her aunt took her hand. "Keep your voice down."

Wrena glanced around, noticing a few stares.

"Dear Wrena, you must uphold the dignity of the queendom." She ran a soothing hand down Wrena's arm. "Now go out and mingle with the guests. I do believe your fiancé is waiting to dance with you."

Wrena absently backed away from her aunt and spun into Eleazar. He caught her by her elbow, a look of concern on his face.

"Are you all right?" he asked.

"I don't know. I can't presume to know anything anymore."

"Come," he said, "let us dance before the citizens begin to speculate." He led her out onto the ballroom floor and took her hand, his other hand at her waist. "If it makes you feel any better, I wasn't given the option of contributing my opinion either."

She blinked and looked up at him. "You're being forced to do this too?"

He locked gazes with her as they spun together among the other dancers. "Yes."

"You know where my heart lies, Eleazar." He had known for months. As her oldest friend, she knew she could tell him anything and was pleased when he did not judge her.

"I do," he said. "But perhaps we can make it work for the sake of the queendom."

She let the thought roll around in her head for a moment, and then she lifted her chin. "I can't. I'm leaving."

"Leaving?" He searched her face and must have seen that she was telling the truth. "When?"

"Now, actually. There is a ship waiting for me and Aurora."

"Now?"

"There is no reason to wait. My mother is obviously not getting better, and though I value myself a good actress when I need to be, I do not think I could go through with something as big as a sham of a marriage."

He seemed to stiffen. He stopped dancing and took her hand. "I understand. And I wish you well." Leaning down, he placed a gentle kiss on the back of her hand. "Please take care of yourself, Wrena."

"Thank you," she said, squeezing his hand. "I promise."

CHAPTER FORTY

BRAM STOOD WITH LOGAN and Azalea, watching the guests enjoy the party. When Lady Maescia had announced that the Queen might be joining the festivities, Bram actually reconsidered his decision to leave Avarell. But once Lady Maescia declared the Queen too ill to join them after all, he knew there was no hope left and no reason for him to stay.

There was only one thing that would keep him in Avarell, but that was a wasted dream. He gazed at Tori from across the room as Logan and Azalea lovingly fought about which one of them was the worse dancer. He couldn't take his eyes off her as his best friend gossiped about how Lady Jasmine seemed to come out of her shell tonight, what with Lady Raven sulking in the corner and staying out of the spotlight.

Excusing himself from his friends, Bram adjusted the cuffs of his coat and strutted to Tori with confidence. It didn't matter to him anymore that she was a High Priestess; he wanted to dance with her. Perhaps he could never be with her, and his plans would take him away from Avarell anyway, but he could at least dance with this woman he'd been admiring since she arrived. He could at least hold her in his arms once more before he left. Every step that took him closer to her made his pulse race faster and his skin tingle with hope and fear simultaneously.

He bowed when he reached her. "You look lovely tonight, Lady Tori."

She blushed. It was the loveliest thing he'd ever seen. "Thank you very much, Master Stormbolt."

"I wondered if you've had a chance to consider my offer."

"Your offer?"

"To dance with me. Just once?"

She let out a small laugh. "No, I couldn't."

"Why not? Is it forbidden to dance?"

"No, it is not."

He presented his hand to her. "Then dance with me. Do you not enjoy music?"

"I do."

His hand remained outstretched. Every second that passed was torture. Until finally, she placed her hand in his and made his heart sing.

Her insides grew warm as Bramwell led her out onto the ballroom floor. What was she doing? She was supposed to be keeping her eye out for the perfect opportunity to slip away to the high tower. But for some reason, she couldn't resist Bramwell's insistence on dancing with her. Besides, what was two or three minutes spent dancing going to do to change her plans? She certainly could afford the luxury of an innocent dance, couldn't she?

But if it was so innocent, then why was her stomach fluttering?

He placed a hand on her waist as he held the other out to prop her hand. They were firm but gentle hands, and Tori felt invigorated at such a simple touch. And though she was caught in his gaze, she knew she had to look away or else be lost in his eyes forever.

"I feel I must tell you how you light up the room, Lady Tori," he said.

"You are too kind. This is a special gown, worn for such ceremonies as the birthdays of royals or weddings, so I don't wear it often."

"It's not the gown that's caught my eye."

She wasn't sure how to respond. She was sure if he could hear her heart pounding, it would be response enough.

As he spun her slowly to the side, Tori caught sight of Raven staring at them, her mouth slightly agape. A pang of guilt stabbed through her, especially when Raven pressed her lips together and charged from the ballroom.

Though she had done nothing wrong, Tori found the moment with Bramwell ruined by Raven's display of disapproval. Luckily the song ended, and Tori immediately took a step back from Bramwell. But he still held her hand in his, a soft smile playing on his lips and an almost sad look in his eyes.

"Thank you," she said, attempting to prompt him to release her hand.

"No, thank *you*." He held on a moment longer, and there was a look in his eyes as if he had something he wanted to say.

Inexplicably frightened by the intensity of the moment, she pulled away gently. Placing a hand on her stomach, she realized that the uneasy feeling she had was not because of Bramwell, but because of the fever. Her joints hurt and her throat ached. Her head was so heavy that she almost couldn't keep it straight when she bowed it.

Trumpets sounded, making her start.

The crowd turned to the front of the room, where three young dancers in matching outfits lined up. Their curls were piled on top of their heads with ribbons, and their long legs moved in unison, even before the dance began. Upon closer inspection, Tori realized they must be sisters, for their facial features were so similar.

Tori stayed beside Bramwell as they watched the trio perform their graceful dance. When she found herself swaying, she reached out to keep her balance, and Bramwell was quick to catch her hand.

"Are you all right?" he asked her quietly.

"Yes. I think I may have had too much wine."

He smiled at her. "I'll escort you out for some fresh air."

"No," she said quickly, not wanting to be trapped with him somewhere when she had a task to do. "I'm fine. I don't want to miss the end of this act." She gestured to the dancers, who finished their dance while the crowd erupted in applause.

The eldest of the dancers, who appeared to be just a few years younger than Tori, stepped forward. "We were hoping to perform for the Queen," she announced. "But in lieu of her absence, we have a song dedicated to Lady Maescia."

The crowd was full of nods and smiles, and one of the younger sisters fetched a rebec, and the other lifted a flute. The older sister closed her eyes and began to sing, her lovely voice carrying in soft waves through the ballroom. But halfway through the song, the melody dropped into a minor key, and the words the young girl sang held a bite that even Tori couldn't deny were meant for the queen regent.

"And the children do weep,
At the injustice she keeps,
We believe every lie,
That she tells as we die,
And our voices fall to silence,

In a realm that ends in violence."

Tori's eyes went directly to the queen regent, whose jaw was clenched, visibly upset by the song.

There was minimal applause overpowered by mumbling and whispers. The duke whispered instructions to his nearest men—Tiberius among them—and in the next moment, the soldiers forcefully escorted the trio of performers out of the ballroom.

The duke then whispered something to the queen regent, and in response, Lady Maescia's expression changed. She blinked, her frown becoming a forced smile, and she took a step forward to address the guests.

"Please," she said, holding her hands out at her sides. "There is still much to be celebrated. Musicians! Play a merry tune!"

Her subjects obeyed, musicians quick to fill the room with gaiety, as Lady Maescia clearly wanted.

Tori's gaze followed the guards who hauled the three young women away. She knew things would not end well for them tonight, unless she intervened. "Master Stormbolt, would you please excuse me?"

Bramwell bowed his head to her. "Yes, of course. I do hope to see you later in the evening."

She didn't respond save to bow her head in return, and then she hastily departed from the room.

The three girls struggled, the oldest one shouting at Tiberius as he yanked on her arm, bringing them in the direction of the dungeon.

"This is an outrage," the oldest one said. "We've done nothing wrong."

"Your little song was an act of defiance against the throne," Tiberius said. "That, according to the duke, is an act of treason."

Tori followed silently as the corridor grew narrow. There were four guards. Tori calculated her strategy.

As she got closer, the oldest girl managed to wriggle out of Tiberius's grasp. She tried to push him away so she could help her sisters, but Tiberius reached out and seized her neck, slamming her against the wall. Tori didn't have time to think. The first shuriken flew into the lamp, snuffing out the light. Next, the kunai flew, and though it was dark, Tori could see well enough to spot it piercing Tiberius's arm, causing him to release the older sister. The second and third shuriken struck the necks of the guards holding the two younger sisters.

The sisters reached for each other in shock, backing away from the two guards who had dropped to the floor. The one guard who was untouched spotted the shadowed figure that was Tori and charged toward her. She flung the last shuriken, which caught him right between the eyes. He fell back and crumpled to the ground.

Tiberius, sneering as he yanked the kunai out of his arm—his axe-swinging arm, Tori noted—clutched the kunai in his fist and came after her. She set her jaw and ran toward him, quick to duck and snatch the shuriken out of the head of the fallen guard, and whipped the weapon at his thigh. He stumbled, falling to one knee and dropping the kunai, and when he was down, Tori seized the blade and rammed it into his chest. He reached out as he groaned in pain, his fingers clutching at the sleeve of her dress and ripping it, but when Tori pushed the blade deeper into his torso, the life faded from his eyes.

She retracted her blade, wiping it off on his coat, then stood to look at the cowering girls backed up against the wall.

"You'll need to leave," Tori said. "I can get you out of the castle." She could tell the girls were too frightened to move. She made sure not to raise her voice. "The other guards will be wondering why these men haven't returned. It would be best if you left *now*."

The older sister finally nodded and grabbed her sisters' hands. Tori led them to the nearest secret passage, and they travelled in silence as she weaved through the hidden tunnels that led to the stables. They came out of the tunnels, the girls shivering from cold and fear. Tori rushed to the back gate and used her tools to pick the lock.

"Aren't you the High Priestess?" The oldest asked.

"There's no time to speak of it," Tori said. "You will need to go through this gate and continue on through the woods until you reach the city. From there, I hope you can find safe passage."

The oldest took Tori's hand. "Thank you."

"It was a brave thing you did," Tori said.

"Cate," the oldest said, taking her hand and shaking it. "My name is Cate."

"It was brave, Cate. I wish you a safe journey."

Cate's younger sisters came forward and hugged Tori. For the smallest moment, Tori smiled.

"Go now, before you're caught."

She watched as the trio ran off, then scanned the courtyard to make sure they weren't seen. Gazing upon the castle, she realized that this was the moment she'd been waiting for. The majority of the guests—and the royal court and the servants—were gathered in the ballroom. Even most of the guards were stationed in the banquet hall or at the entrance to the castle. It was the perfect opportunity to slip away to the high tower. She didn't have much time, because once the dead guards were discovered and the duke realized the trio of performers had gotten away, the duke's men would start searching the grounds. But they wouldn't be searching the secret passageways.

CHAPTER FORTY-ONE

WRENA SHIVERED ON THE SHORE, despite the sheepskin lining of her cape. It wasn't the cold winds that bothered her; it was the agonizing wait for Aurora to appear. They had separated at the party to gather the things they needed to bring with them, each of them promising to meet at the shore where the hired boat awaited them. The spot was far from the docks so they wouldn't be seen, and Wrena worried that Aurora might have gotten lost.

Or that she had changed her mind. After all, the risk was extreme, and they would be giving up everything they knew.

A shuddered breath escaped her lips as a shadow moved toward her. She almost collapsed in relief when Aurora came into view. They ran toward each other and embraced. Wrena wondered if the tightness of Aurora's hold was due to happiness in seeing her or fear for the journey on which they were about to embark.

"I thought you weren't coming," Wrena said.

"How could you doubt me?" Aurora stroked Wrena's cheek.

"I'm just afraid."

"Do you have everything you need?"

"I only need you."

Wrena turned to the man she hired, who stood by the small rowboat that would take them to the waiting ship out on the water. He bowed to her, holding the rowboat for them to climb in.

As Aurora settled onto the small wooden plank that served as a seat, Wrena took one last look at the castle, its lights shining in the distance against the city skyline. She wished she had said a proper goodbye to Theo, but she knew he would be taken care of. With her gone, he would be named King when he became of age. No harm would come to him. She had to believe that was true.

She climbed into the rowboat next to Aurora, their fingers entwining as they shivered in the dark of night. The man Wrena hired began to push at the boat, getting it in the deeper part of the water before he could climb in.

"Cease!"

Wrena gasped, and Aurora's body shook with a jolt.

"Return the boat on order of the captain of the Queen's Guard!" Duke Grunmire shouted.

The man Wrena hired had wide eyes, his mouth agape. He glanced at Wrena, and whispered. "I'm sorry, Your Highness."

Wrena's heart dropped, her head screaming in protest. She thought about taking Aurora and jumping in the water to escape, but she knew they would never get far.

The guards accompanying the duke marched forward and grabbed Wrena and Aurora. Aurora's shrieks carried on the wind. Wrena struggled to free herself from the soldier's hold.

"Let me go, I demand you! I am the Princess of Avarell!"

"You would be wise not to struggle, Your Highness," the duke said. "You wouldn't want your dear lady-in-waiting to be beheaded for treason, would you?"

"Treason? For what? She's done nothing wrong!"

"That's where you're wrong. She causes a threat to the royal line of succession. That is a crime against the crown."

Wrena froze. Tears flowed down Aurora's cheeks as their gazes locked. They would arrest Aurora for this. If she was accused of treason, she could be beheaded. Or worse. Wrena lifted her chin, glaring at the duke.

"You will pay for this."

"I'm afraid you are confused," the duke said, mockery in his voice. "It seems that I have the upper hand—just as I have the upper hand with your aunt."

"My aunt? What do you… Have you been blackmailing the queen regent?"

"The bigger concern here," the duke said, motioning for one of his guards to deal with the man Wrena hired. He continued to speak as the guard ran his sword through the man's chest. "—is what you will do to ensure that your lover survives."

Wrena swallowed hard, her eyes darting between the duke and Aurora. "What do you want from me?"

The duke stepped closer and pinched a lock of Wrena's hair between his fingers. "I believe my son deserved an award for alerting me that you would be here, attempting to make an escape."

"Eleazar told you—?"

"I believe the award of becoming the future King would do nicely. Don't you?"

Wrena stiffened her jaw. "I'll never marry him."

"You will if you don't want to see your little play thing here harmed."

Wrena felt like screaming. She felt like spitting in the duke's face. But the fight dropped out of her as she watched the way the guards held Aurora. She couldn't let them do anything to her.

She would do anything to keep Aurora safe and alive. Even if it meant marrying the duke's son.

CHAPTER FORTY-TWO

SHE FIT THE KEY INTO THE LOCK and turned it, holding her breath until she heard a click. Her heart drummed in her chest as she twisted the knob and gave the door a gentle push. Was the Queen really in this room? Was she being held prisoner? Or was she really ill as Maescia had said?

The room was dark, save for the moonlight breaching the window. When Tori's eyes adjusted to the lack of light, she spotted a figure lying still on an enormous bed. The Queen? She had to know for sure. Risking someone spotting the light in the window, she flipped the switch to illuminate the room. Heavy curtains draped from the canopy of the bed, blocking out most of the light.

Tori kept her footsteps silent as she approached. She'd seen portraits of the Queen, but she couldn't quite tell if this woman was her. The woman's skin lacked a healthy color, her eyes shut but her mouth slightly agape. Her breaths came at a labored pace. Whoever this woman was, she was alive. But who else could it have been? Another step closer, and Tori spotted the Queen's ring. There would be no reason for someone else to be wearing it. And she knew Lady Maescia had been in this room on more than one occasion, so if this woman was not the Queen, Lady Maescia would surely have confiscated the royal jewel.

The Queen's raspy breaths grew louder. Tori wondered if this was part of the Queen's illness or if Maescia had drugged her into some oppressed physical state that made it hard to breathe. Coming closer, Tori noticed chains on the bed. They were slightly hidden by the heavy blankets. Her brow furrowed, following the length of the chain to the Queen's body. She gently pulled the covers back, then gasped when she saw the leather straps bound tightly around the Queen's wrists.

Goran's suspicions were correct. The Queen was being held against her will.

Panic lodged in Tori's throat. What was she supposed to do now?

Rescue her, Goran had said. Tori hadn't thought this through. If the Queen was drugged or not well enough to walk, how was Tori going to get her out of the high tower?

She reached for the leather straps, figuring that whatever her plan was, it had to begin with taking the restraints off the Queen. The Queen stirred slightly as Tori removed the strap from her right wrist. And as Tori undid the buckle from the strap on her left wrist, the Queen's eyes opened wide.

Tori gasped and took a step back. Those eyes were not full of life. In fact, as the Queen shifted her head, her teeth baring and a snarl escaping through her rotted teeth, Tori stumbled backwards in shock. The Queen was not alive. She was an Undead.

The Undead Queen suddenly shot up from the bed and pounced on Tori. Tori threw her arms out to stop the Queen, fingers prodding into the Queen's shoulders as she fought to keep the Queen from biting her.

Tori managed to get her knee up, then jammed her foot into the Queen's midsection and gave a powerful kick. Queen Callista toppled back, groaning and snarling. Tori scrabbled to get to her feet, automatically reaching for her kunai. The Queen hissed as she got to her feet, her Undead eyes trained on Tori. Tori held out the kunai, but could she really use it? Even though she had qualms about killing, she found stabbing Tiberius and taking out the guards a necessity. But killing the Queen? The consequences were much more extreme. And who would believe her if she claimed the Queen was an Undead when she killed her? No, this was not an option.

A noise in the hall stopped them both. Queen Callista, in a hunched stance, swiftly turned her head toward the noise. Before Tori could think to move, the Queen bolted for the door and tore it open. Tori wanted to scream for her to stop, but her voice stuck in her throat. She ran for the door, but the Queen was nowhere to be seen. And the secret entrance to the hidden passageways was open.

Tori scampered to follow, unaware of what she would do if she caught up to the Queen. But the Queen was dangerous. She seemed stronger and more aware than the Undead Tori had come into contact with in the Rift. The only thing she could deduce was that whatever medicines and cures her sister had apothecaries give her did something to her. Lady Maescia may have been trying to cure her, but instead, she had created an even more dangerous Undead.

She had no torch or candle to light her way through the tunnels, but she pushed herself forward anyway. Her skin burned and her stomach was in knots, but she continued on, taking lefts and rights in search of the Queen. Her head swam, her vision failing, sweat fell into her eyes, and she stumbled more than once. Her heart felt as if it were about to explode. But she could hear the uneven footsteps of the Queen up ahead. She couldn't stop now. If the Queen were to get out of the tunnels and find her way into the main part of the castle, there was no telling what might happen.

Bram didn't know where Lady Tori had disappeared to. He checked the chapel, but she wasn't there, and when he happened to run into Lady Tori's handmaid, she claimed she hadn't seen her since she left for the party.

He decided to try the west wing, though he had no idea why Lady Tori would be in that part of the castle. As he rounded the corner, Lady Maescia suddenly appeared before him.

"Master Stormbolt," she said. "I've been meaning to speak with you."

Bram hesitated, trying to read her expression. "Your Grace?"

"I take it you are enjoying the festivities?"

"Yes, Your Grace. It is a lovely party. It is sad that the Queen could not join us, but you have thrown a praise-worthy celebration in her honor."

"I did notice that one of my ladies was not enjoying herself."

"Oh?"

"Lady Raven. In fact, when I went to console her, she shared with me some news that proved quite upsetting, even to me."

Bram braced himself. "What news is that?"

"She said you are leaving Avarell."

He blanched. He opened his mouth to speak, but the queen regent cut him off.

"Is it true you are deserting your post in my queendom to join the Queen's Guard in Gadleigh?"

"I… I am not deserting, your grace. I had planned to hand in a written resignation to Duke Grunmire tomorrow. I decided to wait until after the festivities, so as not to spoil the mood."

"You didn't wait to tell Lady Raven." She cocked a brow. "I'd say her mood is spoiled for certain."

Bram shook his head. "I only meant to spare her feelings."

"Master Stormbolt, I don't really care about you breaking poor Raven's heart. What does concern me is how your loyalty has changed. You know entirely too much about Avarell, the inner workings of the queendom, and Duke Grunmire's most proficient strategies. And now you are to run off to Gadleigh, where you could divulge our court's secrets to an army that might very well become our enemy?"

"Your Grace, my father served in Gadleigh. They only want—"

A horrific scream tore through the castle halls, followed by a human-like growl.

Lady Maescia's jaw dropped, her hand flying to her mouth. "That sounded like—"

Bram didn't wait for her to finish. His hand flying to the hilt of his sword to assure it was there, he sprinted down the corridor. Lady Maescia was surprisingly fast on his heels. A servant boy ran past them, looking horrified.

When they rounded the corner, a body lay crumpled on the floor. Bram gasped as he neared and found it to be Lady Jasmine, blood oozing from what looked like a bite on her arm. Lady Maescia trembled, her hand jittering by her mouth.

"What was that?" Logan shouted, running toward them, Azalea in tow.

Bram crouched down to check if Lady Jasmine was breathing. "I don't know," he said. "It looks like an animal bite."

"No," Azalea said, hunching over Lady Jasmine, who moaned and began to writhe in pain. "Those are human teeth marks."

"Who would do such a thing?" Logan asked.

"Take care of her." Bram stood. "I'll alert the duke."

He marched back the way from whence he came, and Lady Maescia followed quickly behind him. Once they were out of earshot of Logan and Azalea, Lady Maescia grabbed Bram by the arm.

"You can't get the duke," she said.

"Someone dangerous is in the castle. We must alert the Queen's Guard."

"No." She pulled harder on Bramwell's arm. There was terror in her eyes Bramwell had never seen before. "No, this isn't what it appears to be."

"But we need to get the duke. We need men."

"No. I forbid it." With a shaky breath, Lady Maescia released his arm. "They'll kill her."

"What? What are you talking about."

"I'm… I'm fraught to tell you."

"You must."

She shook her head, her shaking fingers pressed against her cheeks. "You have to trust me. I'll make a deal with you. If you help me, I will let you go to Gadleigh, free of any retribution or castigation, immediately. But you must keep this a secret, and you must not let anyone kill her."

"Kill… kill who?"

"My sister."

"The Queen?"

Lady Maescia nodded, tears filling her eyes.

"Your Grace, if someone has come to kill the Queen, it is my duty to protect her. Are you saying someone has entered the castle to attack her? Was that servant a casualty of the attack?"

"No, no. The Queen—my sister—*she* attacked Lady Jasmine. I've seen what she can do. It must have been her. She hasn't been sick all this time, not in the way that everyone thinks."

"Your Grace, I'm afraid I'm lost, and we're running out of time."

"She's become… an Undead." Lady Maescia looked as if she were holding her breath.

"What? You must be mistaken."

"She's an Undead. I've been trying to save her, trying to find a cure. But now… now it's too late. She's escaped."

Bramwell struggled to wrap his mind around this information. He shook his head, his mind spinning. "How could you have kept this a secret? All this time?"

"I had to. You don't understand. No one knows what's really going on here."

Another scream ripped through the castle. "Even if we don't alert Duke Grunmire, they're bound to hear the screams."

"Then we have to find her before the Queen's Guard does."

"Come on, then."

They ran toward the source of the screams. At the end of their search, they found a handmaiden flattened against the wall, the candle flickering in her shaking hand. Her eyes were trained on a secret entrance to the tunnels, which stood ajar.

Bram took a few paces closer to the entrance, when a pair of small eyes looked up at him. A fox appeared, gekkering at him. Bram unsheathed his sword.

"No, don't!" The small voice of Prince Theo came out of nowhere. He stepped forward and stood between them and the fox.

"Theo, what are you doing here?" Lady Maescia crouched down, hugging the child. Bram suspected she was glad he hadn't come across his mother.

"I was following Takumi," Prince Theo said.

"Who's Takumi?" Bram asked.

"Lady Tori's fox." Prince Theo pointed at the fox, who was pacing in circles near the entrance of the tunnels.

"I have a hunch of where to find the Queen," Bram whispered to Lady Maescia so that Theo wouldn't hear.

"What? The fox? For all we know he was the one who bit Lady Jasmine."

"No. You said yourself you know it was the Queen. Are you coming with me or not?"

She drew her lips into a straight line and nodded. Takumi let out a squeal and bound into the secret passageway. Bram took the candle from the handmaiden. "Prince Theo, I need you to stay here."

Prince Theo nodded. Bram turned to Lady Maescia, taking a deep breath, then turned toward the passageway entrance.

"This way," Bram yelled, running after the fox.

"What? Where does this lead?"

Bram didn't bother answering her, taking the twists and turns of the tunnel, attempting to keep up with Lady Tori's fox. He didn't know why he trusted the animal to lead him in the right direction, but something in his gut told him it was the right thing to do.

They ended up in one of the old tunnels, and Bram grimaced as he realized that this way led to the area that should be blocked off. Silently berating himself for not checking earlier as to whether or not the wooden boards sealing off the dangerous part of the tunnels were intact, he picked up his pace.

There was movement and noise up ahead. As Bram got closer, he spotted the magnificent gown Lady Tori wore to the birthday celebration.

"Lady Tori!" he called.

She turned, her face pale and full of pain. She spun away and continued toward the door up ahead. There was someone in front of her, someone in a long nightgown, staggering and moaning. Lady Tori stumbled, but managed to grab onto the hem of the woman's nightgown.

When the woman turned around, Bram could have sworn he recognized her.

"Callista!" Lady Maescia called.

Bram was in shock. The Queen *wasn't* simply ill. And the queen regent had told the truth; Queen Callista was an Undead.

The Queen growled, then turned and ripped the remainder of the wooden planks off the supposedly-sealed doorway. Her strength astounded Bram, who was at a loss for words.

Bram and Lady Maescia rushed forward to the place where Lady Tori had fallen.

Lady Maescia clenched her teeth at Tori, who lay clutching her chest. "What have you done?" She glared at her for a second, then rose as if to follow her sister.

"No!" Bram grabbed Lady Maescia, pulling her back. "Don't!"

"I have to," Lady Maescia screamed.

"No, you can't go that way. It leads to the Rift. I'm sorry, Your Grace, but it could mean your death."

Lady Maescia stopped, watching as her sister disappeared down the tunnel, and clapped her hands to her mouth. She shook almost violently, pulling at her own hair. "No. No, this can't be. I've lost her."

Bram could not stop Takumi, however, who jetted down the tunnel after the Queen, fading into the darkness.

Bram bent over Tori, who clutched at his coat lapel. She looked as if she were struggling to breathe. Bram placed his hands upon her arms. "Lady Tori, what is it?

Tori gasped, her breath labored. "My h-heart. It's failing. I have… the phoenix fever."

Bram's eyes widened. Tori rolled farther onto her back, her legs falling slack on the ground. Cringing from what Bram assumed was the pain of movement, she pulled out a syringe from her satchel. She could barely lift her arm, but she held the syringe out to him. He took her hand, the syringe cradled between them. With her other hand, Tori pointed to her heart. Her eyes began to glass over, her breaths nothing but rasps.

"What am I supposed to—?"

Again, she pointed to her heart. Lady Maescia drew nearer, her face pale.

He shook his head. "I can't."

She pushed the syringe into his hands, her breath coming out in gasps. He took the syringe, staring at it as if it was poison. Could he do this? What if it didn't work? What if he killed her?

"You must do as she says," Lady Maescia said, leaning over them.

Tori's eyes searched his face as she struggled to breathe. "I… saved you once. Now… it's your turn."

His brows furrowed, but understanding set in. If he thought his heart held panic before, it was nothing compared to the torture it endured now.

"She'll die for sure if you don't do it now," Lady Maescia said, her voice a harsh whisper as she hunched behind him.

Tori gasped for breath, her hands clenching Bramwell's tunic. He held his breath and adjusted his grip on the syringe. "May the Divine Mother forgive me," he whispered. His jaw rigid, he plunged the syringe directly into her heart. Her eyes widened as a weak moan escaped her lips. Her gaze landed on Bramwell, her hand reaching for his face, and then, on a shuddered breath, her eyes closed.

Coming Fall 2018

PARAGON RISING

Curse of the Phoenix

Book Two

ACKNOWLEDGEMENTS

There are times when you can only get through the trials and tribulations of what life throws at you by having wonderful people who support and believe in you.

I want to thank my agent, Italia Gandolfo, for taking me under her wing and being a fierce mama bear who promised to fight with me in the trenches. Thank you, Italia, for all you do for me.

A big thank you to Sarah Howell, who so generously and lovingly takes my drafts and makes them into something legible. You are a star, Sarah! I appreciate you so much!

I want to thank Lyssa and everyone at Snowy Wings Publishing for your guidance and support, as well as a thankful hug to my author groups, whose talents are astounding. A special thank you to Jessica Gunn, who cheerleads me when I need it. And thanks to Cheree Castellanos, who not only edited my book but also raved about it with enormous enthusiasm.

I'm grateful for my friends and colleagues—let's go Monkeys!—who always have great things to say. Thanks especially to my home base team: Bonnie, Sasha, Carol, Rose, Cassie, Holly, Kyra, Renee, April, Nikki, and my loving Aunt Barb and Uncle Vic.

A special thanks to Megan Murphy, who entered and won the "Name a Character" contest with Azalea's name. Love the name!

And, of course, thanks to my mother Rebecca, my dad Dave, my brother David, and my extended family: Charlie, Hilde, and Darlene. Last but not least, all my love to my husband Stephan for letting me live my dream, and my grown-up kids: Kirsten, not only super talented herself but also probably my biggest cheerleader of all; and Zachary, who doesn't seem to have a doubt that I'll make it big one day.

ABOUT THE AUTHOR

Dorothy Dreyer is a Philippine-born American living in Germany with her husband, two teens, and two Siberian Huskies. She is an Amazon category bestselling author of young adult and new adult books that usually have some element of magic or the supernatural in them. Aside from reading, she enjoys movies, chocolate, take-out, traveling, and having fun with friends and family. She tends to sing sometimes, too, so keep her away from your Karaoke bars.

Visit www.dorothydreyer.com to learn more.

ALSO BY DOROTHY DREYER

ENTANGLED SOULS: A Runes Universe Novella

Under the Surface: A short story in the FRAGMENTS OF DARKNESS anthology

BALL GOWNS AND BLOOD STAINS: A newsletter subscriber exclusive dark paranormal novella

MORE FROM SNOWY WINGS PUBLISHING

Made in the USA
Middletown, DE
15 February 2018